WHEN WILL IT STOP!?

WHEN you DO

A Novel

Diane C. Shore

DCShore Publishing
dcshorepublishing.com

1.9

ISBN-13: 978-1-7326785-1-4

DEDICATION

Jesus, You are the Healer and Deliverer to all those who call upon Your
Mighty Name. With You, and You alone, we can rise up as if we had eagles'
wings. This book is dedicated to Your Father, and mine; to the Holy Spirit
given to all of us who do believe; and to You, who makes all things new.
Jesus, You are the answer when we cry out, "When will it stop?"
You make a way. Let us always choose You above all else in this life.
You are the freedom we are all searching for. You are the peace and joy we
all long for. Your name holds all the Hope we will ever need.
Thank You Lord Jesus!

1

PRESENT DAY

Tracy Lynn, better known as TL to many, barely slept the night before he hit the road for New Mexico in the spring of 2018. When he did doze, it had been a fitful and disturbed sleep once again. There had been far too many nights like this.

Rising before dawn, TL couldn't stop thinking about the answer that came to him when he cried out, "God, when will it stop!?" God swiftly and clearly answered, "When you do." It surprised TL. It wasn't even really a question of sorts, but more a plea for help. And yet, there it was...the plain, simple truth— just stop. Stop it. Stop allowing the wounding. Set up healthy boundaries that will put an end to the torture. Stop being the scapegoat. Stop being the excuse for misery. But God...stop being there at all? Is that what You mean? How do I do that? Don't You ask us to love our brother? Love our neighbor? Love even our enemies? How did I get to this place filled with such desperation?

With stomach churning, and head spinning through all the agonizing about Vic, TL pulled the car out of the driveway just as the sun was coming up over the hills. It seemed a hopeful sign...to leave in the darkness felt cold and uncaring. But then, there it was again...the pull—the wondering what he was doing wrong to cause this. Victor was seemingly TL's drug of choice. His very own brother. It was time...and TL knew it...but it was so hard.

After a lifetime of being there for Vic, TL knew he had to get away. His mom told him it might come to this. Physical escape seemed the only answer at this point. But would he be able to shut off his own brother? He doubted it. He knew the calls would eventually come from Vic. Could he resist them? He wasn't so sure. His thoughts kept focusing on, "What am

I doing? What if Vic needs me?"

Stopping at the first red light up the street, TL almost turned back. But if he did, he feared it just might kill him. He already felt dead inside other than the painful knot in the pit of his stomach that seemed to never go away. When would it stop? TL heard it again, "When you do." Had he been feeding off Vic, as much as Vic was feeding off him? Maybe. Maybe he was more part of the problem than the solution? Had he helped to create this monster?—this insatiable creature that grew in ferocity with each passing month he lived with him?

When the light turned green, TL stepped on the gas, and drove out of town. He knew he had to...for his own sanity. Maybe this could possibly wake up his brother, too? A verse came to him from Matthew 15:14 in that moment, "...if one blind person guides another, they will both fall into a ditch." TL said out loud, "I always thought I was the one seeing clearly. Maybe I've been duping myself all this time?"

Thinking back, as he drove forward, TL recalled the day he simply met his brother at Charlie's Brewery...

2

ONE YEAR EARLIER

"Hey, Bro, how about we get a place together?" Vic asked, drumming his fingers on the table as he sat across from me.

I looked at him before answering. With my job being shaky, and Vic seemingly heading toward a divorce, it appeared to be a good idea at the time. Vic always depended on me when we were kids.

"Maybe that could make it easier on the both of us," I answered.

"That's cool, Bro," Vic said, taking a sip of his beer. "Let's scout out some places this weekend."

"Sure. Let's do that," I agreed, although something inside of me did question what was happening.

Looking at a few locations, we finally agreed upon a small house. Normally it would have cost us more than an apartment, but the owners made us a special deal. We moved in two weeks later.

"I'll take this room over here. I like the view out the front window," Vic said, not really asking me as much as telling.

"Okay. That's fine, although it would have worked well for my furniture."

"Well, that room there will work, too. Don't worry about it. It will fit," Vic said.

I looked at the smaller bedroom at the back of the house and remembered when we were boys. Vic always got his way. I thought for many years it was because he was Mom's favorite. Maybe that was true...maybe not. Vic had a way to get what he wanted.

Carrying in boxes, we didn't talk a lot—although Vic suggested what was left of my stuff, when we got done, I could sell at a yard sale, or on the internet. In other words, Vic's stuff would be placed first, and any space remaining, I could have. I didn't care all that much, so of course I went along with Vic's ideas for furniture placement.

"How about I run and get us a pizza for dinner?" I suggested, after we'd been working a few hours.

"Oh, I don't know. I'm feeling more like Chinese. Let's have that instead."

"Uh. Okay. I'll go to that place around the corner from here. I've been there once before. It was pretty good," I told him.

"That's not such a good place. I like the one over by the grocery store. You know the one, with the big red sign out front. Get it from there."

"I know the one," I simply said, as I headed out the door.

Returning after about 45 minutes, I came through the door to a barrage of angry words from Victor. "Where have you been? I had questions about some things here! Did it really take that long to get food?"

I just stood there, bags in my hands, and a look on my face that said it all...if Victor would have been listening. "I haven't been gone that long," I said under my breath.

"Let's eat. I'm hungry." Vic said, taking the bags and heading toward a kitchen full of boxes. "If you'd emptied these out earlier, we'd have some dishes to work with."

I followed Vic into the kitchen but wished I hadn't. Once again, it was my fault that there were no dishes out for us to use. "I got us some paper plates and forks at the Chinese place. I knew we wouldn't be able to find the dishes yet," I offered, hoping to appease him.

"I don't like plastic forks," Vic complained.

At that point, we mostly ate in silence, unless Vic spoke up about how his furniture wasn't fitting perfectly in his room and maybe he should take a look at my room again. "I wish Mandy hadn't left me with that bedroom set. No wonder she didn't want it when we split. She probably got herself something that works better, and she left me with this junk. I think I'll sell it as soon as I can. This egg roll is cold. That place is disappointing. I won't go back there again."

"I sure like this egg foo young though," I said, trying to change the mood. "They really know how to make it."

"I guess," Vic said with a grunt, and then quickly added, "We need to set up the stereo system. I don't want to wait to do that. I like listening to music pretty much 24-7."

We fell into bed that night exhausted as the questions from Mom ran through my head. "Are you sure this is a wise choice?" She wasn't so sure about it when I told her of our plan. Vic probably went right to sleep. All I know is I laid awake, rolling over from side to side. The demands of Vic from earlier kept going through my mind. Maybe it was just because Vic gets stressed out moving, I remember thinking, looking for some excuse. He couldn't really be this way all the time, could he? I hoped not. I tried

4

to pray, but I was so distracted, it seemed God was a million miles away. When I finally got to sleep, it didn't seem like any time at all and I could hear music coming from the living room. Opening my eyes, I noticed the sun was up, but I surely wasn't ready to be yet.

Sitting on the side of my bed, I rubbed my eyes open, and walked lazily into the living room. Vic was sitting on the couch, head back, eyes closed, and nodding to the music. He didn't hear me come into the room. I was glad as I walked to the kitchen. Finding a glass, I got myself some water, and then went back to my room, dressed, and started to unpack the boxes. I knew I'd need something to eat soon, but I wanted to get a few things done first.

Vic appeared in my doorway. "I didn't hear you up."

"No. Probably because of the music. You seemed to be enjoying it, so I didn't want to disturb you," I answered him, with a bit of sarcasm.

"What do you mean by that? I told you I like music. I kept it low."

"Yeah. It was low. Don't worry about it," I said, trying to sound more sincere.

Vic turning and muttering under his breath said, "Don't worry about it...This is worse than being with Mandy..."

That was all I heard as Vic made his way back toward the living room. I hoped it would be a better day. Maybe once we got settled in, Vic would lighten up a bit.

"Have you seen my screwdriver?" Vic suddenly yelled from the other room.

"No. I haven't," I called back.

"I thought you had it last night," Vic said.

"I didn't," I answered.

"Are you sure? You had it before you left to get the Chinese food."

"What?" I said, confused.

"Yeah. I'm sure. You had it, and now I can't find it anywhere."

"I'll help you look. I don't remember using it. But maybe I did," I said, shaking away any morning cobwebs that might be blurring my thinking.

"You did. Now help me find it," Vic said in a commanding voice.

"I'm looking. I'm looking," I sighed, already exacerbated by how the morning was getting started.

"Oh, here it is. On my dresser," Vic exclaimed.

"I didn't think I had it," I muttered to myself, as I got back to unpacking boxes in my own room. What's wrong with that brother of mine? Is he in his right mind? I'll be glad to get back to work on Monday, and get a little space between us.

Around ten, Vic came into my room saying, "Run and get us a breakfast burrito! I don't want to leave right now. I'm in the middle of something."

I looked up at Vic from my position on the floor where I was going through things. I would have had a few choice words for him if he'd still been standing there. But he was gone again—back to doing what was important to him. No use arguing, I thought, I'll just keep him happy. I don't want to deal with the wrath of Vic. Not this early in the morning.

Returning from the breakfast shop down the street, I handed Vic his burrito.

"This feels cold...it better not be cold. They're always doing that. They make these up ahead of time, and then sell them like they're fresh."

"Vic, I saw them making ours while I stood there. I'm sure it's just fine on the inside. Unwrap it and see."

"Yeah. It's okay once I got all this paper off. Is this onion on here? It looks like they put onions in here. You didn't order it that way, did you?"

"No. No, I didn't. I know you're not a lover of onions," I said.

"Oh, maybe it's just some white cheese," Vic said, taking a large bite off the end, and sitting down on a box, now wanting to talk. "TL, this place is a too small. I wish we'd gone for that large apartment we saw. I'm not sure this will work."

The rest of what Vic said, I wasn't sure of. I stopped listening after the first few comments, and concentrated on eating my burrito. By the time I was done, Vic had gone on to other things, not really noticing that he wasn't being listened to. I was glad for that, and went into my room, shutting the door behind me.

3

Looking at the light traffic up ahead, it seems a good idea to be on the road before most of the commuters are up and running. Since quitting my job on Friday, I feel God opening this door for me to "escape." The last year has been brutal...on my soul, on my spirit, and on my body. I could feel the knot in the pit of my stomach getting worse with each passing month, and I'm wondering if it could cause actual physical harm? Enough is enough! They say sometimes disease comes from dis-ease...I'm beginning to see how that could be true.

Stopping for coffee, I look around at others who are out so early in the day. What are their reasons? Are they escaping from something...from someone? How crazy it is to think I have to do this? It's my little brother, after all. What harm could he cause? And yet, here I am. After loading what belongings would fit into my car, and getting rid of most of the rest of it, I'm running away. A grown adult. Crazy!

I remember a catch in my spirit when Vic suggested moving in together. There were too many memories of our childhood, and even early adult years, where things were rough. He was really reminding me of Dad. How had Mom put up with this for so many years? When I first talked to her, she didn't want to say a whole lot about Dad, or Vic. As the year went on, she opened up and even talked more about getting healthy herself. I'd never heard her talk like that before. I'd really like a good sit-down with her, face to face. I hope there's time when I get there.

Since Vic and I had been living in different cities for a number of years, we hadn't seen as much of each other, and I didn't give moving in together enough thought. I should have. Maybe I hoped his wife helped him grow up a bit. Now it didn't seem so. Vic was not exactly like I remembered him, he was worse. The incessant complaining, and bursts of anger. Everything was wrong, and none of it was his fault. And no one, and nothing, existed except what was important to Vic. The house that started out small, turned into a crackerjack box that felt like a prison cell. Coming home each night from work, there would be Vic, on the couch, listening to music, waiting for me to be at his beck and call. After all, isn't that what I lived for? Well, it seemed so to Vic.

"TL," the barista called out. "Coffee mocha, extra hot."

"Thanks," I answer, wrapping my hands around the cup, looking for some sort of comfort, I hope maybe this will soothe the ache I feel, and the worry that's consuming me. I know I need to get out of town. But everything inside of me shouts, "STAY!" When Vic gets home and tries calling me, I won't answer it. I can't answer it. What will I say? "I've left town. You're on your own. I can't do it anymore!" Oh no, that's not happenin'. Duck and avoid, at all cost right now. As much as I tried to discuss things with you before I left, there was no getting through to you, Vic. You gave me a "last straw," and I'm taking it!

Getting back in my car and turning out of the parking lot, I know what awaits me in New Mexico might not be perfect, but it will be better than what life with Vic contains. With some family there, maybe it will be a good landing place. How did this all get so unbearable? What did I do to cause this constant one-sided relationship? Why didn't I speak up for myself right from the beginning? Why did I let it get so bad? Wait...wait!! There it is again, thinking it's all my fault—that I caused this. That I should have been different, better, more understanding...more there for him. I did everything I could do, and so much more. But it was never enough for Vic. He took, and took, and took. I have to remember, this is not my fault. No wonder women stay in abusive relationships. They must get so depleted they can't see a way out. I'm just about there, with just enough left of me to make my escape. I'm feeling so depleted, and I'm a strong guy. Capable. But it seems less and less so, as Vic tore me down each day. I gave him any power I had. I let him be all that and a bag of chips. In his mind I wasn't worth the garbage can the empty bag was thrown into. Enough is ENOUGH!

After Vic finds out I'm gone, what will he do? Will he be sad? Will he understand I've left for good? I warned him, but he didn't listen. He thought I would never leave. But I have now. Is the ache that I feel just me needing a fix? Am I already thinking of missing the interaction that left me feeling weak and used? That makes me laugh, but it's not funny. It's truly sad. I'm wanting to call Vic, see if he has a way home, tell him I'll change my mind if we can only work on some things. Vic might agree to that. But even when we tried that in the past, it never lasted. It was only a ruse to get me to stick around. This is sick. It's my own brother.

When he calls, I'll have him leave a message. Then I'm not going to listen to it. I know him...he will talk a good talk, or he won't. He could be vicious, trying to convince me how this is all my fault once again. Or he could act all nice and beg for another chance. Keep driving, I say to myself, as I head out onto the I-5 going south toward Los Angeles. I reach over and turn my phone off, just feeling safer that way. I need some time to think before seeing my parents in Chino, and I need to talk this over more with Mom when I see her.

4

With a lot of unpacking left to do, I still left early for work that first Monday morning after moving into the house with Vic. I didn't want to be late to my job. They were letting people go all the time, and I didn't want them to have any reason to look my way. I spent a lot of my life staying under the radar, as I called it, and then moving in with Vic, I was realizing where I learned it. Through the years, I had become a professional *egg-shell* walker. I knew the right "lane" to stay in to avoid an "accident." It was always best to stay out of Vic's way, and give him that *way* as often as possible.

"Hi, TL. How are things with you this morning?" Butch asked. My manager was a friendly sort of guy.

"It's going okay. How're things with you, Butch?" I didn't want to go into the move, or my brother. There again, keep things simple and smooth. The less I was noticed, the better.

Butch answered, "Had a good weekend. Took the wife to the coast. She enjoyed that. Me not so much. I'm more of a mountain guy."

"I getcha," I said, trying to make it short and get on with sorting through the boxes in the warehouse. Working at a distributor of electronics, there wasn't a lot of time for chit-chat anyway.

"Have a good one. I'll see you at the meeting later," Butch said.

"Meeting?"

"Yeah. Didn't you hear about it? All departments. Five o-clock. Mandatory."

"Okay. Thanks." It's not what I wanted to hear, but I was glad I knew. Missing a meeting right now might give the company the excuse they were looking for to let me go.

Five o'clock came around fast that day. The meeting didn't contain any news that stood out in particular that concerned my position. I was headed home by quarter to six. Coming through the door, I could hear Vic in the back of the house. I startled him when I found him. Not a good thing...

"TL!! Don't do that! Let me know when you're coming in! My God, you just about gave me a heart attack! Where have you been? Do you always get home this late!?"

"Sorry, Bro. Didn't mean to scare you. Just getting home from a meeting after work. How's your day been?" That question was a mistake. I should have gone right to my room.

"The cable guy was here. What a jerk! He asked me questions I didn't have the answer to, and then looked at me like I was the crazy one. I couldn't get him out of here fast enough. I guess we're all set now, though. So be it. I'm hungry."

"What's for dinner?" I asked.

"Heck if I know. I've been working here all day. You're the one off galivanting around. Why didn't you bring us something?"

I just turned and walked away at that point. It wasn't what I needed to finish my work day. Big mistake. Vic followed me and let me have it!

"Why are you being so rude? You never listen to me!" He yelled.

I turned and looked at Vic, hoping he would maybe understand my job was exhausting, but then thought better of saying anything. He would have told me how exhausting his day was, always needing to one-up me. And he was on unemployment for the time being.

"I'll get us some dinner. Just give me a few minutes to relax," I said.

"Don't take too long. Time's a wastin'," Vic said, "and Mandy might be stopping by later. She wants to talk. I hope I don't have to listen to her whining."

Mandy did come by, and after she left that night, I asked Vic, "What's up? Another tough talk?"

"Yeah, man, she just doesn't get it," Vic answered. "I'm willing to work on this, and all she can do is complain. She wants to tell me all the things I'm doing wrong. Did you see the way she just left? I was in the middle of telling her something, and she gets up and leaves. She won't listen to me."

Vic began to tell me all the things Mandy wasn't doing to help what was going on. She seemed to make him crazy. From the way Vic described it, she was like a lead weight to him. Everything she did made it worse in Vic's eyes.

Vic went on talking... "She took the car in for repairs. What did she go and do that for? There's nothing wrong with that car. She just doesn't know how to drive it right. I don't know who taught her how to drive. I don't know how many times I've talked to her about it, and she doesn't listen."

"I hear what you're saying," I commented, although Vic was the one not listening as he veered off into other frustrations he had with Mandy. I eventually started to tune him out—we'd been down those same roads so many times. I knew I should be there for Vic. But whenever I tried to interject some bits of wisdom, or so I thought, Vic really wasn't interested. Vic needed to talk about Vic, plain and simple. He didn't want to hear a way out, he just wanted to sit in the midst of whatever it was and complain.

I went to bed so tired that night, but with hopes for a better tomorrow. I looked for my Bible among the things that were scattered around my room. Finally finding it in a stack of office supplies, I sat up in bed, trying to find some solace in God's Word. Where should I read? Instead, I prayed, "Father, I'm so tired and spent. Life shouldn't be this way, should it? I know moving is in the top five of stress causers. It will get better, right?" I felt led to the Psalms that night. Poor David, he was always pouring out his heart in distress. "Oh Lord, thank You for giving us David as an example. He found his peace in You when the day was done. I am trying here, Lord. Good night."

5

As hard as it is to leave, I'm feeling a new sense of freedom as the miles add up between the Bay Area and New Mexico. Could this really be it? Could I be free of my brother? Maybe he is sorry? NO! Don't even think that!

Ahhh...a rest stop up ahead. I think I'll take a break there, walk around a bit, and breathe. Yes, breathing would be good here. It seems like I haven't been able to really breathe for a year. I never thought anyone could be so suffocating. Vic, Vic, Vic began to absorb my every waking moment. Even at work all day, my phone would ring. Vic needed something. On the drive home each night, it seemed like I was heading into chaos, but I didn't even know what it was yet--just that it would be there, waiting for me.

I know I really need to do even more research about all of this. There's things I'm still missing. How does a person get so caught up in another person? Maybe with a husband and wife...I saw Mom deal with similar stuff. But with a brother? I just don't get it. How did Vic obtain so much control in my life, and in my thoughts? Even with everything Mom and I talked about. Why is this so hard to comprehend? It doesn't seem real. Maybe getting some space is the only way I'll be able to clear out my head.

Pulling out my phone after getting back into the car, I know I shouldn't turn it on, but I do. Ding, ding, ding, ding, ding...the text messages go on and on. Vic must have made it home and plugged in his phone. "I'm NOT going to look at these," I say to myself after seeing the words of the first one before looking away. "WHERE ARE..." I'm gone Vic, GONE! I say to myself, as I click on the internet, remembering again when Sue at work mentioned the word narcissist. I wasn't even sure what that meant at the time, but I did consider she was on to something. She seemed to understand what I didn't the one day I brought up the difficulties with Vic in the lunch room with her. Thankfully, it was just the two of us. She was kind, listening on that day when I couldn't help but spill out my frustrations all over the table. I remember her nodding a lot and saying some things that sounded way too familiar. Sue told me there were umpteen number of videos to watch as people talked about every aspect of narcissism. I'd been learning about it, and talking to Mom about it, but I needed to know more. This is a strange place to continue my search, in a rest stop. But it's time to finally stop and rest...and breathe.

Feeling the warmth of the sunshine through the window, watching cars come and go, and families taking bathroom breaks, I can feel my eyes getting heavy while scanning through some informational videos. That's okay, I'll just nap a bit. What's it going to hurt? No one knows where I am; or is expecting me to be anywhere at a certain time. I didn't give Mom an exact day or hour I'd be arriving, just that I'd be driving through their way soon. My time is mine, I think, drifting off into the sleep I missed out on from last night.

Waking a couple of hours later, I pull up that video I was looking at before falling asleep. But I wonder, do I really want to further educate myself about this right now? In this rest stop? Can't I just run away and never think of it again? Probably not. That's not realistic. I know better. There's no healing in that. I've already lost too much of myself in Vic, and I need to find out how to recover me—the peaceful, once fun-loving me. I've become a shaky shadow of myself, lacking confidence, and hope. And all this while knowing Jesus? Really God! I'm so sorry. I put Vic's needs above even You, maybe even playing You in Vic's life. I once was closer to You, God. Now I feel like I'm rolled up in a ball, trying to protect myself and just survive. I should have gotten out months ago. I should have gotten away, and been with You, finding my identity in You alone. Please forgive me, Father. I'm coming back to You now. Thank you that each day Your mercy is new. I know You can renew my mind. You've been there for me before, and I know You will be again. I need to turn my focus on You. It may take time to heal. I know it will take a lot of prayer and being in Your Word. I'm willing, Lord. And when I do want to give up and give in to anyone who mistreats me like Vic has, please help me to resist that. Please, don't let me turn back to the darkness, no matter how tempting it seems, no matter how pitiful they sound. Remind me what You said, it will stop, "When You Do." Thank You, Jesus. I'm stopping.

Oh, here's another good one to listen to...it's asking is my brother a jerk or a narcissist? Wow! Honestly, I don't know. As I listen, I learn some things, finding out that not all jerks are narcissists, but all narcissists are jerks. Okay, then. What is Vic? I know something has been wrong with him. What is it? Sometimes he does act mostly normal, especially when we are with other people he's trying to impress. It seems like I bring out the worst in him. So maybe it's been me? There's so much more I need to learn about this. I've let Mom do most of the research and fed off her. Now it's my turn. Maybe I can bring something to her, too?

Yes, Vic can be mean, rude, and untrustworthy, but he can care about some people in his life. He seemed to care about Mandy when they were first in love. He has a couple of friends, not many, but they seem to think he's an all right guy. Oh wow, this says that narcissists see themselves like kids see themselves—it's all about them and their needs. But how can a grownup man act like that? Doesn't Vic know that I will, or would have done anything for him? Why did he have to be mean about it? This is saying they will cut off their nose to spite their face. I wonder what that really means? Cutting off a nose to spite a face...it says here it's a "needlessly self-destructive over-reaction to a problem," or "causing problems for yourself by trying to punish someone else." I guess I was the nose.

Could Vic be reasoned with? This is a good question. Hmmm, jerks can be reasoned with, but narcissists can't. To me, this is really putting Vic more in the narcissist category. There was no reasoning with Vic, he would just put up a wall if I "invaded" his emotional space. Sometimes that came out as anger, sometimes he went totally silent—he was sort of predictably unpredictable. I laugh to myself, although this isn't funny, when I hear, "They don't seem to be grounded in reality." No wonder we couldn't ever get into a deep discussion about anything, he always skirted around everything. Was he afraid to go there with me? And why? All I wanted to do was talk with him, come to some sort of agreement that would work for both of us. It's sounding here like Vic wasn't just being rude, he was delusional. I think I'm just at the tip of a huge iceberg. I have a long way to go, diving deeper under the water to what lies beneath. Maybe I'll find myself under there, too, and find out why I put up with this for so long.

I want to sit here for a few more moments, God. I want to feel Your warmth. You created the sun that brings this comfort. It can seem a simple thing, but it isn't. I don't want to take anything for granted, not ever again. And Lord, I know with You, nothing goes to waste. All this pain will be used for good because I love You. Once You have brought me through this, maybe, just maybe, there is someone else I can help find his or her way out of the darkness that the enemy pulls us into, using whatever means necessary to steal, kill, and destroy our lives. Sadly, I think I'm finally realizing those things can even come through a brother that I love. I hate leaving my life behind, and the people I care about, but my true life may lie further down the road in New Mexico.

6

After a couple weeks, most things had been put away, or gotten rid of. Vic seemed to calm a bit, and I had high hopes that the storm had passed. Yes, I was still the one listening and doing more of what he wanted in our relationship, but as long as I did, there was peace. I could live with that. I was good at it. Not rocking the boat, giving away my choices for the choices of another never seemed to bother me all that much. What did I care? I was pretty much happy with whatever was going on. Or, was I?

"Where are you, Vic?" I said out loud to no one but me and God. It was Friday night, and I arrived home from work, ready to hang out. Vic and I talked about maybe going out to eat together. But now he was nowhere to be seen. I texted him. I got no answer. In fact, it looked like his phone was shut off. Where could he be? Oh, he'll be here soon, I thought, he's done this so many times before. But by nine, I gave up and went to my room. I couldn't get ahold of Vic, even though it looked like he started to receive my texts, he didn't answer. I felt bad. My stomach was in another knot. I wanted to spend time with Vic, but I never seemed to be a priority to him. Couldn't he be more considerate? He knew I was here waiting for him, didn't he? Those were the questions I would ask myself, and never really get any answers to. It just wasn't worth the fight. Vic would be home when he was ready.

I was up early the next morning, wanting to go on a run before getting some other things done. In the kitchen, while filling up a water bottle, Vic sauntered in...

"Mornin'," I said.

"Yeah. Okay," was all Vic muttered while getting some juice. "My head hurts."

"Why's that?" I didn't really want to know the answer, but it seemed right to at least ask.

"Too much fun last night," he answered.

"Oh, really?" I said, starting to feel sick inside. Didn't he know? Didn't he care?

"Yeah. Rob and I went over to the coast earlier in the day and ended up staying later than we thought. Found some people there to hang out with. Listened to some music. It was all good."

"All good, huh?" This wasn't feeling *good*. Did I matter at all to my brother?

"What's up for today. Want to do something?" Vic asked.

I made him wait a bit for a reply, but I couldn't stay quiet long. He would know something was up, and there again, dealing with that just wasn't worth it. Plus, I thought if I appeased him, maybe eventually I would matter to him. He would see that I'm a good guy, too. I didn't know it at the time, but my people-pleasing side was overruling logic. Vic wasn't going to change because I appeased him. I needed to change. I didn't know that back then, but God was trying to help me learn it. I was the one all this was making crazy. It didn't seem to be bothering Vic at all. Could it have been I was just a step he walked on to get to where he really wanted to go? Probably so.

"Uhh, I'm going on a run right now." I said. But I could feel myself backing down with my response to Vic that day.

"Well, that won't take a lot of time. In fact, why don't you just skip it and we can go to the hardware store and get some stuff to fix that piece of furniture in my room?"

"Well, I'm ready for my run and really would like to do that first," I answered, trying to stay strong. But I could feel myself cowering even more.

"I have to see Mandy later. I can only do it this morning, so let's do that now. I'm sure your run can wait."

Taking in a deep breath, while not letting Vic see it, I put my water bottle on the counter, and went to change my clothes. Another morning devoted to Vic. Why not, what else is new? I thought to myself. Why am I such a wimp?

"Okay, I'm ready to go!" I called out, looking around for Vic, and finding him on the back porch on the phone. He sort of nodded to me when I opened the door, like yeah, yeah, I'll be done in a sec. Forty-five minutes later, he was finished with his call. I so wanted to say something, but I didn't. I just got up and drove Vic to the store. He said his car wasn't working so well.

"This place never has what I need. Do you think these handles will work?" he asked me.

"Looks like it to me. If you like them," I answered, not wanting to add much more.

"I don't know. Let's ask a sales person if they have anything else that would work," Vic said, getting the attention of the guy at the end of the aisle. "Do you have any other handles? Your selection here is so small. Who does your buying? It's pretty despicable."

The salesperson looked at Vic, and then at me, probably wondering at the rudeness of my brother. "That's all we have there. Can I help you find something else that would work for you?"

"NO! I've looked, and I don't like any of it. We'll just go down the street to your competitor until you start getting some better things in here. You must have poor management here."

Before the guy could answer, Vic stomped out of the store, with me trailing slowly behind, giving my apologies to the sales guy—after all, it wasn't his fault. Why did Vic have to be so obnoxious to him?

"What took you so long?" Vic said, rocking back and forth by the passenger door of the car.

"Vic, that guy was doing the best he could. It's not his fault what kind of selection they have. He doesn't do the buying. Don't be so hard on the guy."

"Me? Hard? He wasn't even doing his job. He didn't come over to help us when he saw us in the first place. I had to track him down. I should have reported him to the manager! What a jerk! I should have gotten his name and had him written up."

"WHAT? Oh, come on, Vic..."

"Come on!?! You always side with the other person. Why can't you ever support me in what I say? It's seems like to you I'm always in the wrong, and the other person is always right. I get so tired of it, TL! You make me crazy!"

My choice at that point was to either let it all blow up, or blow over. Of course, I chose the latter. Trying to get Vic to agree on most anything was nearly impossible. There was Vic's way, or the highway.

7

It's intriguing thinking back on that part of living with Vic as I drive speedily down this highway. I'm making my choice, and I'm happy with it. The highway it is! And it's looking darn good to me right now. I've got my own music playing, and the open road ahead of me. What I left behind is a sad state of a person.

Pulling into a huge cattle ranch and restaurant beside the freeway, I'm ready for a good cut of prime rib. I remember being here years ago, and it was the most tender prime rib I'd ever eaten. Taking a seat, I order what looks good, and pull out my phone for more research. There's a lot more to learn, and I've got plenty of time to do it now. With Vic in my rearview mirror, maybe I'll be able to see what's ahead without it being over-shadowed with his selfish, self-centered self. There! I like saying that! It feels good! It's all about self with Vic. It's high time I realize that! If Vic's never going to change, no matter how nice I can be to him, then I'm the one that needs to move on and find a new way of being in this world. I've never met anyone quite like Vic. Oh, uh, "That's not true," I hear in my head, "What about Carl?" Oh. Carl. Was I missing something there, too? I ask myself. God, are You "pinging" me?

Taking the first bite of prime rib, I'm reminded of just how delicious it is here. The smell may be terrible while driving by all the cows, but it's well worth it when they raise beef to be this tender. As I chew, I think back on Carl, my buddy from night school. He was such a social guy, and he seemed so pleasant to everyone. I was drawn to him the minute I met him. He and I started spending a lot of time together. He was fun, and he seemed well-liked. Looking back now, I can see the progression...downward. It dawns on me why we're not friends anymore. Oh, he was fun and helpful to all on the outside, but when we hung out, just the two of us, that's when things got harder. I remember Carl dating this girl, Kate. Their relationship didn't progress well either. And he was so wrapped up in her, that nothing else mattered once they met, not even our friendship. I tried to be supportive, and listen, listen, listen. Those were the only times we spent together then, when he had a problem. Otherwise, he was with Kate, although he was miserable. I was ignored, forgotten, really not even thought about unless I reached out to him. Kate moved on, and so did Carl. I didn't hear from him for years at a time—not until I would give him a call. The conversation was usually good, and we would agree to talk again soon. He'd tell me he felt bad about not getting ahold of me, and I would believe him. But future calls didn't happen, unless I called him. I wondered why I kept at it? I eventually stopped, and I haven't heard from him since. Was it really even a friendship? Or just a draining of my energy when we did talk, so he could keep going in his life? Maybe this is exactly what God wants me to learn about in this new season without Vic? Thanks for reminding me of Carl, God. I'm gonna order some desert and see what I can find out about all this. I'm in no hurry, as long as they don't need their table here. Maybe I'll make it to the Grapevine tonight and stay there.

This cake tastes delicious—now, what can I find? What's this about a wolf in sheep's clothing? This is sounding sort of like Carl. He appeared so nice in the beginning, and really played the role well. I think he played me, too. Why has it taken me until now to clue into these things? This is like opening a can of worms. God, is this what this move to New Mexico is all about? I think I need to look back on a lot of my relationships and see what was happening, starting as a child. It's good I'm stopping in to see Mom and Dad before heading east. Maybe living with Vic wasn't such a bad thing? It might be the very thing that's waking me up to what's actually gone on for years—not only with Vic, but with other members of my family, and even some of my friends. Even in talking with Mom, I've still been so blinded. In the midst of things, maybe it's harder to see what's happening...to see the lack of empathy from others I've spent time with. Or maybe the hardest thing is to make a change, so the abuse will stop? That's probably a big part of it.

There's so much information here, where do I go now? I'll look for what sounds like Vic and me. Oh, here's something talking about how to get rid of a narcissist in your life. Hmm... It's talking about limited or no contact. So, I guess what I'm doing is in line with that? I've tried to spend time with Vic, doing it his way. Maybe his way is sick? That's probably what's making me sick. It's contagious! I almost laugh out loud to myself, although it's not funny. It says here that it can be confusing. Realizing how confused a narcissist can make you is important. I sure feel like I'm crazy when I'm around Vic. He seems to know what's what and doesn't hesitate to tell me. But don't I have a right to say what I think and feel? Not with Vic, obviously. What else does it say here?

I'm a victim of a battle in a war? Interesting. It did seem like there were landmines everywhere I stepped with Vic. Hence, the egg-shell walking. I had to know where I was stepping at all times, and veer far away from anything that would cause an explosion. There was that time when Vic was planning a party at our place. I don't even know how he got people to come, his friends were dwindling, especially after separating from Mandy. Some only put up with him because they liked her, I suspect. But it was his birthday, and he wanted a party, so he planned one. About three guys were coming over to play poker. It wasn't a good night as Vic sat at the table talking non-stop about whatever seemed to fly into his head and out of his mouth. The beer was flowing, too, and that didn't help as the evening got late. It's like he couldn't see anyone else in the room but himself and how important all his stories were. I was so uncomfortable. But I kept quiet, too. Why doesn't someone speak up? Why do we let the narcissist have so much control? Fear? Certainly, some from me, I'm realizing.

Reading on, this says to stop rejecting myself, that maybe I fear rejection because I reject myself. What? I've spent so much time focusing on Vic, but I need to focus on me? That seems so wrong, God. Shouldn't we be focused on others? I don't know how this lines up with Your Word? I hope to get more time in New Mexico to read my Bible. I need to make it a priority. That makes me laugh...am I a narcissist with God? Is it always about me and my problems, and not enough about God and His goodness and blessings? I need to work on that, too. Boy, I have a lot to do in New Mexico, and I haven't even arrived yet.

With the cake gone, I know I better get up and move to a different place for more research. I think I'll sit on this couch here in the lobby for a while. There's a bit too much cow smell to sit out of doors. Must be the way the wind is blowing today. It's good to not be in any sort of hurry. What a concept! Not rushing around like it talks about in Psalm 39, "All our busy rushing ends in nothing." I want this trip to New Mexico to end in something. Interesting, that I'm headed toward "New" Mexico. God, You're fun, as You renew my mind. Maybe that's why You left me some family there to meet up with during this season of my life? It doesn't feel like I've been walking in my real identity for most of my life, from what I'm reading. Who am I? What is important to me? I want You to be important to me. I know my relationships are important to me. Are my likes and dislikes important? It doesn't seem like they rate high on the scale. Uh oh, this one is interesting...it talks about our families. Wow. It says that when we grow up in our family environment, we are so used to how it is we don't even think about it. If there was narcissism in the home, it feels normal to us. I know it wasn't all roses and candy. I remember silent treatments being given by my dad. I remember conditional love, especially from him, now that I think about it.

This says narcissists target people who can be made to feel a certain way. Wow! That's me! And it's Mom, too. She knows that better than I do now. She's learned a lot about this part, saying we need to separate thoughts from feelings. I'd never heard of such a thing. I think I've mixed them up my whole life. Instead of thinking, am I feeling? I know when I get hurt by someone, I try to dismiss it. I've actually done quite well at forgetting about the harmful actions of others. That doesn't seem healthy to me now, as I sit here. Isn't that what I've done with Vic for years? He was the bully brother. Was I his punching bag? And I didn't even say "Ouch!" when he "hit" me. That's crazy! I should have spoken up for myself and told him to stop, that he was being mean. But instead I stuffed my feelings and didn't think about it long. I just wanted it to pass by unnoticed, so we could be "friends." This says that people like Vic don't mess with people who can basically defend themselves. They recognize there's a strength in that person, and they go on and find a more willing, weak, victim to abuse. It says if I'm unwilling to put a distance between myself and my abuser, I am too deeply enmeshed with them. What does that word mean?

*Clicking on the word "enmeshment," I read the definition in Wikipedia. "**Enmeshment** is a concept introduced by Salvador Minuchin to describe families where personal boundaries are diffused, sub-systems undifferentiated, and over-concern for others leads to a loss of autonomous development."*

That's a lot to take in, and I'm not sure I understand it all. I better break that down. Personal boundaries are diffused. That seems clear enough, sort of intermingled, not knowing where one stops, and another begins. There again, who am I and what do I want and like? Yes, I can see that getting swallowed up in a home as a child. Just do what you're told, and don't ask questions. That old, the child is to be "seen and not heard." So totally different from today's generation. I think we've gone too far the other direction, but a healthy balance between the two seems to be needed here. And now this sub-systems thing, how our families function, perhaps, and not separating thoughts and feelings in all of that? I definitely see the over-concern for others leading to a loss of who I am.

Looking up, I see a flock of birds flying overhead outside the window in a V-shaped pattern. Oh, Your timing is so good, God. Look how they all follow in line behind the lead bird. They know their place, as I knew mine with Vic. As long as I stayed in that "lane" I could make that world work. But it needed to stop. How did I know? Probably because when I even attempted to disagree with him while I was with him, he went bonkers! I need to be the bird that breaks away from the family of birds for a while and finds a better way with You God. When birds are injured, they do that, and another bird flies with them for a while. Maybe my cousin, Bobby, will do that with me in New Mexico? Flying in formation works perfectly for birds when they are healthy, but they know when to rest. Being created in

Your image, God, You have provided ways for us to rest and heal. You are to be the One in control, not a family member, not a friend, not a co-worker. You, and You alone. That is the newness I long to walk in, or drive in, I should say. Speaking of which, I think I'll drive on down the road.

Shutting down my phone and getting into the car, I know I have a long way to go, both to get to New Mexico, and to get to the bottom of it all. Is it really possible to find a new way of being at any stage of life? I believe so. God is never done with us until our time on earth is done, and even then, maybe the newness continues on in Heaven? This is a scary journey because I don't know what I will find at the end. But I am willing, Lord, to travel it with You.

8

What do you mean you're not going to work today?

"I've got a bad cold," I said to Vic.

"Hmmph, okay. Well, I'm going out for a while." Vic said, as he turned to go, with no offer of a glass of water, or even a bowl of cereal being brought to me.

As I laid in bed that day, I didn't feel good. Not only the cold, but my relationship with Vic. I couldn't understand my brother. Why was he so thoughtless? And yet, he could be nice...sometimes. There was that day he brought home a new TV. I knew he didn't have the money on his unemployment, but it seemed like he wanted to be a good guy for once. We set it up together and enjoyed a movie that night. He even offered to make us some dinner. That's the brother I wanted to do life with. Sadly, he was soon back at it...and even worse. He had a plan to use me all along.

"Hey, TL, I need a ride to Monterey on Saturday. You know my car isn't super reliable. My favorite band is giving a concert, and I don't have a way to get there other than you."

"Vic, I have plans for Saturday," I responded, knowing I was stepping on an egg shell.

"Plans? What plans? You didn't say anything about that!"

Knowing I was pushing it, I was trying to stand firm when I answered, "Vic, we're two grown men here. We don't have to check with each other with everything we do. I want..." That was the end of anything I was able to say in the moment.

"You gotta be kidding me!" Vic yelled, and his eyes looked like fire might shoot out of them at any moment. "We live here together. You think you are so important that you can just hide stuff from me! I can't believe you would be so selfish! I don't want to talk about this anymore!"

I sat there looking at Vic, knowing the fight wasn't worth it. I could cancel my plans, do them another day. I didn't say anything at first, because I couldn't. Vic stomped out of the house, and I didn't see him for a few hours. I sat at home, worried, anxious, and feeling trapped. If I stood up to him, I paid the price. If I bowed to him, I paid the price. I had nowhere to go with Vic. He was in control.

When Vic eventually came home and wasn't speaking a word to me, it was my "job" to make peace. That's what I thought. It was the only way I knew to be. It seemed I would do anything to please him, when all he was doing was stepping over me to please himself. Why couldn't I just tell him no? I was the one going crazy, and he didn't seem to care about me at all. I couldn't turn my feelings off for my brother, but he couldn't turn his on. But I relented, once again, hoping it would make him happy.

"Vic, look, I cancelled my plans on Saturday. What time do you need to be in Monterey?"

"By three," Vic said, barely looking up from the book he was reading.

"Okay. I'll take you." I said, upset with myself and Vic.

"I want to leave by one." No apology, no thank you, just a command. "Did you get your wash out of the machine. I need to do some laundry this afternoon," he said.

"Yeah. It's out." I didn't want to talk with Vic, so I headed toward my room as he called out, "You didn't finish off the chicken, did you?"

"No, Vic. It's there." Why did I feel like a whooped puppy? Maybe because I was.

I gave Vic the silent treatment for the rest of the day, but he didn't seem to notice. He didn't seem to care about anything but his music. So much for the new TV and watching it together. It would stay off, that I knew, until Vic was ready to turn it back on. He was in control of that, too. No wonder we call the remote the "controls." They were in power, just as Vic was.

Saturday came much too soon, as far as I was concerned. Vic was busy around the house getting ready. I was trying to stay clear of him. I liked the band he was seeing, but there weren't any tickets to be had. He hadn't gotten one for me. He hadn't even asked. He was going by himself, for all I knew. I didn't want to ask that either. If he was going with a buddy, it would only make me feel worse. I decided to make the best of the day and go to the beach. I needed to be alone. Vic was busy, and I could relax.

The waves were good, so I enjoyed watching the surfers after dropping Vic off. I would have liked to have gotten out there and joined them, but I'd only surfed a few times when I was younger. I knew I'd make a fool of myself even trying now. Later in the day, I made my way over to Canary Row, and enjoyed some good eats there. It turned out to be a decent day, and my resentment toward Vic mellowed. I remember thinking, oh well, he wanted to see this band, and I don't really mind giving him a ride here. What I had to do wasn't all that important. He probably just doesn't realize what he's doing. He gets a little absorbed in himself, but he doesn't mean it. There are times he can be a decent guy. I need to focus on those times. That's how it usually played out in my mind.

By the time I got the call to go pick up Vic, I was in a good mood, and all was forgiven. He came out of the concert a bit drunk, but in a seemingly happy mood. We had a good drive back home, and he fell into bed satisfied with his day. I decided to do the same. I remember thinking, why make this bigger than it needs to be? Vic's not giving it a second thought, why should I?

9

"Hi, Tara!" The door swung open revealing my high school friend.
"Tracy Lynn! So good to see you! Come on in. Would you like something to drink? I didn't expect you this early, but it's nice to see you whatever time."

"Yeah, well, I'm not really on a schedule, and when I remembered you lived in Bakersfield, I decided I could cut over this way and see you."

"I'm glad you did!"

"How about we go out and get some ice cream somewhere?"

Tara was quick to agree, and before long, we were seated and digging into a large banana split.

"I haven't had one of these in so long. Thanks for sharing it with me, I couldn't eat this whole thing," Tara said this with a big smile and a large portion of vanilla ice cream with caramel sauce piled on her spoon.

"I haven't either. How are things with you? Do you like living in this area?"

"It's okay. Bakersfield is not exactly where most people want to end up. But the people are nice, and the price is right. How about you? What are you up to? What brings you by here?"

"Oh, I'm on my way to New Mexico. A big move for me. I was living with my brother, Vic, in the Bay Area. He and I moved in together about a year ago. My job was a little shaky, and so was his marriage. I'm beginning to understand why."

"You mean with your job? Or Vic's marriage?"

"Vic's marriage. He's not an easy guy to live with. You've been married, Tara, and I'm sorry to hear about your divorce. Do you mind me asking what happened?"

Tara sort of mixed together some chocolate and caramel while delaying her answer... *"I don't mean to pry if you don't want to talk about*

32

it."

"*It's not that. Well, maybe it is. Liam was abusive, TL, verbally and emotionally in the beginning, and eventually physically abusive. It's not something I'm proud of. I saw red flags early on in the marriage. Sadly, I didn't see them while we were dating. He seemed to be the greatest guy ever. Attentive. Loving. Encouraging. He was always faithful, remembered to treat me well on my birthday and at Christmas. He even impressed my family with his generosity. But then, it was like once I had the ring on my finger, he changed. I've never known anything like it. I've been doing some looking into it on my own, and I've had some counseling, too. Turns out, I'm not the only one to experience something like this. He was what my therapist calls a Covert Narcissist.*"

"*Oh man!*" Setting my spoon down and leaning on the table, I shake my head. "*I can't believe what you just said. I'd never really paid much attention to that word before this last year or so, but it seems I should have.*"

"*What word?*"

"*Narcissist. I've been dealing with the same thing in my brother. A lady at work mentioned it to me when I told her about Vic. She said I should research it. I've been looking into it. It seems like all arrows are pointing to my brother, and even my dad. It's some tough stuff to live with. I'm sorry it happened to you, too.*"

"*Yeah. It's a sneaky business, I guess. I mean some are way out there— much more recognizable like the overt ones. But with the covert, it's just like it sounds. You don't know it's coming until it hits you. Sadly, it hit me. I was living a horror story. And I mean, it changed instantly. We had just gotten married and were on our way to our honeymoon. He told me he just wanted to stop off at the place we rented. When we got there, he said, 'There's a surprise in the bathroom for you.' I was excited. I thought it was some sort of wedding present. It wasn't. I hate to say what it was.*"

"*You don't have to tell me if you don't want to.*"

"*I think the more I talk about it, the better it will be. I went into the bathroom, and there taped above the toilet was a letter from an ex-boyfriend. I didn't even know what to think about it. He came up behind me and glared at me in the strangest way. Then we hung around for a bit, and I was changing my clothes, getting ready to leave. I had on a white slip, not revealing, but his friend stopped by. They were sitting and talking in the living room, and he had me come and sit on his lap. I felt uncomfortable, but it was almost like he was showing off his prized possession. It was weird.*"

"*Oh, Tara, that's a sick person. I'm so sorry.*"

"*I'm the one who's sorry. I stuck around far too long. He got meaner and meaner, almost killing me twice, literally. But here's the strange thing, I loved him. And when the times were good, they were really good. I just never knew when it was going to flip to bad. And when it did, they were really bad. Thankfully, we never had children together. I don't know what kind of a dad he wouldn't have been."*

"How did you get away?"

"It wasn't easy. I had a friend who was encouraging me and helping me in other ways. But I would leave, and then he'd coerce me to come back. He was so sweet on the phone. I couldn't resist him. I would go back, time and time again. Finally, I guess I'd had enough, and stopped believing his lies. I'm still healing from it all, and it's been three years. And here's the sick side of me, I have to be careful to not hook up with another guy just like him. It seems like I'm fly-paper to them. And it's not always them, it's me. That's why I've sought out counseling. There are broken things in me that attract broken things in them. They can 'smell' that I'm what they're looking for, it seems. Almost like I put off a scent of being an easy mark. I don't know. I'm still learning."

"Wow. I know why I stopped in here to see you. God seems to want me to get the message that I need to get far away from Vic, and not look back until he's ready to change."

"Don't hold your breath, TL! They can promise to change, but it's a lie. I wouldn't believe a word of what Vic says without at least a year of steady improvement and work on his part. They can lovebomb you. That's a word I've learned. And then turn mean again very quickly. They have tactics we aren't even aware of. I don't know if they even are."

"You mean they don't know they're doing it?"

"I guess some do, but some don't. They've been that way so long, it's all they know. And they go from person to person, finding anyone who they can feed off, until their victim wises up and says enough. Some never do. I know people who have endured these relationships their whole life, until the day they die. Then the narcissist finds a new 'supply' to satisfy their needs."

"Interesting, Tara. I finally cried out to God, 'When will it stop?' It seemed He quickly answered, 'When you do.'"

"It makes sense. I had to stop, too. It didn't appear Liam was at all interested in changing his ways."

"Let's finish up our ice cream, and I'll drive you back home. Would you mind if I crashed on your couch for the night? I was going to try and make it to the Grapevine tonight, but it's getting late."

"I'd love to have you stay! Absolutely!"

"Thanks. There's more I think we need to talk about."

"I agree."

After talking late into the evening, Tara has gone to bed. My thoughts began to wander as the hours tick by. This couch isn't super comfortable, but at least it's a place to lay my head. And it's good to spend time with an old friend. I wonder what Vic is doing. Is he sorry? Looking at my phone, there are a few new texts from him. They are slowing down. Reading through them is so bothersome, but maybe I need to.

Scrolling up, I see one from about noon. "You're being so selfish. Only thinking about yourself." Then the next one, "You need help, Bro!" I need help? Vic writes, "If you hadn't been so weird about everything." On and on, until he must realize I'm not going to say anything back.

Since I'm awake, I might as well look up a few things. See if I can make some sense of this nonsense. That's the perfect word for all this because it's without sense. It seems there was nothing I could do right.

10

Mandy stopped by one Sunday afternoon. Vic was out. I wasn't sure where. I hadn't talked with her for quite a while. I'd try to stay out of the way when the two of them were discussing things. Answering the door, and inviting her in, led to some interesting discussion.

"Have a seat, Mandy. Want anything to drink?" I asked.

"Oh. Thanks. No. I don't need anything. I thought Vic was going to be here. Do you know where he is?"

"I don't. Did you try calling him?"

"I did. Seems like his phone is shut off," Mandy answered, shaking her head in frustration.

"Yeah. He's known to do that," I said.

"Mandy, can I talk to you about some things? If they're not too private. I'm having some troubles with Vic, and I haven't lived with him for a long time...not since we were younger. I guess I expected him to grow up and out of whatever it was that made our getting along so difficult when we were kids."

"Sure. I'm not opposed to that. Vic wouldn't like it. But I'm really not too concerned about that any more. His times of making my life miserable are ending."

"It was really that bad, huh?" I asked.

"Bad? Let's just say it got to the point where it was tortuous. Oh, I wanted to make it work. I wanted to make some sense out of our relationship. Vic has some really good qualities, and I tried hard to hold onto those things...those moments. But in between, I thought sometimes that I would lose my mind."

"In what way?" I asked.

"His control. He was, I don't know, obsessive about things being his way. He couldn't even hear me, it seemed...or even cared to."

"I sort of get what you're saying," I replied. "Can you give me an example. I'm trying to put my finger on what's going on here, between us, now. It seems elusive at times."

"It is elusive. You try to put a finger on it, as you say, but it seems to slip away before you're there. There's so much manipulation involved, and control issues. One time, Vic and I were going bowling and I was happy to spend the time with him. In the beginning, he seemed happy, too. But I got more uncomfortable the longer we bowled. I couldn't do anything right. I walked wrong. I held the ball wrong. I kept score wrong. I just wanted to have a good time. He wanted to be in control. That's no fun for me."

"True. He definitely likes to have things his way," I agreed.

"And that same day, we were meeting friends for dinner. He talked non-stop at dinner. No one else could get a word in. And it was all so negative. Everything that was wrong with the world, his life, his job, even our marriage at one point. I know it was making our friends uncomfortable as he complained about the way I made the bed, how I cooked, what career I had chosen. He even tried to control the way I ate. They didn't say anything. But I know they were anxious to get the evening over with, and so was I."

"Was Vic always like this? Since you met him?"

"Well, I guess he was. But I didn't say anything. I just let him be who he was. There were good times in there, too," she said.

"Do we dismiss the junk by hanging onto the good stuff, ya think?"

Mandy answered, "I think we do. Maybe because the fight isn't worth it...with the anger, and the silent treatment and all. They are like a Dr. Jekyll and Mr. Hyde. I tried to pretend I was living with one, and not the other, just to survive."

I interjected, "But I keep hoping things will get better. If I just keep in line with Vic, we can sort this out."

"Oh, I thought that for years," Mandy said. "And then, I'd had enough. I know divorce isn't right. I mean, I'm not a super religious person, but my parents did take me to church when I was growing up. I believe in God, and I know I don't follow Him closely enough. Maybe if I did, He could have saved my marriage. I don't know."

"I don't know either, sorry to say. I've found myself trying to read my Bible, but it was easier before living with Vic. Even though I am more desperate for it now because of him, I'm also distracted. I know the *only* way I can refill is by reading my Bible and praying. But I wish I didn't struggle so much. I wish it was more automatic."

"Yeah," said Mandy, "I would like to think that if there is a God, He can heal my heart from the damage Vic caused."

"From what I know of God, He can heal most anything. Even Vic could be healed, right?" I asked, not really sure of the answer. "But it's a choice we make, don't you think? Maybe Vic doesn't even realize he needs help? Maybe he does, and he doesn't want to change?"

"Well, my free choice was to say 'enough' about Vic and move on. I mean, I'm still coming around and trying to see if things can be mended. But I have to tell you, the more time I spend away from him, the better I feel, TL. I'm sorry for that. But if he's not willing to change, then I have to change what I do. I don't want a divorce, but it seems that's the way we are headed. I don't think he's all that interested in mending things, other than bleeding me dry emotionally when I'm around him. That's probably the only reason he would want me back. And for all I know, he's already got someone that he's spending time with. My counselor said that's a normal pattern for people like Vic—even though he may want to be done with me, he won't let go of me until he has someone else in line that he can use. It's sick."

"It is. It's strange to think about it...that my brother is like this. I wonder where it started? Perhaps with my dad? And where did my dad's tendencies begin? Is it passed through the generations? Do I have it, too? Or did I somehow escape it?"

"I'm no expert, but I'm sure if we asked them, those that are better educated could give us some idea," Mandy answered. "I know I'm part of the problem. When I would try to leave, foolishly, I would always open the door for him to come back when he beckoned me. A counselor told me that it makes him feel powerful, when I take him back. It means he sort of has a god-like status. He knows I'm waiting for him, while he's out having a great time with someone else. He knew there was always an open door for him. But, no more. If he and I can't work this out in a new way, then these talks with him about getting back together are going to finally come to an end. I mean look, he knew I was coming here today, and where is he? That's passive aggressive behavior if I've ever seen it. Funny thing is, I didn't see it before. Maybe it is God opening my eyes? I don't know. A good God would want us to love one another, wouldn't He? But Vic's not loving, and it started to make me sick, physically. That's not good."

"No, it's not," I replied, understanding how my own gut felt too often these days.

"Sometimes, TL, it feels impossible to get away from Vic. He's had that much control over me. My self-confidence got so low. I couldn't see anything but him, being with him, and being controlled by him. Slowly, but surely, he was cutting me off from everyone else I know. If this doesn't get better, even separated, I'm going to have to have nothing to do with him at all. And I wonder who that will make crazier? Him or me? Probably me! He will probably just move on to someone new."

"Maybe he's moving on to me," I said. "It seems that with you not living with him anymore, I get the wrath a lot of the time."

"Oh, I'm sorry, TL."

"NO, no, don't be sorry. I need to be talking with you today about this because I need to learn what you are learning. I don't care if he is my brother. The Bible says, 'Who is my mother? Who is my brother? It's those that believe and follow the Word of God.' Jesus said that. Maybe God was trying to tell me something about how loyalty to a brother works? Those in the family of God are true family. I read that those who don't believe in Jesus can't call His Father their Father. Their true father is the devil. That's bold! Jesus isn't even trying to be PC there!"

"Well, I don't know where that leaves me. Like I said, I've got some religion in my background. Maybe you're saying that to wake me up?" Mandy was gazing off while saying this...and shaking her head.

"Maybe. I don't know. And what if people who act like Vic are demonized?" I replied. "I don't know about this whole possession or oppression thing, but maybe Vic has a demon that's controlling him, and through him that demon is controlling those in a relationship with him? And trying to destroy us?"

"That's an interesting and scary thought. I hadn't put those pieces into the puzzle." Mandy said, looking at me again. "Satan is a bad boy, isn't he? And what if he's who makes Vic a bad boy? I'll have to think about that."

"WHAT'S GOING ON HERE!?" Vic practically yelled as he suddenly came through the front door and saw us both sitting there, talking."

11

Even though the night is getting late here at Tara's, this is some fascinating stuff on narcissism I'm finding—how a man can be comfortable detouring the life of another. It makes me think about how a train is derailed. It seems to be moving smoothly along a set of tracks, but something on the track ahead can cause so much damage. What has brought me here tonight, Lord? What is it You would have me learn? Has the enemy really been trying to derail my life? Is Satan trying to steal what has been planted deep in my heart? Your light? Does Satan really work through people who are willing to be used as his instrument of destruction?

Reading further, I know I don't want to be the prey of another. I once heard, "Pray or be Prey." I choose to pray tonight, Lord, and seek Your help. It seems Tara has seen some dark days. It seems this whole narcissism thing is more wide-spread than I would ever have guessed. How many lives are being ruined or tormented, and it's not even being identified so much of the time. If people, if I, can't put a name to it, how can we call it out of the dark? I'm thinking we need Your help bigtime here, God.

Wow! What I'm seeing here in 2 Corinthians 6:17, "'...come out from among unbelievers, and separate yourselves from them,' says the Lord." Maybe it's really okay that I have pulled away from Vic? At least for now, until he is willing to stop the infliction of so much emotional pain in my life. It asks here on this site about the possibility of converting a wicked man? Of course, there's always hope in Jesus. That's why Jesus came to this earth, to die for our sins, to set us free. But we have to choose that, don't we, Lord? Otherwise, should we partner with those who are destroying us?

Oh man, I'm getting so sleepy, I don't have to rush this....

--*-*-*

"*TL?*"

Opening my eyes, I see that the sun has come up, and Tara is probably wondering why I am lying here still fully clothed with my iPad on my chest.

"*Oh. Good morning, Tara. Sorry, I fell asleep last night doing some research. I hope I didn't bother you?*"

"*No. Of course not. I hope you slept okay on that couch. It's not the most comfortable.*"

"*Well, it must have worked for me because once I shut my eyes, I didn't open them until just now.*"

"*Would you like some coffee. I can get some going?*"

"*Sure.*" *Pulling myself up to a sitting position.* "*How much do you know about the Bible, Tara?*"

"*Not a whole lot. I'm not opposed to it. But I've never really studied it like I saw my grandma doing.*"

"*I was seeing some interesting things last night. Mind if I run some stuff by you?*"

"*Not at all.*" *Tara took a seat nearby.*

"*It says here in John 8:32, 'And you will know the truth, and the truth will set you free.' I so wanted to be set free from all that Vic was doing, but confrontation is so difficult for me. Being around someone like Vic, I knew confronting him would only lead to chaos. It never seemed worth it. I just wanted to live in peace, so I would walk the straight and narrow to be able to at least have a façade of peace. I'm starting to see how confrontational Jesus was. Maybe it isn't wrong to call things as they are. Jesus told the people who believed in Him that they were His true Disciples.*

"*Jesus doesn't pull punches?*" *Tara asks.*

"*No, He doesn't. When I read this, Tara, it makes me want to pray, 'Make me bold like You, Jesus.' But it's so hard for me. Why? Probably because of what it says here. It says, 'At that point they picked up stones to throw at him. But Jesus was hidden from them and left the Temple.' Vic would do the same. He picks up verbal stones and throws them at me. And I would probably take the brunt of them, believing some of the lies he was spewing at me. That's who I was.*"

"*But it's not who you are now, TL. Did you see what it said there?*"

"*What?*"

"*They picked up stones to throw at him. At the very end, it says He 'left the Temple.' That's what you did. You left, Vic. You got away. If it's good enough for Jesus, it should be good enough for you.*"

"*Oh, man. I didn't notice that before. Thanks for pointing that out. Confrontation is not my strong suit. But I can learn. If Vic isn't willing to change, I am willing to leave."*

"Good for you! That's what I had to do with Liam. I loved him. You love Vic. But it doesn't mean we have to stay there and take their abuse!"

"I'm so glad I stopped in to see you. You are helping me process some new things. Thanks, Tara."

"It's always good to see you, TL."

12

As Vic flew through the door and dropped his coat on the couch next to Mandy, he was boiling mad. "I go out for a bit and come home to find my wife here all cozied up with my brother!?"

"VIC. Come on. Mandy came by to see you and you weren't here. Don't..."

"DON'T BE TELLING me anything I already know," Vic was yelling now. "I see how you two are conspiring against me!"

"You have no..." Mandy tried to say before Vic laid into her.

"MANDY, don't try to defend yourself. I know you've probably been cheating on me for years. And probably with my brother here."

"Stop it, Vic!" Mandy responded sharply.

"Stop it? You stop it! I wanted to have you come over today so we could talk, and now it seems there is no need," Vic said, storming out of the room.

Mandy looked at me and shook her head, whispering, "This is a lose-lose situation. I've been here too many times before. There is no reasoning with him when he gets like this. I think I'm just gonna go."

As Mandy got up to leave, Vic suddenly reappeared. Seeing that he was about to lose one of his punching bags, he took a seat over in the corner chair. "Where do you think you're going? I thought we were going to talk today?"

"Vic, you're in no mood, and neither am I. I think we should save this for another time."

"I've got the time now!" Vic said sternly.

Taking in a deep breath, Mandy stood her ground and told Vic she'd be back another day. As the door closed behind her, I knew there was only one place I wanted to be, and that was anywhere where Vic wasn't. I started to get up and go to my room. But I was trapped, or so it seemed at the time. Vic started in talking to me, and I just couldn't walk away. He may be rude, but I just couldn't be. I wished I could have been as strong as Mandy. She had learned.

"That Mandy," Vic said. "She always gets so upset when I'm just a little bit late. And she's always late to everything. Seems like all I've done is wait for her in different places through the years. I finally feel like I've found someone who will be there when I need them."

I looked over at Vic. I shouldn't have been shocked, but I was. Mandy was right, he was seeing someone else. "You what?" was all I managed to say in the moment.

Vic looked at me in disgust. "Why not? There are people in this world who appreciate me. Mandy never did."

"Bro, you are messing up any chance you may have of getting back with Mandy."

"Mandy has nothing I want. I don't think I want her coming over here anymore. She's a screwup. Always thinking we'll get back together, when really there's no chance for that. I've tried, man, but she just doesn't have it going on. Lydia is something different."

"Lydia, huh? You think someone else is gonna be able to make you happier?" I asked.

"Definitely. Lydia is helping me get on with my life. She tells me how strong I am, how smart. She sees my good qualities."

"Whatever, Vic. I really don't want to talk about this," I said, getting up and going to my room at that point. I heard the music turn on behind me. I knew Vic was already dismissing the whole conversation the minute I walked away. My heart went out to Mandy. My heart went out to me. We had only been sharing the house for two months, and it already seemed like two years.

13

It feels good to be back on the road. And Tara felt like a breath of fresh air. "Jesus left the Temple"...she encouraged me that sometimes leaving is the right thing to do. I appreciate that so much.

Dialing Mom, I hear her answer, "Hi, Tracy Lynn. How are you?"

"I'm good, Mom. I'll be at your place later today. I stopped to see a friend in Bakersfield. You remember Tara, right?"

"Oh, yes. She was such a sweet girl. Your dad will be out golfing in the afternoon. You know it's good for him at his age. To get out and walk. But he shouldn't be too late."

"That's fine. I'd kinda like to talk with you before he gets there anyway."

"Oh. Okay. I think that would be good," Mom agreed.

"Yeah. Kinda what we've talked about before, but in more depth. I've been learning some things."

"I understand. We'll talk. See you soon." Mom is sounding a bit tense.

"No worries, Mom. I'll see you soon. Bye."

"Bye."

Driving up the hill into Valencia, I see the familiar site of Magic Mountain. How many times did we go there as kids? I loved the big roller coaster, which now seems dwarfed compared to the new rides that have gone in.

Dad is difficult. I know I haven't given it enough thought...what Mom has put up with for so long. And the years haven't helped. Dad has gotten more cantankerous. Mom is always so gentle and kind. She softens, but he hardens. I think this time living with Vic, and my talks with Mom, have caused both of us to look into this more. We both are on a healing path.

Pulling in to get a burger and some fries, I sit a while and bring up more information. It's time I really dig deep about what a narcissistic parent might look like, and their effects on the children. Wow, this is almost funny. It talks about breaking the family trance. It says if I think things have changed, just go home for the holidays. Am I heading into a hornet's nest by stopping and seeing Dad and Mom this time? Now that my eyes are really being opened? Will things show up that I never paid much attention to before when I was with them? I should really take this time to brief myself on this before I get there. I want to go in more prepared!

It says we don't notice the trance until it's broken. I think mine is breaking as I drive south. I surely hope so. What kind of a trance have I been in? The parent's feelings become the child's reality, and that's part of the trance process. What does that really mean? It says, fear states, guilt states, what is normal or not, emotional patterns, the meaning of love, are all part of the trance. It's like a pig in a mud pen. They don't even notice it. It's not easy to see the mess we are in. We get stuck in patterns, wrong patterns. But how do we break it if we can't see it, I wonder? We have to take apart the family rules or beliefs. This says that some have to "de-self" in a family to make others happy. To not be who we really are. Wow, that sounds familiar. How many times have I done that with Vic? And how many times, now thinking back, did I do that with Dad? And I see Mom does it, too. I need to take a step back from them when I am there and see what's happening between them. There wasn't much peace in our home. Lots of arguing. But then it seemed as I got older, Mom got quieter to try and keep the peace. Dad didn't change much though, from what I saw.

I'm seeing here if I stand up for myself, it seems like it will hurt everyone. I guess that's true, we all pay when a narcissist's feathers are ruffled. I am really going to watch this time. It's like we don't see something until we know it's there, and then we see it EVERYWHERE! But I don't know if I'm looking forward to this visit now, or not. I do want to find out some information about our relatives in Las Cruces from Dad. I contacted Great-Aunt Martha there, Dad's aunt, and she suggested I stay with my cousin, Bobby. She gave me his contact info, and he was happy to hear from me. He always seemed like a nice guy. Even though he's Dad's cousin, he's only about ten years older than me, and we always got along well. It will be good to spend some time together until I find my own place there in New Mexico.

Back in the car, I think I should read some Scripture before arriving at my parents' house. I want to go in with the full armor of God on. I'm not one-hundred percent sure how that's done, but I would have to guess reading God's Word is a big part of it.

Second Timothy 3:17 looks interesting. People are "lovers of themselves." Well, Vic sure is. And now I'm thinking, maybe Dad is, too. That one site talked about people being influenced by demons, and not recognizing it. Mandy mentioned months ago that Vic seemed evil at times.

It says when in a battle with a narcissist, there can be an amused look in their eyes. The more upset they get others, the more satisfied they are. That's kinda scary to think about. We can so easily fall into the trap of getting upset, and then that's just what they want? It sounds like in second Timothy, that this will be even more prevalent in the end times. It's been two thousand years since Jesus walked on this earth. We must be getting close?

"Lord, I don't know what You have in store for me with this visit. I think I've been changing inside, no longer willing to just put up with verbal and emotional abuse. I don't know how this will look when I'm with Dad. Help me figure it out as I go. Sometimes he can be okay. Sometimes, not. Help me take a step back from my family and see things in a new way. If we have been wallowing in a mud pen, I ask You to wash me off with Your Living Water. Clear my eyes so I can see what's true and right. Help me be strong yet loving. I had to leave my brother behind. I'd really rather not have to do the same with my dad. But I will follow You through this. In Jesus' name. Amen."

Hours later, pulling up in the driveway, I can see Mom sitting in her chair through the front window. She heard my car...

"Hi, Mom!" Giving her a long hug, I can feel a tension that I maybe never paid attention to before. "Is Dad home yet?"

"He should be here in an hour or so. Come on in. Did you get something to eat?"

"I did. Had a burger on the road."

"I'm so glad you came to see us on your way to New Mexico. I'm sorry to hear things got so rough with your brother."

"Oh, Mom, it's nothing all that new. I'm just waking up to more of it. You know some of the stuff we have talked about since I moved in with Vic. I think it runs deeper than I've been fully aware of."

"I believe you're right. There are many layers... Come on in, you can put your bag in the guest room there. I cleared out some stuff. I wasn't sure how long you were staying. You know how an empty room can easily become a closet," Mom said.

"Yeah. I do. It's like if we don't keep a car in the garage, it will quickly fill up with everything and anything."

"Exactly!" Mom is quick to agree.

After taking a seat, Mom wasn't one to mince many words. "Tell me, is your brother doing okay? How are you now?"

"Health-wise, Vic's just fine, Mom. Don't worry about him. He's as strong as an ox. For me, it's the emotional turmoil that happens with him. I just couldn't be around him anymore. He sucked me back in big time even as late as this last Friday, and that was a mistake on my part. I should have listened to you months ago about all this."

"What all has happened since we last talked?"

"I'm fully waking up to some things, Mom. Living with Vic brought so much to the surface. I can see why Mandy can't be with him anymore."

"I'm so sad about their divorce situation. She is such a sweetheart," Mom replied.

"Yes. She's a nice gal. But Vic is hard to live with—for a wife or a brother."

"And a son," Mom added.

"You see it, too?" It seems in some ways I'm seeing Mom for the first time as I sit here with her, as an equal, someone who struggles with the same things I do.

"Oh, TL, I have for years. He so takes after your dad. I've done my best to try and see their goodness when it does peek through. It gets harder though."

"Tell me about it, Mom. Why have I been so blinded to it over and over again?"

"You're not blinded to it, TL, you're just very accepting. That's who you are. You don't like to make waves, you never have. I saw that when you and Vic were just young boys. But as we get older, those traits we are born with come out more and more. I can see it in your Dad's lineage. I saw it in his Aunt Martha. And in his Grandpa Bart. It's interesting to watch it weave its way through the generations."

"What is it, Mom? Does narcissism explain it? All of it?"

"Well, I've been researching that, like we talked about. But there's more to it... There's a co-dependency side, too. We have our part in this. Early on, I guess I just saw it as their pessimism or grumpiness. Let's just say they don't light up a room when they come in."

"Yeah. I get that. After a year with Vic, and watching what was happening with Mandy, and God knows who else, I've been looking into some things you and I talked about. Like I told you, a co-worker mentioned this narcissism thing some time back. It's hard to pinpoint, exactly. But I did learn that a jerk can be reasoned with. A narcissist cannot. It's more of a mental illness. Maybe you've been mainly looking at Dad and his relatives through the years as jerks, or 'not nice.' But if they really do fall into the spectrum of being narcissists, then that's something different."

"Now that we can talk in person, tell me what more you've learned, TL."

"I still have a ways to go, Mom. But in looking at some things about being married to a narcissist, I know these things will ring a bell with you. You've done so much research."

"Go ahead," Mom urged.

"Before any of your research started, how were your personal boundaries with Dad? Did you feel like you were intertwined with his life and his activities and had forgotten what's important to you? I'm just going to throw some stuff out here that I've made note of in my phone. You *can take it or leave it. Were you disrespected or ignored? Did you ever leave your thoughts and awareness behind? Were you harsh with yourself—blaming yourself for things that probably weren't your fault? Did you have chronic anxiety? Did you find yourself trying harder to keep the peace? Did you settle for crumbs? Did even just a little effort on Dad's part seem to go a long way with you? Did you fear confrontation? Should I stop here?"*

"That's a lot, and sadly, I do relate to a lot of it. Not all of it. Your dad has his own activities, like golf. I don't join him in that. But through the years, I see myself in a lot of what you're saying."

"Well, what I'm describing here is more the 'supply' for a narcissist."

"Right. I remember learning about being 'supply,'" Mom responded. "That's the codependency part."

"Yeah. Narcissists need a 'food' source, sort of like a bed bug. When we sleep, or maybe we could call it sleepwalking through these relationships, they suck the life/blood out of us. Leaving us wounded, and uncomfortable. I hadn't thought about it that way until just now, about the bed bug. But they are nasty little creatures that I don't have a clue why God would create!"

Mom laughed. "Yes, they are. And HARD to get rid of. I don't want to be the 'supply' in this, and I know you don't either. What course of actions have you found to take for yourself?"

"That's a very good question, and those are some of the answers I'm searching for as I drive toward New Mexico. I've found myself to be the 'supply' for Vic, and I had to get out of there before there wasn't anything left of me. He was eating me up alive! Now, I know you don't want to leave Dad, and that's not what I'm here to tell you. But if we can recognize these traits, maybe, just maybe, we can start to live with better boundaries."

"You can leave Vic behind. But you're right, I'm not leaving your dad. Not after all these years. I feel like I'm making some progress here with him, or at least with me. We talked about that. He's been a good husband in many ways. I'm finding there are changes I can make to help this situation. I'm learning about self-differentiation"

"What is that?"

"It's about separating your feelings and thoughts. I read that thoughts are everything from the neck up. Feelings are from the neck down. I guess when we get so involved in these relationships, we can't tell the difference after a while. I've also learned about the beast?"

"The beast?"

"Yes, TL. We are to stop feeding the beast. What we are doing, being their supply, is only making them stronger, and us weaker. We have to stop putting our heart out there for the narcissist to pound on. Sadly, they tend to want to harm. I don't know why. I guess it's the brokenness in them."

"Something has gone wrong..."

"Our trauma is real. Spouses of narcissists are known to be survivors, TL. We should spend time with healthier people and try to take care of ourselves. That's hard, to make it more about me. I've been giving it a try, and it feels strange. But I made a new friend recently, and she is a God-send. It is such a mutually caring relationship. I believe God is really trying to shed a light on the darkness so I can see it clearly. Sometimes we just get so used to the junk."

"I know. But I believe that's why we're having this discussion. We do know how Dad is, and how Vic is, and others that we know. And we aren't going to change them. But we can change us, with God's help. And sometimes, like with Vic, that means putting a lot of miles in between. I'm going out to New Mexico to recoup and see what God might have for me there. I don't know what the..."

"Hey there, TL! Good to see you!" Dad practically shouts as he comes through the front door. "How are you?" he asks, giving me a hug and a big pat on the back, but not waiting for a reply. "You're earlier than I thought. Evon, why didn't you tell me what time TL was getting here?"

Mom quickly answers, "I didn't expect him this early, I..."

"Well, you should have known, with the way TL drives. He's like a maniac on the road!"

"Dad, I..."

"Did your Mom get you something to eat? Evon, see if there's any of that cake left from last night. Get the boy a piece!"

"Dad, I don't need any, really."

"Nonsense!" Dad responds, looking at Mom, and giving her a wave of his hand toward the kitchen. Looking at me, Mom does as she is told. Obviously, we both still have a lot of work to do.

The rest of the afternoon went like that. Dad was in control through most of the conversation. By late evening, I was finally able to get into a discussion with Dad about our family in New Mexico.

14

I remember the first time I went to that church near our new place. I'd been wanting to try it. There were always loads of cars in the parking lot. I wasn't disappointed. I found a place toward the center and listened close as the pastor preached about many good things. And then I heard it, the verse that spoke directly to my heart. Looking back, I knew God was with me that morning in a way that I never had before.

"All of you, look at me," the pastor suddenly said, pointing to his eyes. "I have a word that someone needs to hear. It's in Proverbs 4, verses 14-15, 'Do not set foot on the path of the wicked or walk in the way of evildoers. Avoid it, do not travel on it; turn from it and go on your way.'"

That was probably the day I should have started planning my "escape." It seemed God was giving me the go ahead. I should have left the very next day. Sadly, I stayed another nine months or so. I don't know what took me so long to wise up. I guess all in God's timing.

When I got home from church, Vic was waiting for me. I had invited him to go with me. He said God was for people who felt weak, and he wasn't one of them. He told me to go ahead and get my fill of whatever it was they were dishing up there. But don't serve any of it here in this house.

"Hey, Vic," I said casually, as I walked through the living room where he sat listening to his music.

Vic glanced up at me and pushed pause on his music. I stopped, thinking he was going to say something. He didn't. So, I went on back to my room to get changed. Then I heard it, the blaring of a song so evil I couldn't believe even he would listen to it. The lyrics ranted about Satan and his powers, using the most vulgar words ever. What had gotten into my brother? I shut my door, but it didn't begin to keep the darkness out. I knew I needed to talk to Vic, tell him to turn it off. This was a confrontation I couldn't avoid.

Walking back into where Vic was, I looked him straight in the eye. What I saw was shocking! It seemed I was looking into the face of evil like I'd never experienced before. It didn't even look like my brother. Under my breath, I whispered, "Jesus. Jesus. Help."

"Vic, you gotta turn that down, or better yet, off," I practically had to yell.

"WHAT? I can't hear you!" Vic shouted back.

I walked over to the stereo and pushed the off button.

"WHAT DID YOU DO THAT FOR!" Vic was the one now yelling, and it wasn't because he needed to be heard above the music.

"Vic. I live here, too," I said. "I pay my half of everything, and I don't want where I live to be invaded by that."

"By what? I don't know what you're talking about."

With a loud sigh, and fear in my gut, I continued to tell Vic, "This isn't good for either one of us. These lyrics are...evil...and..."

"NO, THEY'RE NOT!" Vic interrupted. "You and your churchy, do-goodie ways. You think you know it all, and that I'm some bad guy, and you're just oh so holy!"

I waited. I knew, arguing right then would do no good. I stood silent, and let Vic rant a bit longer, hoping for a calming that could be talked through. It never came. When Vic was finished, he left the room, and left me standing there once again. I felt like such a failure. It seemed Vic always had the upper hand. But then again...the music was turned off. Maybe I hadn't lost this battle after all.

I felt so confused, and even though the message that morning had been good at church, it didn't seem to stick with me long. There was such a heaviness on me, and Vic's presence was disturbing. He left later that day to meet up with someone, somewhere. I didn't really care. I was just glad he was out of the house so I could have some peace on my own. Phoning Mom that afternoon, we began to really get serious about some previous discussions. It was time. She attended church that morning, also, and God had us on the same page. She said Dad was particularly difficult when she got home, too—she knew she was coming to the end of what she could endure. What I didn't know then, was that Mom's investigation into her own healing was so very helpful in me finding mine, also.

I remember telling her, "I can't take much more, Mom. I never should have moved in with Vic. He's just impossible!"

"TL, I understand," she said, tenderly. "There are things I've lived with through the years that I never wanted to burden others with. I still don't. But one thing I'm discovering is, that waiting it out hasn't changed a thing. I need to really look into who I am. Who did God design me to be? I don't want to miss all that He has for me. I've really been reading my Bible, and it's helping. I find my comfort and wisdom in God's Word when I can't find it anywhere else."

"I'm trying to do the same, Mom, but I can't seem to focus," I lamented. "Vic's presence in this house, and he's still looking for a job, is so overbearing. My shut bedroom door isn't nearly enough to shut him out."

"Keep on, TL," Mom encouraged. "Keep searching for God in all of this. I think you and I can learn a lot together. But we have a long way to go. I've put up with too much for too long. Something has to change. If not in my surroundings, then in myself. That's what I think I need to learn and apply to my life."

"Thanks, Mom," I said. "I'm glad I have you to talk to about these things. I'm not ready to move out yet. But I might just have to one day. I hope you will understand that I still love my brother if that should happen."

"Oh, TL, never worry about that. I know your heart. You have a very kind and giving personality. I've always seen that in you. You would never hurt your brother on purpose."

"Thanks, Mom. I hope to talk with you again soon. I gotta go now."

"Okay. Let's talk soon. Read your Bible. Sorry to be such a 'Mom,' but it's the best thing both of us can do."

I laughed, agreeing with Mom as I hung up the phone that day. She was always such a source of comfort to me.

At dinner that night, Vic and I pretty much ate in silence in front of the TV. That was fine with me. The less he talked, the easier it was for me. I didn't want to talk about Mandy, either. Knowing that he had Lydia in his life, there wasn't much I wanted to get into with him. I knew trying to talk him out of seeing her, and making things work with Mandy, wouldn't be happening. It was like talking to a brick wall. Maybe it was better for Mandy to just move on. Maybe God wasn't doing this so much to her, as He was doing it for her? Vic was being unfaithful. That was a deal breaker.

15

With Mom gone off to bed, I want to move the discussion to New Mexico.

"Dad, I'm really looking forward to learning more about our family in New Mexico. I'm so glad cousin Bobby has agreed to let me stay with him a while."

"You better find a job fast," Dad shot back. "Don't be free-loading off anyone while you're there. I don't want them thinking I raised a loser of a son."

"Dad. Don't worry about it."

"Well, I do worry about it. You're in your thirties. You should be full on into a career of some sort by now. I don't know what you've been doing all this time with your life."

I'm already feeling suffocated from this discussion, but I try to continue on. I want to learn more about our family history in New Mexico. I've heard there was a Sanatorium there in the Organ Mountains that was part of our history. I am trying to get through Dad's negativity, so he can give me some info on that.

"Dad, tell me more about your dad's Great-Grandma Minnie."

"What? Why do you want to hear about her? That's so far in the past."

"I know. I know, but I love history. And since I'm going to Las Cruces, I think it would be fun to look into some of our family stuff."

"Most family stuff is better left in the closet," Dad says, obviously wanting to change the subject.

"Well, how are we gonna know who we are if we don't know where and who we came from?" I respond.

"TL, you're just wanting to stir up a hornet's nest there. Just leave it as it is. Go to Las Cruces, and do what you gotta do. But leave the family history buried in the hills where it belongs."

Dad isn't opening up about anything, which is nothing new. He only has one focus right now, my job.

"TL, what sort of work are you going to be doing when you get there? The longer you're out of a job, the harder it will be to get back into something. They will see your resume' and not want to hire you. They will wonder why you haven't been working."

"Dad, come on. I have a good track record with my jobs. It was just time for me to leave. A new place will understand. These things happen all the time in business."

"Don't waste time though, TL. You start the minute you get there...go out knocking on doors."

"Doors?"

"Yeah, get in contact with people. Have Bobby help you. He probably knows some people."

"Actually, I might take a whole different direction when I get there. From the way Bobby talks, the restaurants in that area seem to do a good business. I'm thinking of maybe opening up some sort of taco place..."

"WHAT!? Oh, man, TL. You're crazy. That will never work. You don't know enough about that sort of business. You should do what you know. Don't try to venture into anything new!"

"Dad, it's just me. I don't have others depending on me. I can give this a try."

"You have you depending on you. If you free-load off Bobby, I'm never going to hear the end of it from my Aunt Martha. I don't want her calling me and complaining. I better not hear..."

"You won't. Don't worry about it. I'll do what I need to do. I'm tired, Dad. I think I'm going to go to bed now. Good night."

"Okay. We can talk more tomorrow," Dad says.

I know he's not happy with me, but I'm happy to be done with our conversation. I don't know why I thought it would be any different than it ever was. Dad usually just told me what he thought, and wasn't interested in what was important to me. I will miss Mom, but I gotta get out of here tomorrow.

16

I remember the day I was out washing my car and Vic pulled up...with Lydia.

Looking up, I saw the two of them getting out of his car. I didn't really want to be involved, but I knew there was no way around it. When I met Lydia, she seemed nice enough. My heart went out to her. Vic was being his out-going fun self, and she was buying into it, hook, line, and sinker.

"Lydia, this is my brother Tracy Lynn. We call him TL for short. Because he is." Vic laughed, thinking he was being funny. Lydia looked a bit uncomfortable.

"Hi. Nice to meet you," Lydia said, reaching out her hand to shake mine.

Drying my hand off on my pants, I shook hers. She seemed tentative—just the kind of woman Vic likes, I thought.

"Lydia and I are going to grab a bite to eat before we see that war movie at the theater."

"Do you like those kind of movies?" I asked her. She just smiled and said nothing.

"It's supposed to be good. She'll be fine," Vic said, defensively. "I've been wanting to see it, and you always seem too busy, TL."

"Uh, you never really asked me about it, Vic. I would have g...."

"We're going in now. Did you finish off the bread?" Vic interrupted, per his usual way of skirting around an issue.

"No. It's there," was all I cared to say. My heart went out to Lydia. She had no idea what she was getting into. I wish she could sit down with Mandy and get a head's up about Vic, but there was no way that was happening.

As I was drying my car, they both came back out, headed to the movie.

"TL," Vic said sharply, "I just left our stuff there in the kitchen. You had it such a mess, I could barely find what we needed."

I could tell he was embarrassed at the way *he* had left the kitchen that morning and was not wanting Lydia to know he was such a slob. I let it slide once again, figuring it wasn't worth it to confront him on this. And I didn't want Lydia to feel more uneasy than she already did.

"Vic, I'll get it. Just enjoy your show." Why was I always so willing to accommodate him? I could feel the anger rising up in me, but the last thing I wanted was to deal with his wrath. It just didn't seem worth it.

"Do you have twenty bucks I could borrow? I'll get it back to you tomorrow." Vic never had money on him.

"I loaned you..." Never mind, I thought, and said, "I do," pulling out my wallet. Reminding him that I just loaned him money again the other day wouldn't go over well. I handed over a twenty and watched as they drove off. I stood there shaking my head as I heard the phone ringing on the front step.

"Hi, Mom. How are you?" I asked, still frustrated by this latest encounter with Vic.

"Good, TL. Just wanted to see how things were there."

"Oh, well...I don't know." I didn't really want to go into it at that moment.

"You don't know? Or you don't want to talk about it?" Mom asked.

"Probably some of both. I hate to complain. I need to be stronger, to stand up for what I know is right. Why is it so hard?" I asked, not really looking for an answer.

"What's happened? Is it your brother again?"

"What else? He is just so self-centered. And now he's got...well, this new woman in his life."

"Oh, I'm sorry to hear that. Poor Mandy."

"I don't know, Mom. I think it's more like poor Lydia. That's the new gal's name. She seems nice enough. Not that I really got to talk with her. But I think she's in for trouble with Vic. I don't know that he's really capable of loving anyone, or treating them with respect. I'm sorry to say that."

"No, no, that's okay. I'm listening. And I've been doing some research in that area with your dad. I think Vic is a chip off the old block...I hate to say. But you know, we have talked some about this. I do think it's time for both of us to maybe, I don't know, step up a little. Stand our ground. I don't want huge battles to ensue, but..."

"I don't either, Mom. But I'm tired of being his doormat and his excuse for all his bad behavior. He just accused me of leaving things a mess here, not wanting to look bad in front of Lydia. And I just let him get away with it. It's making me crazy. But if I said anything, I would have had to deal with his anger, and it's just not worth it."

"But maybe it is, TL. Maybe by us speaking up and setting some better boundaries with those who act this way, we could make some progress...feel better about ourselves?" Mom didn't sound like she was fully in, but I could tell she was trying.

"I don't know. I'm thinking I really shouldn't have moved in with Vic."

"Yeah. You have that option. I don't. I'm with your dad; and will be here until death do us part. That is my decision. But I shouldn't have to be his doormat either. I mean, I guess if he decides to leave because I am changing, that will be his choice. I surely hope not though."

"I understand. How are things going with you then?"

"It's about like it was. I think both you and I have a lot to learn about all this. I'm glad we can talk about it. Sometimes things come to a head for a reason. That's where it gets more painful to stay where we are than to change. Then we are more willing to take some needed steps forward."

"I sure hope so, Mom. I'm going to try and hang in here. I have a job, and a place to live for the moment. It's not that easy to find a new roommate, and it sure helps with the bills, even though it's just Vic's unemployment for now. But so much of the time I just want to avoid Vic. And that's no way to live."

"No, it's not. Oh, your dad just came in from his errand. I need to go now. But let's talk again soon. And let's really look into this whole thing and grow in this together. It's time," Mom said.

"It is. Have a good rest of your day. Say hi to Dad."

"I will. Bye now. Love you."

"Bye. Love you, too."

17

Being awake early is good. I don't want to waste any time this morning getting out of town. I can hear Mom in the kitchen already. She seems to be saying good-bye to Dad. I hear the door shut, and then his car drive off.

I grab my bag and go into the kitchen. "Good morning, Mom."

"Hi, TL. You're up early. I was just having my second cup of coffee. Your dad had to leave for an appointment. He should be back by 11:00."

"Mom, I think I'm gonna head out before he gets back. Last night wasn't an easy conversation with him. He just doesn't listen and is still treating me like I'm a teenager. I want to try some new things in New Mexico, and he's not for it at all. All he can talk about is me getting to work so I don't make him look bad to Bobby and the rest of the family out there."

"Oh, TL, please don't worry about that. I know you'll do fine in whatever you choose to do. I'm glad you have a place to go when you get there. But I know you won't take advantage of that help. Your dad just worries."

"He does. I know we've talked a lot about changing ourselves, since it doesn't seem like Dad and Vic are much interested in change. I don't think they even realize there is a need."

"I don't think they do. But maybe by you and me changing, it will make things better. I'm sorry you were not able to stay with Vic. But I understand. You're probably going to feel guilty, but please don't. I know you did your best. Vic will be fine."

"Thanks, Mom. Will you be?"

"Yes. Don't worry about me. It's a long process, but at my age, I get that. I've worked through a lot of different things through the years. As you can tell from last night, your dad and I have a ways to go. I learned

that when some feel weak, they tend to manipulate. When they feel strong, they will more intimidate. It can fluctuate, but the ultimate goal is to dominate."

"Wow," I said shaking my head.

"I know your dad gets more riled up when others are around. He seems better when it's just the two of us. What's coming to me, little by little, is that there are broken things in me that need healing. I'm praying a lot about that. Walking and talking with God has really revealed some interesting things to me. Places where I feel less than, if you know what I mean—where I might allow people to be mean because I think I don't deserve better than that. This isn't something that seems to be able to be rushed, but more something I need to cooperate with God about."

"Tell me more about that. Maybe it's something I should do."

"Sure, TL. Anyone can. We know that God is our Healer. And without using money that I don't have for a counselor, I am going to thee Counselor known as the Holy Spirit, in a way I never have before. I am talking to Him about my feelings and asking Him where those feelings came from. He is showing me. I'm learning more about that term, self-differentiation...separating our thoughts from our feelings."

"Oh yeah. It's pretty powerful stuff, it seems. You mentioned that."

"It is, TL. So what I do on these walks is I talk to God, and He has been bringing up a wound from my childhood. I ask Him, 'What should we look at today?' And something comes to me—a situation that was painful to me. Like...let's see. Which one should I share with you? Okay, I was in the seventh grade and I had this friend, Nancy. We were very close, but then another girl came into our group, and her name was Susan. Susan basically stole my friendship with Nancy. Until just recently, I didn't know what had happened. But when I took it to God, and I separated my thoughts from my feelings, many things came out of that. I told God I thought that was unkind of Susan. That it was mean. That it was selfish...and a number of things. Then I asked myself how I felt about that? I felt sad. Lonely. Rejected. Abandoned, and so on. I acknowledged it all, and then I asked the Holy Spirit to nurture that young girl in me and heal that wound. To bring His healing balm of love to that broken part in me. To clean out any infection, and strengthen my foundation in Him—to wrap His loving arms around my younger self. And I have been healing through many such memories in this way."

"That sounds like a good plan."

"It seems to be helping. And then what God revealed to me really surprised me. Long before I knew anything about all of this narcissism stuff, God showed me that Nancy was a co-dependent type of personality, and Susan was a narcissist. Nancy became her 'supply.' In the end, it really had nothing to do with my worth, but everything to do with Susan targeting Nancy for what she needed. I realized that Nancy didn't dislike

me. She just got pulled away by Susan, unknowingly, really. I can see this in a better light now and be healed from it. By identifying my thoughts and feelings, other things get revealed that I never expected. It seems to be working. God loved me so much that He sent His Son to die for me. And Jesus loved me so much that He did die for me. I want to start to see that my worth is found in God alone and should not be determined by anyone else's actions or inactions toward me. We are all broken people in need of Jesus. I want my thinking to be healthy and not operate out of a warped way of seeing the past as a child. It's time to put away childish things. That's Biblical!"

"That's powerful, Mom! Thanks for sharing that with me. I'm going to try doing the same thing when I head on my way. I can't afford a therapist either, but I think we've both needed one."

"We probably have. I mean, life hasn't been all that terrible. But it can surely be better."

"I believe that. I'm going to load up now, and head on out. I hope this doesn't cause any problems between you and Dad when he returns."

"If it does, I will deal with it. It will just be another way I can grow and learn if he gives me fits. I have to remember God delights in me."

Laughing and giving Mom a hug, I'm so thankful to have her in my life. She helps me make sense of things. She's so open to talk with me about stuff.

After saying good-bye to Mom, I'm ready to see what lies ahead of me now. From what Mom is saying, it's important to look into past wounds with God, and cast out the lies of Satan. With healthy truth operating, we can move forward into our future relationships in a better way. I don't think it's easy, but I believe it's possible.

18

After the morning's interaction with Vic, I was glad he left to be with Lydia for the day. Mandy was pretty much out of the picture now. He seemed to be so absorbed in his relationship with Lydia that nothing else much mattered. It was nice *not* to have his music playing. A quiet house was so peaceful. I still had a strange mixture of emotions, though. I was glad to have him out and busy, but wondering why we couldn't get along better and have some fun, too? Why was my mind constantly jumping back and forth between never wanting to see him again, and hoping we could be close as brothers?

I made myself a burrito and took a seat on the couch. Taking a look around, it was a nice place we lived, although small. At first, I tried to ignore the pain in my chest, thinking it was just a bit of normal discomfort that happens in the body from time to time. But the longer I sat there, feeling it radiate even into my back, the more I couldn't just pass it off anymore. I knew I needed to get some help. Calling Vic, he didn't answer.

I wondered if it could possibly be a heart attack? At my age? Probably not. Calling my friend, Andy, from work, he came right over. I didn't know him super well, but he was a good guy. He arrived about 20 minutes after I called, and by then, I was really in bad shape.

"Come in!" I called out, weakly, when his knock came on the door.

Andy took one look at me there pale and sweating and loaded me into the car for a trip to the ER. He wanted to call an ambulance, but I insisted that he could drive me. After arriving at the hospital and trying to get ahold of Vic over and over, I knew I was pretty much on my own. Andy had plans that he couldn't cancel, so I found myself laying there alone. Vic wasn't the brother that I hoped he would be, and I needed to face the truth about that. I called my mom.

"Hi, TL. How are you?"

"Mom, I'm in the ER. They are running some tests on me."

"Oh, no. What's wrong? Are you okay?" She was more than concerned.

"All was well. Vic was out, it was peaceful, and then my chest started giving me fits. I had a guy from work drive me to the ER. I couldn't get ahold of Vic. Still can't."

"What can I do? Should I catch a flight? I don't know if I can get there until tomorrow. But I will get there as soon as I can."

"Mom, I don't know yet. Let me get some test results back, and I'll let you know."

"Okay. I don't want you to tire yourself out on the phone, so I'll let you go. But please, call me back as soon as you get word of anything. And I'll try to get Vic."

"Okay, Mom. Bye."

"Bye. Please call me...I love you."

"I will. Love you."

Hanging up, I knew that Mom would be there anytime I needed her. She told me later that when she told Dad what was going on, he wasn't empathetic at all. He was more interested in what she was making him for dinner. She hated to tell me that, but she knew I wouldn't be surprised. Dad didn't do "sick." We were all supposed to pull ourselves up by our bootstraps and carry on. He figured it was just some indigestion, and I'd get over it. When I called Mom later with the news, Dad had already gone to bed.

"Mom, the doc said I might have had a mild heart attack. He knows I'm young for this, but with the stress I live in, it could be contributing to it. They still have some tests to run to fully know the extent of it. They're going to keep me for the night."

"I'm booking a flight..."

"No. Don't do that. Let's wait until morning, and then we'll see," I said, trying to sound strong.

"Are you sure?"

"Yes. And Vic finally did get back to me. He's not coming to the hospital. He's at home. But maybe if I do need something, he'll be around tomorrow."

"Oh. That son of mine. I'm sorry for your brother's lack of care. And your dad's," Mom said.

"Mom, I've got you. And you've got me." I really didn't want her to worry.

"And we've got God, TL. You're right. We will be fine."

"I'll call you in the morning. Get some sleep. I'll be okay."

"You, too. Talk to you soon," Mom said, sounding like she might cry.

After talking to Mom and being moved into a regular room, I laid awake late into the night. Not because I was worried about my heart. But more that I was thinking about what I was doing living with Vic, and when and if I should leave? He was preoccupied with his life and causing stress in mine. Was God giving me a warning signal, a word, that I should move on? I prayed but didn't seem to get any sure answers. But then, wasn't a near heart attack a sure answer enough?

The next morning brought good news. But also a warning from the doctor. I needed to take it easy and lower the stress levels in my life. I knew I couldn't quit my job, but how much could I pull away from my brother while still living with him? That was the question. When I called Mom to tell her the news, she was so relieved. Dad, not so much. He pretty much indicated I was over exaggerating my condition from the start, and I should buck up. That was a typical response from my dad. I didn't take it much to heart. But then, maybe that was my problem. I should take these things to heart and deal with them. By shoving this stuff deep inside all these years, sweeping it under the rug, it hadn't helped my psyche any, or the *physical* condition of my heart.

When all this happened, I wondered if I really even knew myself? I seemed to get so lost in those around me, and their needs... I needed to pay more attention to what was going on now. But mostly, I continued to live with what was, always hoping for the better things to come. That was craziness. I heard if we continue to do what we've always done, we'll get what we always got. It's so true!

19

Driving out of Chino, I am enjoying the green hills and the snow-capped mountains behind them. It's not usually this clear here. It's nice to see it this way from time to time. It feels strange to be leaving California, and all that it includes behind me. A part of me is so sad, knowing the good things I had were very good. But the bad...so difficult. I am excited about the adventure that awaits me in New Mexico. Giving Bobby a quick call, I'm happy to hear that he is looking forward to my arrival. I drive along, thinking about the things Mom and I talked about, and things I've been looking into. I start to run it all through my head again. I hope one day, I will get more clarity and healing.

How come Vic seems to make sense to himself, but I can't do that for myself? He seems so sure of what he says. Maybe he's a bunch of hot air? Looking up some things last night after I went to bed, I'm seeing a side of me that I'm not pleased with...something Mom and I talked about these last months, but I couldn't really grab hold of—the co-dependent part of me that feeds into Vic's narcissism. It's not all his fault. I play right into his hands, in a sick sort of way. And so much of it comes from the wounding we have experienced as children. Mom is probably right by going back, asking God about certain situations she went through, and then seeking God's healing there. I never thought that much about it. I had a pretty good childhood. My life hasn't been terrible. But still...

"God, is there something hidden back in my past that I need to deal with?" I say, wondering what might arise. I'm surprised when something does. My memory takes me to my fifth-grade report card. At the beginning of that year we had moved to a new city. I had gone from being one of the most popular kids in the class to feeling totally out of place. From the top of the dog pile, to a pile of you know what.

God, help me think about this. Help me go through the steps that Mom was talking to me about. What was I thinking in all of this? I was thinking...I'm dumb. I'm ugly. I'm lacking what all these other kids seem to have in this new school. I'm thinking something is wrong with me. Okay, and how did all that make me feel? It seems we are to separate the thinking from the feeling so I'm trying to do that. This is challenging. I guess I felt...lonely, scared, odd, panicked...like this wasn't going to work for me. And then what? Now what did Mom say she does? Oh, she prays and asks for healing and comfort.

God, I need healing in this wound. Help me know what was really going on here. Oh, I hadn't changed? I was the same person before and after the move? That's an interesting development. The kids around me were just being who they were, there wasn't a plan to make me feel this way? They didn't notice how out of place I felt? They were only ten, too. And then what did my teacher tell me? What did he write on my last report card in his class? That was something that stuck with me. He wrote, "I wish all of my students were as sincere, helpful, and diligent as TL." Wow, that's how he viewed me? That's certainly not how I was viewing myself.

What's that God? How did my dad react to that comment from my teacher? Oh yeah, he sort of pooh-pawed it, making me feel like I was putting myself into a lofty position because of it. Why would Dad do that? Why wouldn't he tell me how proud he was of me? He probably told everyone else how great I was, to make himself feel better. But not to me...to me, I got shunned by him. Was that his insecurity? Probably so, huh, God.

Okay, so I'm a young kid, feeling awkward in a new school, and the teacher writes these words that stick with me all these years later. God, I think that was You speaking through that teacher. Maybe for today, You're showing me what was happening that I didn't see at the time. Interesting. I needed encouragement from that teacher. And to have a male teacher, too, to make up for the lack from my earthly father. You are a good God.

Lord, heal that place in me that was wounded at the time. Pour Your love into that wound and help me know that You loved me enough to die for me. That You believe I'm worth dying on the Cross for, to save me for all of eternity. Clean out the infectious lies of the enemy that have plagued me all these years unknowingly. Thank You for loving me so much and for bringing me healing on this day. In Jesus' name. Amen.

I wonder if that did anything? I'm feeling a bit more peace as the miles add up. I need to do this with each thing that is brought forward from my past. Mom has shown me something good here. My narcissistic dad was having an effect on me long before I ever knew it. It was subtle, just his little way of shunning those teacher's words. He probably didn't even realize what he was doing, or how much I needed that encouragement. Dad was probably working out of so many wounds from his own childhood, it was the only way, it is the only way, he knows how to be.

This may be why I've become such a people pleaser. Trying to get others to like me...to see me. It may have started back in these moments. I have been working so hard through the years trying to make peace with Vic, and others, when that's not what was needed. I needed to make peace with myself. I'm loved by my Creator in Heaven, just the way I am. God designed me this way for a reason. Lord, You saw me all along. You know every hair on my head. My teacher saw me as sincere, helpful, and diligent. That's who I am, I'm not what my dad says about me, or even the loser I might picture myself as. I have to believe there is a reason for me being here and being who I am. I'm going to look for that in New Mexico...I'm going to find more of God's healing, and more of me when I get there. I'll be digging up more bad "roots" there, and tossing them out of the field of my life. I want pure soil to plant a new life in. I want to get rid of my twisted thinking and bring in more of God's thinking.

Passing through Palm Springs, I see the browns and tans of the landscape ahead of me. The desert certainly has a beauty of its own. I'm ready for the change. After hours of driving, I'm starting to see things we don't have in California. The signs make me laugh, although it's probably not a laughing matter. In New Mexico, it's telling me about the dusts storms, and what to do. "Pull over. Stop your engine. Take your foot off the brake. Stay buckled." Wow! This must be serious business. And sure enough, what is that up ahead? I see a lot of dust blowing around. I wonder if I'm going to get caught in one of these storms? It looks like I'm going to be able to get through before the majority of it crosses this road. The cars behind me might not be so lucky. I wonder how that would be to sit and wait it out?

At long last, I see the city of Las Cruces down at the bottom of this sloping highway. It's bigger than I expected it to be. Bobby has given me his address. I look forward to spending time with him and getting to know one another better. His mom, my Great-Aunt Martha, is a crazy kind of lady. Maybe she and my dad have more in common than I think? I'll have to talk to Bobby about that and see what it's been like for him growing up. Bobby was born to her pretty late in life, so he and Dad aren't close in age. He and I are more like first cousins. That will make it nice.

Those mountains behind the city there look very interesting. Those must be the Organ Mountains I've heard about. I want to find out what happened in those hills that my dad wanted me to stay away from. Yes, they will be one of my first stops on this journey before I settle down into any kind of real job. I hope Bobby can go with me to the mountains.

20

After taking a few days off to rest, I knew I had better get back to work. Losing my job would not be good. Vic's unemployment was only going to last so long, and then who would be paying the bills? Vic didn't seem concerned about getting a job any time soon, as he spent lots of time with Lydia. But even that relationship was growing tiresome to him.

"Hey, Vic, your phone is ringing!" I yelled from the kitchen, back to the bedroom. Vic was avoiding Lydia's repeated phone calls now.

"I hear it! Just leave it!" he shouted back. "I'm in no mood to talk to Lydia."

I could have told her this would happen, that Vic couldn't stick with a relationship that required anything of him. As long as she was giving, giving, giving, he would continue to take from her. But lately, she had some medical issues of her own, and that required a little TLC from Vic. It wasn't in his wheelhouse. He pretended to be busy looking for work. It wasn't true. I could clearly see that.

When the doorbell rang later that day, no one was more surprised than me to open the door to Vic's friend, Kevin. The look on his face needed few words.

"Where's VIC?" he asked firmly, looking past me into the house. "I need to talk to him!"

With no "Hello," no "How are you, TL," I knew trouble was brewing. And the last place I wanted to be was in the middle of it.

"Come on in. He's in the back. I'll get him." I knew Vic wasn't going to appreciate my *Open-Door Policy* toward his "friend." But what did I have to lose? Vic was always upset with me for one thing or another. Why not another thing to add to the list.

"Vic!" I called out, walking back to his room.

Knocking on his door he shouted, "I told you! I don't want to talk to

Lydia right now!"

"Uh, it's not Lydia. Kevin is here."

Opening the door and looking me straight in the eye, he said, "Tell him I'm not here."

"He's already sitting in the living room waiting for you," I said, almost with a tone of satisfaction.

"You idiot! What did you go and let him in for. You should have told him I wasn't home!"

"Vic, your car is out front. I'm not gonna lie for you."

"You never do anything for me!" Pushing me out of the way, Vic went to face Kevin.

Kevin hadn't taken a seat. He was standing, ready to face Vic when he entered the room. Vic actually put his hand out to shake Kevin's. Kevin pushed it aside, saying, "I didn't come here to be friendly!" That stumped Vic. He wasn't used to people being so bold with him.

"You know what I'm here about, don't you, Vic?" Kevin wasted no time getting into it.

Vic stood silent. I stood in the doorway, wondering if this was what I thought it was? Lydia was Kevin's little sister. Big brothers are known to be protective of anyone their sister would date.

"Lydia is a mess, Vic. What have you done to her!?"

"Done? I don't know what you mean?" Vic sounded genuinely stumped, but I knew it was a game he was playing. Vic knew exactly what he was doing most of the time.

"Don't act so confused, Vic. I've known you long enough to know how you work. I wasn't all too happy when I heard about Lydia dating you. You're not even divorced yet, and now you're using her to satisfy your needs. You disgust me, Vic." Kevin wasn't pulling any punches.

Vic went stone silent. He could feel he had met his match, and he wasn't sure where to go from here. The longer he remained quiet, the angrier Kevin got.

"Say something, you loser! Lydia has been crying for days. My mom is very concerned. My dad wanted to come over here, but I told him I would do it. Believe me, you don't want to come face to face with my dad."

Vic sat down and glared up at Kevin. The look on his face changed from one of confusion, to one of sly satisfaction. Kevin could see it and sense it, and it enraged him all the more.

"You slime bag! I've seen you do this too many times," Kevin continued, "but this time it's personal. This is my sister! And if you ever come near her again, you'll be getting more than words from me. It won't be pretty!"

Kevin left, and Vic remained seated as I walked fully into the room. He looked at me and a smile came to his face that sent chills up my spine.

Who was this brother of mine? Did he actually derive satisfaction from another person's misery? Was this just more fuel being added to his destructive fire in a person's life? When his phone rang again, Vic picked it up. He didn't even say hello.

"How could you, Lydia? I've been busy, and you're crying, and going to your family, and making a mess of things! Then your brother comes over here and lays into me! This is all your fault! If you would just be more understanding of my life, everything would be fine. But no, you go and blather our personal stuff to everyone, and make things so difficult for me!"

I think Vic would have gone on, but I could hear Lydia wailing into the phone, and he probably figured she couldn't hear him anymore at that point.

"Look. I can't take all your emotional outbursts. Go back to your family and tell them they need to stay out of our business, or you won't be seeing me at all. Don't call me. I'll let you know when I'm ready to talk with you again."

Vic hung up the phone, not giving Lydia a chance to speak. I felt sick for her, and sick for myself to see my own brother act this way. This time it wasn't an attack on me. But watching him attack another so viciously started to open my eyes to just what I was dealing with. I wasn't sure what to call it at that point...narcissism, demonization, or just being a total jerk, but this was all bad. My days with Vic needed to come to an end. Why was I stalling?

21

Pulling up in front of Bobby's place I'm a little surprised as I turn into a trailer park. From his address, I thought it was an apartment. He lives in an RV? Wow!

Shutting off my car, I see Bobby coming out to greet me. He looks a little older, but other than that he has the same warm smile and hearty handshake he's always had.

"Hey there, Bobby! How's it going?"

"Great, TL. So good to see you again. Who would have ever thought you'd turn up here?"

"I certainly didn't. But it feels good. That's quite a long drive from my parents' house, but I made it through the dust storms and everything. Even saw tumbleweed blowing across the road. So different than the Bay Area."

"That's for sure! Wait until you get to know this area. I think you'll find it has its own kind of beauty. Come on in, let me show you around the place. Bet you didn't think this would be home for a while. The RV life is pretty good. Lots of nice people, and the facilities here are handy, too. Nice big showers, if you prefer them over the rig here. And there are washers and dryers when needed. This is a 55 and over place, but the owner is a friend of mine. I help him out with stuff, so he makes an exception in my case."

"Sounds great... Wow, this is big in here! I've never been in much more than a pop-up trailer. This is quite different." There's not only a couch, but two easy chairs, a large screen TV, and plenty of counter space in the kitchen. "Is that a dishwasher?"

"Yeah. It is. I'm telling you, this is the life! People think I crawl into a bunk at night when I tell them I live in an RV. Let me show you the bedroom. You can have a king-size bed in here, but I special ordered this with twin beds. I prefer living with someone, and this just makes it easier."

"You don't know how much I appreciate you giving me a place to land. I hope to not out stay my welcome. Of course, my dad is worried that I'm going to look like a leach to you and your family."

"Ahh, yes. Will. Your dad reminds me of my mom. They are both so hard-headed."

"You could call it that. I'm realizing it may run deeper than just stubbornness with Dad, and maybe even with your mom, but let's save that for a later time. How about I take you out to eat? Got any favorites in the area?"

"I sure do. Just get your stuff stowed away in here, and we'll go. The closet there has some room at the end of it, and anything else you have, feel free to find a place where it works for you," Bobby says.

"You are very easy. After what I've been living with, I'm just about speechless."

"What do you mean?" Bobby looks at me more than a little puzzled. "I thought you were living with Vic?"

"I was. You haven't seen him for years, right?"

"Right."

"Well, we'll talk. But let's eat first. A full stomach might help before we get into all that."

Pulling up in front of a little adobe place, I see tables outside. The scent of meat grilling sets my mouth to watering. "Where do you like to sit, Bobby? Wanna sit outside?"

"I love to sit out when it's weather like this. Gotta take advantage of the cooler temps before summer sets in. This place can blister in the heat!"

The chips and salsa are quickly delivered to our table.

"Oh, man. These are good chips. I think I've come to the right place for Mexican food."

"Oh, TL. Yes. Being so close to the border, the food is great. Did I hear right when we briefly spoke that you might like to open up a little taco place around here?" Bobby asks.

"Yes. That's in my thinking. I want to get a feel for the area and do some family history stuff first. And then get to it. I hope you don't think I'm sluffing off while I spend some time looking around. Especially in the Organ Mountains there. I hear our family has some stories to tell from there, and I think they might help me get to the bottom of some troubling...shall we say, personalities, that we have seen through the generations?"

"Well, hey, I've got a few days off. Being a fireman, we work a strange but good schedule. I'd love to hike around with you and learn a bit myself about our family. I don't normally do that, but it sounds like fun. I have to admit, I'm pretty much a home-body when not working," Bobby says, munching on chips.

"I don't want to be a bother, so you do what you do. But it's cool if you

want to go with me! I'd love that. I was hoping you might be interested."

"The steak that I've had here is awesome, but also I've had the pork tacos. They are pretty much to die for," Bobby explains.

"I think I'll go with the steak this time and come back again for the tacos."

"Good choice. I think you'll have plenty of time to try it all. And I want you to know, I don't mind a roommate. I'm used to it. In fact, this is one of the rare times when I don't have someone living with me. It's perfect timing!" Bobby says with a genuine smile.

Dinner with Bobby was relaxing. He's so easy to talk to. I look forward to hiking up the mountain with him tomorrow. Lying in bed, it feels good. Maybe God knew I had to wait it out a bit with Vic until Bobby had a bed open for me? He seems so easy going and helpful. Giving me a lo-down of the area and setting up a time to head out in the morning for the mountains, this seems so comfortable already. Leaving Vic was hard, and leaving my life there was even harder, but I'm encouraged by just how I feel already. They say you don't know what you've got 'till it's gone. Maybe you don't know what you're really living in, until you're not? I feel so free. I can be myself. Bobby is not pushy. He listens and responds in a way that I've missed while being with Vic. Bobby is not all about himself. He actually takes an interest in what I'm doing, what I think, and even when he disagrees, he's accommodating. The good food, the good company, and a place to lay my head makes for a great ending to this trip, and a good start to tomorrow. Drifting off to sleep, I look forward to a new life in New Mexico. What God will have me discover here, and experience, remains to be seen.

22

I knew I needed to give Mom a call after the scene yesterday with Kevin. From that point on, I didn't see living with Vic going anywhere but downhill.

Mom answered her phone quickly. "Hi, TL. How are you this morning?"

"Hi, Mom. I'm hanging in there. How are you? You sound tired," I said.

"I am. A bit. But don't worry about me. I know you need to rest and make sure your heart is okay."

"It's doing fine. I wanted to talk with you about something, though. Vic had an encounter with his friend Kevin yesterday. That's Lydia's older brother. It seems that Lydia has been upset for days, and Vic is totally ignoring her. Kevin laid into Vic, and I don't blame him."

"I'm sorry to hear that, TL. I hate to take a side against my child, but poor Lydia is probably in deeper than she can imagine. What is she upset about? Is there a particular problem?" Now I could really hear the strain in Mom's voice.

"I don't know, Mom. She's had some health issues. Vic hasn't been there for her. Maybe she thought he was more committed than that? But we know Vic..."

"Yes, we do. His commitment level is very low. When trouble's brewing, he's not much help. You experienced that with your heart problem."

"I did," I agreed, but not wanting to worry Mom any more about that than need be.

"You're doing okay, aren't you? I'm concerned about the stress there continuing to be hard on your heart," Mom said.

"Mom, I don't think I can live here much longer. Vic isn't getting better, and now this thing with Lydia. Vic isn't going to change any time soon, but I can. That's what I've started to realize."

"I understand. I love Vic. He's my son. But I recognize so many things that he's seemed to pick up from your dad. I wish there was more I could have done to prevent this." I could tell Mom's voice was cracking a bit with emotion.

"Don't blame yourself, Mom. I read an interesting thing that said we are all born as a narcissist. The question is, will we grow up and out of it? Vic saw it modeled for him with Dad..."

Mom interrupted gently saying, "So did you, TL. And you're not like that."

"I don't know the answer to that. There are probably many layers of dysfunction that contribute to how we turn out. But it's also a matter of personal choices. I have those same things rolling around in my head that escape out of Vic's mouth. I choose not to voice them whenever possible. One other thing that might be a contributing factor is how we handle criticism. When someone points out a flaw in my character, I take it to heart. I want to change. But with Vic, he just gets defensive, and meaner."

"That is true. I saw that even when you were young boys," Mom added. "I understand what you're saying about what escapes out of a person's mouth. We all have those same struggles. Some people feel they have a right to say whatever. We should always be in check with the Holy Spirit, thinking first before we speak. And when we do say hurting things, realizing it and saying we're sorry is so important. Sadly, few are able to do this. If we aren't willing to take a look at ourselves, recognizing our own thoughts and feelings, I'm seeing we are blinded to the wounds that need healing in our own lives. God has had me focusing on the log in my own eye before trying to remove the splinter out of someone else's. I'd love to help your brother, and to help your dad, but first I need to work on myself and make sure I'm coming from a healed place. Otherwise we really are the blind trying to lead the blind. And as the Bible says, then both fall into a pit."

"Wow, Mom, it sounds like you have really been digging into this stuff. I wish I had more time to do that. If I can get away from here, and away from Vic, maybe I can clear my head a bit. I think I should try to move to some place far away. I just have no idea where that might be. With my job here, I would need to save up some money to make a move. I should start this week, setting some aside when I can. I'm glad we're having this talk today. It's planting some ideas in my head that I need to implement. Please don't say anything to Vic about me leaving. He would get so mad!"

"Oh, I won't. And if you need a little extra, I can help you out," Mom said, in almost a whisper. I knew she didn't want Dad to hear.

"I hope there will be no need for that. I can do this. I'm a grown man, and this is my decision. But I appreciate being able to discuss it with you."

"Anytime, TL. Please know that I understand and will support you as best I can. For now, I better go and take care of some errands I need to run. Keep me updated as to how and when you plan to make a move. Vic and I don't talk as often as you and I do. It's always a bit harder conversing with him. We talked more when he was with Mandy. I think she did level him out some. Now with Lydia, and all that...I just don't know what's going to happen to your brother."

"Me either. I'll do what I can to help. But mostly, I gotta help myself get through this time with him. Good talking with you, Mom. Take care."

"You, too. Please get some rest."

"I will. Love you. Bye."

"Bye-bye, Son."

23

It's good to be able to ride with Bobby today over to the Organ Mountains, since he knows his way around. It's a beautiful day—not too hot, not too cold. And the wind isn't supposed to be bad until tomorrow. Bobby said the dust storms can get so thick you can't even see the mountains. That's hard to believe on a calm, clear day like this. It seems like God is on our side for this adventure.

"I really am intrigued by the homes around here, Bobby. They are so different than the ones in California. I would guess it's because of the dust storms? These adobe type homes look like they can take a beating. Look how the windows are so small on the sunset side—keeping out the heat?"

"Yes. It's hard to imagine how hot it can get out here, but it can, and will. They have those large windows on the east side to be able to view those beautiful mountains. But when the sun gets past high noon, it's time to shut it down! Those little windows let in light but keep the afternoon heat out."

"Makes sense. You don't come up here often, Bobby?"

"No. Like I said, I'm pretty much a home-body," he says, chuckling.

"That's fine. You probably get plenty of excitement from your job when the station bell rings! Talk about a hot job in the summer. Fire and heat! Wow! You must drink a lot of water!"

"I do!" Bobby says emphatically.

"It doesn't seem like we're climbing much as we drive, but looking behind us, I can see all of Las Cruces and beyond. What a view!"

"It is amazing up here. I've really only been here once before. There's different trails you can take, but I'm thinking the one you'll be most interested in is the one up to the sanatorium, right?" Bobby glances over at me with raised eyebrows.

"Yes. That's the one I'd like to do. I can come back other days if I want

85

to hike around more by myself."

"Sounds good. Is there something in particular you're looking for TL?"

"I don't know. All I know is what I left behind recently wasn't good, and I'm wondering if there's some answers way in our past that could shed a little light on the situation."

"What sort of answers?"

"Like why my brother is so impossible? Sorry to be so blunt about it. Is it okay if I talk with you a little bit about him on our way?"

"For sure. I'm all ears," Bobby says, almost settling in for a good story.

"Where do I start? Maybe I should explain about some of the research that I've done over the past months or so, and even more on my drive here. I've become familiar with the term narcissism. I'd heard it before, but I never really gave it enough thought."

"I'm with you there, TL. I've heard it, but what exactly is it?"

"I'll try to break it down quickly, although it's hard to do because it's such a wide spectrum of personality traits between different individuals. But...here, let me look at some notes I made in my phone. I want to get this correct. I'll just hit on a few high points, if that's okay?"

"Sure."

"I read how narcissists lack the ability to recognize the problem, and they don't take responsibility, they blame everyone else. They think they are entitled to special consideration and attention. When they blame others, it can start to make that person doubt their own sanity. It can also be hard to detect who the narcissists are, but they are identified by the pain they inflict on others. I find that fascinating! And here's another interesting point; they don't recognize that someone else exists separately from them. They more see others as an extension of themselves and under their control."

"Wow, Really?"

*I can tell Bobby is intrigued. "Yes. And we are only scratching the surface with the amount of notes I've already made. With an overt narcissist, they can charm you, almost into a trance. With a covert one, especially in a parent, they can disguise it with worry or overprotection. By the time you realize what's going on, it can be very difficult to change that relationship to a healthy balance. They can even bring you to a place in your thinking where you're in agreement with how amazing **they** are! Here's something that's hard for me to do. I read, it's important to draw attention to all the unnecessary critiquing that they can spew out and let them know they need to stop it. They may not understand why, but they can learn what you will and won't put up with from them."*

"This sounds complicated, TL. Where did you learn all this stuff?"

"I've had to do some research after living with Vic for the last year.

When I was reading this, his personality hits on so many of these points. The thing is, I'm to blame, too. I don't like confrontation, so I just walk on egg shells around him. That doesn't help him, or me!"

"I guess not. But I've done that with my mom for years."

"It does run in families. Actually, everyone has a bit of narcissism in them. But some are so far gone on one end of the spectrum, they become such a pain in the you-know-what!"

"I get it. I have to stay clear of my mom at times. I mean, I want to have a relationship with her, but she's so full of vitriol...I learned that word because of her—it means cruel and bitter criticism. But all this time, I didn't realize that may be narcissism. Wow! I thought it was just normal for her."

"I haven't spent a lot of time with you, Bobby, but I'm glad you're creating healthy boundaries with your mom. I already notice how you're so different than Vic. I don't feel on edge with you. I didn't set healthy boundaries with Vic, or with my dad, and we don't get along so well."

"I had no choice with my mom, TL, she got viciously cruel. She almost wrecked me. I had to back off and protect my sanity. I test the waters before getting near her now, and if I draw back a stump, I stay away until the waters calm some." Bobby demonstrates with his hand, drawing it into a fist.

"Very smart of you."

"We're almost to the visitor center, but I'd really like to hear more about all this, TL."

"I think we'll have plenty of time. Let's go on in and take a look around before our hike. I'm really looking forward to seeing what's up there in the mountains, Bobby."

24

Although the work week dragged, I felt a new sense of hope after talking with Mom. I knew it was time to start planning an escape—save some money and take a look around at my options. Where would I go? I'd always been a California boy. But distance was needed. I didn't want Vic coming anywhere near me once I made my move.

Coming home on Friday, I was relaxing. Vic was out somewhere, and I was glad for the space. It wasn't the house that lacked peace, it was Vic's presence that sucked the house dry when he was there. Sadly, this peace didn't last long when Vic strolled through the door with a new gal on his arm. The smile on Vic's face said it all, Lydia was out, this woman was in.

"Hey there, Bro! Kickin' back huh? Did you stop by the grocery store on your way home? We're totally out of bread and eggs here."

"No, Vic, I didn't," I said with a concealed sigh of frustration. "Hi, I'm TL. Vic's brother," I added while standing and stretching out my hand to her.

"I'm Abby. Nice to meet you."

"Oh, yeah. Abby, TL. TL, Abby." Vic said nonchalantly, walking away into the kitchen. Poor girl didn't know which way to turn. Should she follow him, or stay with the brother she just met?

"Have a seat. He'll be right back," I said, not knowing if that was the truth or not. Sometimes Vic could disappear on a phone call. I hoped I wouldn't have to stall around too long for him.

"Thanks."

Once again, Abby seemed sweet, shy, and at a loss. More "food" for Vic's empty soul to feed on.

"You live around here?" was all I could think to ask her.

"No. I live in Pacifica," Abby answered, glancing nervously toward the doorway Vic disappeared through.

"Can I get you anything to drink?" I knew I shouldn't, but I couldn't help but once again pick up the slack where Vic left off.

"No. No thanks," she answered.

Abby was not one for conversation, so this was getting more uncomfortable by the second. I turned on the TV for a distraction as I heard Vic on the phone on the back porch. His voice was raised, and the few words I did hear, sounded like trouble was brewing in Vic's life again. Suddenly I heard a door open and close, and Vic stomped back into the room. He told Abby they needed to go, and out the front door they went. It wasn't but ten minutes later the doorbell rang. When I answered it, there stood Lydia. Tears streaming down her face, hands shaking with emotion. "I need to talk to Vic," she sobbed. Of course, I asked her to come in.

"Is Vic here?" she asked timidly.

"He's not, Lydia."

"But I just talked to him. I told him I was coming over. We need to talk."

"Well," I sighed outwardly this time, "he's gone out."

The sobbing was pretty much uncontrollable at this point. I went to get tissues to soak up some of the mess Vic was leaving me with. I liked Lydia, I did. But I was tired of seeing the debris of sadness that my brother caused in the lives of so many, me, being one of them. I could feel for Lydia. Sure, my pain was different—Vic didn't say he loved me. But I don't know that Vic could love anyone at this point in his life. I first thought that my being nice to Vic could solve what was happening here. It was becoming evident that no amount of kindness or love could solve what Vic didn't see as a problem. He skirted away from the consequences of his actions. And here I sat, staring his abuse square in the face again. Handing Lydia a couple of tissues, I knew I had to say something.

"I don't know what to tell you, Lydia. My brother...he...he's a hard one to pin down. I want you to know, this is not your fault. Whatever the problem is you're having with Vic, don't take all the blame on yourself, if you are. Maybe I'm overstepping here...I don't know what you're thinking."

"But if I could only have a chance to talk to Vic, I know I could make him understand."

"Don't be so sure of it," I said. "I don't think Vic can hear past his own voice. I don't want to burst your bubble here, or hurt you worse than you already have been..."

Lydia interrupted, "But he thinks I lied to him. I need to explain."

With a grimace, and a shake of my head, I tried to let her know I wasn't so sure. I knew Vic was the liar most times. But she didn't seem to hear me either.

"I just need to talk with him. Where is he, TL?" The hysteria was growing now, and I knew something needed to be done.

"Let me get you something to drink, and I'll see if I can get ahold of Vic for you."

"Oh, would you? Thank you!!"

Walking into the kitchen, my anger was rising to a new level. First, he leaves me sitting with Abby. Then he races out the door before Lydia arrives. What next, Vic!? I've had it.

"Here's some water. Now let me go call Vic."

"Okay," she said with a slightly hopeful tone.

Of course, Vic didn't answer his phone. I knew I was only stalling for time by calling him. Reentering the living room, Lydia looked up at me with a deep longing in her eyes.

"No such luck. I didn't get ahold of him. Is there something I can do for you in the meantime?"

"Can I tell you what happened, so maybe when you see Vic again you can plead my case?" Lydia asked in the most pathetic tone I'd probably ever heard.

"Well, I guess so." I really didn't want to hear it, but what choice did I have?

"TL, I haven't been feeling well. Migraines have always plagued me. And when Vic wanted to go to the coast for the weekend, I just couldn't get myself out of bed the morning we were to leave. I wanted to! I would have given anything to go with him. He was so upset with me when he left, saying he'd just go by himself then, that I was always thinking of myself first. I told him I could go another time. That I'd pay for it all. He just wouldn't listen. He accused me of ruining his fun. Oh, TL, what happened then has made me physically sick. Later that afternoon, I finally got to feeling better. I thought the best thing to do was drive over to where we planned on staying and surprise Vic, let him know how much I really did want to be with him. When I got to the hotel, I saw his car in the parking lot. My heart was so happy! He was here, and I could make this all up to him. I got a spot to park right next to his car, and I went in through the lobby, so glad that my headache had cleared. When I got to the front desk, they wouldn't give me Vic's room number, so I tried his phone. He didn't answer. They agreed to phone his room, but he didn't answer that either. I didn't know what to do, so I took a seat in the lobby. After some time, I heard laughter coming out of the elevator. When I looked over, Vic came out first, with a couple of other people behind him. I started to get up to let him know I made it, we could be together after all. Then I saw him turn to the woman behind him and...and...he KISSED her!"

The sobbing was back to uncontrollable now, and I knew this is probably where Abby came into the picture. What could I say? My brother. Can't live with him...well, can't live with him. Period. Male nor female. What a mess!

All I could say, which sounded stupid, was, "What did you do then?"

"I couldn't move. I couldn't think. I just sat there. It's a large lobby, so once Vic was done...making out with this woman in front of the now emptied elevator, they started to walk in my direction. Vic spotted me. The young woman didn't have a clue who I was. The look on Vic's face wasn't one of remorse, or shock...it was one of a cold, unmoving, inhuman stare. Where were the feelings he had for me? Could they be gone that quickly? Vic walked toward me, and in anger said, 'What are you doing here? I thought you had a headache? Are you checking up on me?' Before I could barely utter a word, he was gone. He and the girl he was with. He left me there in a puddle of tears, shock, and my own remorse."

"Remorse? I hate to break it to you, but Vic is an unfaithful, lying, slug of a guy—my own brother. Don't chase after him, Lydia. Let him go, while you still have any sense left in your head. Vic isn't going to change. No matter how much you talk to him and explain this to him. He didn't waste a minute to hook up with someone else, and you deserve better than that."

"But he loves me, TL. He really does! We have been spending so much time together. I know I mean something to him..."

"I'm going to be harsh with you here, because I want you to get this. Vic doesn't know what love is. He uses people. Plain and simple. He uses me to pay the rent. He uses you to fulfill his needs. We are just people he uses for his own self pleasure. When we fail to satisfy those things for him, he moves on to someone he thinks better fulfills his needs. But in my case, I'm going to move on first." I was sorry it was out once I said it. I didn't want Vic getting wind of my plans. Then again, he probably wouldn't be having much contact with Lydia in the future, so I shouldn't worry.

"I think you're wrong, TL."

"You can think what you want, but we're both the ones sitting here unable to get ahold of Vic. I think we better call it a night. I've had a long week, and you have some thinking to do. I'll let Vic know you came by, although he already knows. That's why he left. You can take it from there. But I'm warning you, this will only change when you do. Vic is Vic. You gotta find yourself before you find him, so he doesn't swallow you up and spit you out any more than he already has. Take a long look at who is apologizing here. It's not Vic. He doesn't even realize he needs to. He cheated on YOU, Lydia! And you're still running after him. For a while, he was addicted to you, you were his supply. Now he's moved on. The best thing you can do now is get over your addiction to his addiction to you. It's a crazy, wild ride, and you gotta get off of it before it destroys you. You liked how he needed you, how he wanted you, no matter how he treated you. You're better than that. Let Vic go, and get your own life back. Sadly, he won't even miss you because you were never you, you were just his to use for a time. Vic can't really be in a true relationship with anyone until he finds his own healing. He doesn't know how, Lydia...he doesn't know how—he's not capable, no matter how much love you bring to the relationship."

"It's just so hard for me to think that someone could be so manipulative and toxic on purpose," she said sadly.

"It's true, and we gotta realize what's going on before it destroys us," I answered.

My heart felt sad for Lydia that night as I walked her to her car. I know I'd been bold, and it was hard for her to hear. She didn't deserve this. She was just another co-dependent in the long line of us, needing to find some healthy boundaries in our relationships. I went to bed that night reading my Bible and praying that I would be able to see myself as God sees me, as a valuable child in His Kingdom so I could be set free also. I never heard Vic come in that night. I was glad.

25

"Nice little visitor center they have here, Bobby."

"Yeah. They even hand out water for free to anyone who needs some. It gets so hot around here; guess they don't want anyone to be without it," Bobby says.

"This place goes way back. This sign says Colonel Eugene Van Patten built the Dripping Springs Resort up here in the 1870's. It was quite the social gathering place. Can you imagine living back in those times with no air conditioning?"

"I can't," Bobby laughs. "Only when my air conditioner has problems on the RV do I get a feel for it. Fortunately, that has only happened once."

"This resort also had a roller skating rink. Wow!"

"So, what's your research up here have to do with our family, TL?"

"I'm not one hundred percent sure what difference it will make. But I do know that my Grandpa Joe had a grandma named Minnie who died in this sanatorium in the early 1900's, right about 1918 from what my dad told me."

"I think I heard something about that. But it is so long ago, what does it have to do with us today?"

"That's what I'm here to find out. Maybe getting a background on this place will help? This sign says that in 1917, Van Patten sold the resort to Dr. Nathan Boyd. Boyd's wife was a victim of tuberculosis, so he used the resort as a TB sanatorium. Wouldn't that be something if Minnie knew her?"

"Seems possible," Bobby says.

"Oh look! Two rock dams, which provided water for the complex, can be seen still."

"Let's head on over then, TL. I think it's about a mile or so up the trail. Not a hard climb, if I remember right."

"I think I'll grab a bottle of that free water before we go. I don't think the old rock dams will be providing us any."

"Good idea! I'll get some, too," Bobby chimes in laughing.

The hike is a gradual climb. Like Bobby said, nothing to complain about. And with the weather being so nice today, I'm barely breaking a sweat. *"I'm gonna take some pics down toward Las Cruces here. Let's stop a few minutes. I love the look of the old horse barns here, or whatever they were."*

"I think you're right, TL. It looks like they were for horses. Oh look, there's some deer running off in the distance! I'm gonna see if I can get some pics of them."

Bobby's personality is calming as he enjoys the terrain and wild life, too. Continuing to hike, I see a sign saying that Van Patten was originally from New York, and attended West Point, serving on the staff of General Stonewall Jackson. There's a bit of history here! It says he settled in Las Cruces in 1872.

"Bobby, this resort is at 6,000 feet, 2,000 feet higher than Las Cruces. No wonder we get the views up here."

"It's a pretty cool area," he says as we continue the hike.

"A stageline came up here from Las Cruces, which is a 17 mile trip. I think our trip here today by car was a might easier than they had it!"

"I believe you're right," Bobby laughs.

"Look here! Indians lived in these areas. It says a large crew of Indian boys worked here and carried water from the springs to the rooms in jugs. Bet their tips weren't too great. Not like working a cruise ship."

"For sure. Let's see, Van Patten sold this all to Boyd who had studied medicine in San Francisco. But he originally came here as an agent for a British company, planning to build a dam on the Rio Grande River. It says that project was stopped by a government injunction. Just think, if it hadn't been, would this sanatorium have ever been built?" Bobby asks. *"Minnie would have never ended up here."*

"Isn't it strange how twists and turns can change a person's path? I think about being here now because of difficulties I ran into with my brother. Who knows what my future will hold since leaving the Bay Area? Let's walk on up further and see what's there."

"Okay, sure," Bobby answers with ease.

It seems even in not knowing my second cousin well, I still feel more relaxed with him than I do my own brother. What a breath of fresh air he is today. It feels good to just be, and not worry about the next thing that might come out of Vic's mouth that will set my guts churning.

"Lots of walls still standing here," Bobby says, pointing out what was left of the buildings. *"Look, you can see where the hallway was inside the resort. Picture those Indian boys lugging the water through there."*

Walking up further, I can hear water. On the left, there's a little *spillway. It must run faster some months than others. I wonder if it totally dries up in the heat of summer? "Let's go up there, Bobby. The sign says, 'Boyd Sanatorium.' It looks like we're getting up into the mountains to a place that's actually tucked in behind those that we can see from Las Cruces. How cool is this?"*

"TL, do you know how old Minnie was when she died here?"

"I think she was right around 40, something like that. My dad has a picture of Minnie. She left something like eight children behind with her husband, James. Your grandma, Lucy, was one of the eight, if I've got this figured out right. Lucy was my Great-Grandma.

"Yeah. I think that's right. I really haven't put a lot of thought into it. Some people love this ancestry stuff. Me, not so much. I think skeletons left in the closet can be best."

"That's something I'm going to find out. But I won't bug you with it if you're not interested, Bobby."

"I don't know. Let's see how this plays out," Bobby answers tentatively as we walk on toward the sanatorium.

I like being here with Bobby. I could have come alone but that wouldn't have been half as much fun. I feel like we're two explorers, digging up old artifacts. Although the signs do say, "Stay off structure...help protect your heritage." That's funny. I do have family history here. Would my Great-Great Grandma Minnie, spending her final days here with TB, have ever thought 100 years later we would be here, seeing the walls left behind that once surrounded her? How sad for the children she never saw again. I wonder if Lucy was one of the oldest? Maybe she had to care for the younger ones when her mom was gone? I wonder what Lucy was like?

"Hey, Bobby, do you remember much about your Grandma Lucy?"

"Oh, yeah. Some. She was a nice lady. She would always make me waffles. She grew apples in her back yard, and I loved to eat them fresh off the tree when I would visit her. She was kind of quiet, but my grandpa sure wasn't. He was...well, gruff, might describe him best. He used to get mad at me if I ate too many apples at once. One day I got my shirt caught on a branch and it ripped. Oh wow, you should have heard him call for my grandma. And she came a runnin'! She knew when Grandpa called, you listened. He chewed her out for what I'd done. Said it was all her fault for not watching me close enough. I felt so bad. It wasn't her fault. Grandma always took careful care of me. But she took the blame, not saying a thing—just taking me into the house and fixing my shirt as best she could while Grandpa stood there and told her how to do it. I kinda stayed clear of the apples after that. At least when Grandpa Bart was around."

Listening to Bobby, I felt his pain. I knew what he was describing perfectly, and it made me think about narcissism coming down through the generations. Is it because it's modeled for us? Or in our genes? Or maybe both? I wonder if anyone really knows?

"Bobby, your grandpa sounds like the kind of person I'm trying to stay clear of in Vic."

"Oh. That makes sense. And I also see it in my mom, right? Do you think it's inherited?" Bobby asks.

"I don't really know."

"I hadn't really thought about all this, TL. I just knew there were people in my family, like Grandpa Bart, and Mom, who were not easy to be around. And you're saying it can be because of narcissism? And what's that again, exactly?" Bobby asks.

"I'm not sure of the most complete definition of it, but it includes some of the characteristics we talked about on the way here. My notes say they are a person who commands another person's resources. They are self-absorbed, and they devalue others. They are manipulative, as well as many other things. You know, it's hard to change if you don't want to, and even if you do, that's still tough. But if you don't even see a need for change, then what? When we see something wrong in ourselves, and want to change it, that can have good results. But when we feel guilty about the bad stuff that we're doing and saying, and shut down from it, not caring about getting healthier, that seems to do just the opposite. I remember once when I said something sarcastic, and someone called my attention to it. It really struck a chord with me. Was I being like my dad? I made a conscious decision to cut out the sarcasm. Yeah, sometimes it's funny, but it seems to get meaner over time. It makes me think, isn't sarcasm really a devaluing of others? Anyway, from that point on, I figured even the little bit of funny it might be, wasn't worth the possibility of hurting someone with my words. I appreciated it being brought to my attention."

"Wow, that's good, TL. I see what you're saying. Do you think that by Minnie dying and leaving all those kids behind, it could be the cause of some of this narcissism stuff in our family still today, TL?"

"Well, wounds from childhood, from what I've read, can develop into a co-dependent nature or a narcissistic one, depending on how we respond to them. And there is a wide-spectrum there, also. It sounds like Lucy was more on the co-dependent side. But did she marry Bart because of that? Maybe Lucy grew up taking care of others, and didn't know anything different by the time she met Bart? He was probably attracted to her because of that, as she was to him with his neediness. That very possibly could have been a root cause of where we find ourselves today with your mom and my dad. Somehow, and I say this hoping, you and I escaped the narcissistic side. But sadly for me, not the co-dependent one. That is something I plan on working on in myself. I put up with Vic for way too long. When I cried out to God, 'When will it stop?' It seemed He answered me, 'When you do.' So I had to do something to change what was happening. Funny thing, Vic has pretty much given up trying to get hold

of me. At first, he was pretty relentless. Now it's totally quiet. I don't know what to think."

"Wow. It can get confusing. You may be helping me realize some things with my own mom. I think we're already discovering some hidden nuggets about our past here in the mountains today."

"Me, too, Bobby. Me, too."

26

Vic's car was out front the next morning, and his bedroom door was shut. He had come in, but I had no idea when. I quickly got dressed and went out for a run. I still felt so bad for Lydia, even though she needed to hear the truth. But now, the last thing I needed was to have an exchange with Vic.

It felt good to get out and be free. I got to think more on the run about what my future plans would be. Sitting on a park bench after about four miles, I took some time to process my thoughts and pray. Prayer was hard, like plowing the soil sometimes, like I heard in a sermon a few weeks back. It can seem boring. But it can yield amazing results. I had recently read that prayer is our best tool against the enemy, Satan. I needed all the tools I could get with Vic. He seemed so cruel at times. But then it made it hard in the moments when he was actually nice—it was confusing. Which Vic was I supposed to believe, and know?

Kids were playing in the park, the parents probably trying to get some outdoor time before it got hot. It was going to be a warm one. I was glad to be out early. An elderly lady sat down on the bench beside me. I didn't think much of it, until she started to talk to me...

"Beautiful day, isn't it?" she commented.

"Sure is. Good day to be out of the house and breathe in the fresh air before it gets hot," I answered.

"Looks like you're a runner? I used to ride a bike in my younger days. How far are you going today?"

Looking over at her now, she was probably in her 70's. It was hard to picture her on a bike. "I ran about four miles," I said. "Just taking some time here before going home." I didn't really want to venture too far into anything with her, but she seemed to want to continue talking.

"Do you live close?" she asked.

"Yeah. About a half mile from here." I almost asked her where she lived, but I stopped and said nothing. I more wanted to be looking at some stuff on my phone than having a chit-chat conversation with this lady, although she seemed very nice.

"It's a pleasant area. Interesting though, as I sit here watching these families. You just never know, do you?" She left that question just sort of hanging there. I had little choice but to finish it with another question.

"You just never know what?" I asked, although not really all that interested.

"You just never know what people are really like." She was the one seemingly willing to stop there. I was the one then more interested in continuing on with the conversation.

Putting my phone away I said, "That's true, I guess. Why do you say that?" I wondered then what her life might be like.

"I say that because of the Scripture I was reading this morning." She paused there and looked at me. "Do you believe the Bible to be true?"

Wow, she dove right into that one. What boldness, I thought.

"I do," was all I answered.

"Good for you. Because it is. It's the only Truth we really have in this world. Everything else seems to be more like a façade."

I was getting to like this woman, she didn't speak too much, but it was obvious she was a deep thinker.

"A façade?" Now my part of the conversation seemed simplistic. I hope she didn't think I was the chit-chatter.

"Yes. I think most people who read the Bible are familiar with the verse about the Pharisees being white-washed tombs in Matthew?" She ended it like a question.

"I guess." I wasn't totally familiar with that, but I had definitely heard it preached about.

"What caught my attention even more is right above that passage. It's about the cup," she said.

"The cup?" I repeated. Now she did have me stumped.

"Yes. In Matthew 23 Jesus talks about the Pharisees cleaning the outside of their cup and dish, but inside they are filthy—full of greed and self-indulgence. Jesus said to wash the inside of the cup, and then the outside would become clean, too. It makes me question how well we really know people? Are we only seeing the clean outside, and the inside is totally different?"

This woman was speaking to me at this point. I began to wonder, did God sit her down here next to me? I sat quiet for a moment when she stopped talking. She sat quiet, too, just watching the children play on the apparatus.

"Mind if I ask you something," I said.

"Not at all," she replied.

"It's almost like you know something is going on in my life. Something that others might not see from the outside." I wasn't sure how to explain myself from that point on, without sharing the total story. So I asked her, "Is there a reason you're sitting here talking with me today? I don't mean to be rude, but..."

"You're not being rude. I love your question. I sensed when I sat down here that you weren't just resting from your run. Your mind seemed absorbed with something. I didn't want to disturb you, but sometimes we just need help processing things. I've lived long enough to know that." She chuckled then, as did I.

"Oh, I need help. Maybe in all your years... Oh, I don't mean to imply that you're old." I stopped.

Laughing, she said, "My name is Sarah, by the way."

"I'm Tracy Lynn. TL for short."

"Nice to meet you Tracy Lynn. I don't want to impose upon you, but if there is something you'd like to talk about, I have plenty of time." Sticking her arm up in the air, she added, "I don't even wear a watch."

"I feel funny telling a perfect stranger what's going on in my life."

Sarah laughed again, saying, "Well, you needn't worry then, because I'm nowhere near perfect."

How could I not give this a try, with her gentle wit.

"Sarah, I live with my brother. My younger brother. And it's not going well. I need to move on, so I have to find out where I'm going and when."

"Where and when? Both very good questions. I'm big on prayer, so I can't help but tell you to start by asking God what your plan should be. He is the great Provider of all things. Both large and small. Sometimes the answers are quick. Sometimes, the answers are very slow in coming. But through it all God is trustworthy. He has everyone's best interest at heart. I'm sorry, I don't mean to push too much."

"You're fine. I'm listening. My mom is a praying woman also. And..." I didn't know if I should really get deeper into this, but I did, "...she is dealing with my dad. He's a lot like my brother."

"Do they both have strong personalities?" Sarah asked.

"You could say that. I'm learning that they may both have a personality disorder called narcissism. That sounds pretty ominous when I say it out loud to you."

"I'm familiar with what you're talking about. It's not all that uncommon. In fact, most people you will talk to have someone they know with similar characteristics. There's no real easy answer. Everyone, and every life situation, is so different. One thing that's important, if you don't mind my input..."

"Go right ahead." I was beginning to trust this not-so-perfect stranger.

"There's a portion of Mark that talks about the demonized man in the cemetery. Have you heard of him?" she asked.

"I guess. I don't know the story all that well," I answered.

"It's not a long story," Sarah said, "but an important one. The man lived an isolated life because what was ruining his life was so powerful—it made him into a naked crazed man living among the tombs. Jesus came along and set him free. But we have to notice, the man was the one that came to Jesus and bowed before him. His pride didn't keep him from Jesus, even though the demonic powers that were controlling him fought against it. He pressed through his demons, seeking healing. We all have those opposing spirits...one part of us wants the fleshly desires, the other part, the spirit, is drawn to Jesus. We have to decide if we want Jesus more than we want other things in this life, like control, alcohol, even worry...worry can truly grip us and change us into people we don't want to be--or being liked by others...that's another one. Being people pleasers is not being a Jesus pleaser. Many involved with people who have strong personalities, like narcissist, are people pleasers. The two always seem to be a perfect, or not-so-perfect match, I should say—it's out of balance. One in control, one being controlled."

"Uh, you are hitting close to home with me now, Sarah," I said.

"It's okay, Tracy Lynn, hitting close to home is where change inside us gets its start. We always sit in church thinking our spouse should be there, or our child should be there, hearing the message. When what we should be doing is taking it in for ourselves and trusting God with their lives. What we want for them, is also needed in us, perhaps just in a different way. We can trust God that they will hear what they need to hear, at the right time. When our own lives change through the power of Jesus, that's when we can, and only when we can, have the greatest impact for the Kingdom of God on those around us. It may not be as obvious as a crazed naked man running out of the tombs. But we truly need to look at ourselves first, seeking healing and change with Jesus. Then, and only then can we do what Jesus told this healed man to do."

"What was that?" I asked.

"He told him to go home to his family and tell them everything the Lord had done for him first. How merciful Jesus had been to him."

"Oh, that makes good sense," I said. "I'm hearing you. God made that pretty clear when I called out to Him one day. It has to start with me. You are definitely confirming that. We have to put our own oxygen mask on first, just like instructed on each plane flight."

"Well, TL. He's not a God that messes around. He will teach those that are willing. This man in the cemetery was willing, and he was healed. When we aren't willing to give ourselves completely to Christ, we will be ruled by dark forces. There is a queen in the Bible named Jezebel. She was married to Ahab. Many today are still affected by the same wicked spirit that ruled her. It is a very controlling and manipulating spirit."

"It makes me wonder if my brother has it?" I asked.

"Perhaps. Many even sit in church, believing in Jesus and thinking they are right with God, but in their hearts they are far from Him. People with controlling personalities sometimes have this Jezebel spirit about them. They have a hard time seeing that change is needed in themselves. They are trying to change and control everyone around them instead...to meet their selfish needs. This is driven by their own insecurity and pride. Only Jesus can help them if they will bow before Him, giving Him their heart for transformation. If they won't..."

"If they won't, then what? This is what I need to know, Sarah. The rest I think is sinking into my thick skull."

"Well, you've probably heard it before...boundaries are key. We have to prayerfully decide where our healthy boundaries will be with people like that. Just like that cup we were talking about, people can be clean looking on the outside, but when we get to know the inside, it can be quite different. Now, I'm not telling you to fear relationships. Just be wise, even with family...sometimes especially with family, in your case. We need to have a sense of self-preservation. And even with someone like your dad, or your brother, you will eventually realize that there is already a loss there if they are not willing to get healthy themselves."

"A loss?"

"Yes, a loss of unconditional love that you will need to mourn."

"Oh. And there's a grieving process even with that?" I asked.

"Yes. Of course, we desire unconditional love, especially from our parents. But that is a rarity on earth. Only God truly gives unconditional love. He is the One who will never leave us nor forsake us. We have to come to terms with our parents' limitations. We all have them...limitations, that is. And when we recognize these limitations, we can begin to find some healing. We idealize our parents, especially the good ones. But we can't make an idol out of anything or anyone. We must have God as our top priority, so all else can fall into place as it should. Some tend to focus on the good stuff and minimize the disappointments with others, forgiving and forgetting very quickly, so they can keep them on the 'throne.' Of course, we are to forgive, as Jesus taught. But ending up with a tangled, complicated set of unacknowledged feelings is not God's plan either. We can have a problem with how to handle certain relationships if we aren't honest with ourselves—sometimes we repress too much. Taking it all to God in prayer when there is a problem, is once again, key. He is most willing to listen and help."

"Wow, Sarah, you just brought this conversation to a place where my mom is at. She's working on recognizing her own thoughts and feelings. It has been helping her. Maybe God sat you down here today to reinforce that in me--that I need to do the same."

"Sounds like your mom is moving in the right direction. Remember, too, a narcissist's cup seems full of self-confidence, but really deep inside they feel like a fraud. They are in fear that others will expose them, so they work hard at maintaining control of everything and everyone by cleaning the outside of their cup. Sadly, they are so wounded and in fear of rejection, that they try to control others so they won't be rejected, and that's exactly what happens. People don't want to be around them. Many times we label them 'Control Freaks.' Our first step in these types of relationships is recognizing what's going on, see the cup for what it really is, and then allow the process of discovery and healing to unfold in ourselves. Which is what probably has you sitting on the bench here today."

"You're exactly right about that. I don't want to keep you much longer, Sarah, and I need to get home, too. But thanks for talking with me today. I don't know how God does it, but He has helped me with your story of the cup and the crazed man. I will look those up in my Bible, and pray about it all. I need to do that more often."

"Your journey has many steps, Tracy Lynn. Keep walking it out. You're on a good path when you're following Jesus. Be at peace, and always pray for your dad and brother. They need your prayers. Forgive them, too. That's so very important. Forgiveness keeps your heart free."

Sarah's voice sounded so soothing. I couldn't help but give this stranger a hug good-bye before I jogged away. When I got to the edge of the parking lot, I took one look back at this sweet lady. I hoped to see her again one day. She was gone. There is really only one way to exit that park...the way I was going. Could she have been...? Nahh, do angels really visit us on park benches?

27

It's not too bad walking up the rest of the way. Bobby is just ahead of me.

"Hey Bobby, I'm surprised how much of this is still standing with the vandalism they've had here. Especially since it says some of these were ephemeral structures."

"Uh...what? You're going to have to translate that word for me. What is ephemeral?" Bobby asks, laughing again.

"Hey, I'm with you. I didn't know either. But it just so happens I ran across that word recently and had to look it up, so when I read it on this sign here, I knew what they meant. You don't hear it every day. Ephemeral means short-lived, lasting for a very short amount of time."

"Oh, okay. I don't know that I'll be using it a lot," Bobby says chuckling.

"From what I read here they are trying to restore portions of the ruins. It's fun walking around all this, but I don't know if we're going to find a lot of answers. Seems like we can get a feel for how isolated the TB patients were though. I don't know much about TB, but once here, I doubt they saw their families again. How sad that one of our relatives actually died here. Even though the illness was isolated in these structures, the effect of it may still run deep through our ancestral line. I'm thinking Lucy was an innocent victim of her mom's TB condition. After being left as the oldest child and raising her siblings, she married Bart, and then gave birth to grandpa Joe and your mom, Martha. Sounds like your grandpa Bart rubbed off on your mom. And my dad and Vic got caught up in it, too. I think I actually read that it's not uncommon for the narcissistic traits to show up in subsequent generations. The Bible says the sins can go through three and four generations. Maybe it's all tied together somehow? I guess our job is to identify what's happening in our lives and put a stop to it. Not easily done, but I've heard with God all things are possible. My mom is

big on that right now. She's trying to set up healthier boundaries in her life. It's hard, but needed. My dad has done a good job of wearing her down, but she's trusting God to make her strong again. She loves that verse about finding renewed strength in Isaiah. She always says, 'They rise up as if they had eagles' wings.'"

"Eagles are so cool. I'm glad you have a good relationship with your mom, TL. I wish I had that with my mom. My dad, Harry, was a good guy. I sure miss him. That cancer took him quick a few years ago."

"Yeah. I was sorry to hear about your dad, Bobby. Really sorry."

"Thanks. What do you say we head down now, and grab something to eat? All this hiking is making me hungry again."

Walking back toward the visitor center, I notice the creek beds are bone dry. Only rocks remain in them.

"Bobby, sometimes my life with Vic seemed so dry--like I was stepping from rock to rock having no real connection with him."

Moving the toe of his shoe back and forth through the dusty trail we are on, Bobby says, "As dry as this, huh?"

"Yes. It felt that way. Parched. But even though I'm in this dry land now, and the greenery of California has been left behind me, I'm feeling more refreshed here. Just spending the day with you helps. You're a good guy, Bobby. You're showing me what a normal relationship can be like with a level-headed relative. It seems we really connect."

"I have my moments, too, TL." Bobby says.

"I'm sure you do. We all do. But dealing with junk from someone day in and day out gets old fast. I could barely make it the year with Vic. He wore on me each day."

"Tell me some of what it was like as we hike. Maybe I will be able to identify some things about my mom and you'll be a help to me to make more of the changes I need to. I can be very good at sweeping a lot of things under the rug and ignoring them. It's just not worth the battle sometimes," Bobby explains.

"I getcha! I'm the same way, although you have healthier boundaries it seems. We don't like ruffled feathers. I've heard that this is a discovery process. It doesn't happen overnight. You could say it's like a story that's waiting to be written. I'm not a writer, but I am living this, so I'm reading and listening to a lot of things. Self-help, self-healing is the way I have to do it. I know counselors are expensive. My mom says the Holy Spirit is our Counselor, so I'll have to work it along those lines. Keep talking to God about things—only He knows what we really need to work on."

Bobby says encouragingly, "I don't know anything about the Holy Spirit. But you go guy! I think you're on the right path."

"There's some stuff I've heard, sometimes even on a park bench, but that's a story for another time... We have to want to heal. And if we don't, I believe we really can hand this stuff down to our kids. If I ever have any,

they will be around their grandpa and uncle, and I want them to know how to draw a line in this dry dirt and say, 'Don't cross it!' If my dad ever talks to my kids the way you said Bart talked to you and scared you from eating any more apples...then blaming it on your grandma—I want them to know it's wrong. That's just sick."

Bobby shook his head saying, *"I better glean some of this stuff from you then, so I don't see that pattern repeated in my life, too. We grow up thinking it's normal."*

"We DO! But it doesn't need to be this way! We try to look away from it, I believe. Like it's not going on, and we start to convince ourselves to the point where we pay no attention. Our side of blindness is as sick as their side of narcissism. They say it takes two to tango...this is the same thing. Narcissism happens because they find their counterpart. If we don't look at it and find healing, we can be our own worst enemy. Not acknowledging that there even is pain in this can be very detrimental."

"I've certainly done that with my mom," Bobby answers. *"My response to my mom's cruelty at times is to hide...to ignore and pretend it never happened is easier at first, but it adds up to disastrous results later on down the line, doesn't it?"*

"I believe so. My dad has no idea how hard it is to have a conversation with him when it's so one-sided and opinionated. I wonder, does he even hear me and see me? I feel invisible to him. Instead of asking me about my trip here, he just belittles any idea of it. It makes me feel small and worthless in his eyes. No son wants that."

Bobby sighs, *"No, of course not."*

"I need to recognize these things, and deal with them now, Bobby. I'm actually starting to feel grateful that I've had such a rough year with Vic. Maybe I needed that for all of this to come to light. Maybe I would have just put up with my dad for the rest of my life as things were. That's not right. Not that I can change him, but I can change me by understanding this stuff. I think I just put up walls and hid behind them. That does no one any good. I need to take down those walls and be who I am. If my dad, or Vic, don't like it, I need to learn to live with that."

"I hear more power coming into your voice, TL," Bobby says looking straight into my eyes.

"I feel it. I've been looking into these things long enough now to at least let some of it start to absorb, not only into my mind, but into my heart. I hope being here, away from the pressure of living with Vic, will help me in that. I want to know who I am, not who Vic or my dad think I should be. It got to the point where I couldn't ignore it anymore, and maybe that's a good thing. I want my life, not theirs!"

"You're a good guy, TL. Although we haven't spent a lot of time together, I always found you to be easy going. I remember getting into a hassle or two with your brother. But I just thought it was kid's stuff. Now

I'm thinking it was more than that. You're opening my eyes. I don't want to remove everyone from my life that may be on the narcissistic side of being, but I do want to be aware of it when I see it."

"That's half the battle, from what I'm learning...acknowledging things. I learned from this one doctor online that we have conscience and unconscious parts of our brain. What we think about is very important. We can actually cause our brain to be damaged by thinking the wrong things."

"What?" Bobby asks.

"Yeah. We have to discipline our thinking, our mind, to protect our brain from stuff. It's tied with that part of the Bible that talks about taking every thought captive to Christ. It actually means what it says. If we don't do that, stop the crazy thinking, we will impact our brains in a bad way. And also, forgiveness is a huge part of all this. It's really not as much for the other person as it is for us. If we don't forgive, then those toxic thoughts of unforgiveness keep us entangled with that other person even though they might be thousands of miles away from us. If it's in our head, it's like they are right here with us. I DON'T want to give someone that much power in my life...an entrance into my head!"

"I sure don't either!" Bobby adds, "This is amazing stuff I've never thought about."

"If we forgive, then they can say whatever they want, and it can't hurt us...or our brain, at least. It can sting our emotions, of course, but then we can reject it and not allow it entrance into our brain structure. I need to forgive Vic a lot to keep him out of my brain."

"That makes me more motivated to forgive. I always thought it was for the other person."

"Bobby, from all I am learning, God is really for us and not against us. I know the Bible says that, but we gotta walk it out to really experience His great plan. I'm so glad my mom has helped me with all this stuff."

"I agree," Bobby says.

"We have to forgive to stop a narcissist from impacting our life, even when they aren't with us. I have to work on forgiving my dad, too, so he can't keep bugging me from California. It takes time for healing, but it is very possible. And I'm happy to know that. When we get to know this stuff, and talk to God about it, that doctor says we can change what was damaged in our brains to healthy brain matter. Isn't that amazing how God designed our brains to heal?"

"It sure is!"

"Some of this stuff that hurts our brains is brought on by things we do, our own sin stuff, but some is brought into our lives by others. Either way, it has to be dealt with. If it's from someone else, we have to leave that with God to deal with. If it's something we are doing, then we have a choice to make to stop it. It's all really up to us. God has given us so much power in all this by some simple steps. But I've been so caught up in it all I couldn't

see straight. Once again, thanks for letting me come to New Mexico and hang with you, Bobby. I think this New Mexico air is good for me. That makes me chuckle, isn't that what Minnie did, heading up into the Organ Mountains for healing? She may not have found healing, but I believe I am finding mine."

"This has been a good hike and talk. I'm discovering a lot with you. Maybe getting off the couch once in a while is a good thing!" Bobby laughs, adding, "I know a great place in town to grab a burger. Let's head there. But after that, I will be ready to put my feet up again."

"I'm with you! Feet up and all! Thanks!"

28

Vic was gone when I got back to the house. He probably wanted to outrun Lydia. The bench talk with the wonderful lady had delayed me long enough to award me an empty house to come back to. I wanted to call my mom after showering. Things seemed out of hand with Vic, and she was usually pretty good at leveling me out again. She would be intrigued by this lady, too.

Getting out of the shower, I heard a commotion. Cracking the bathroom door, I knew it wasn't good. Vic had come back, and Lydia must have been waiting for him. She was trying to push her way into the house, and Vic wasn't having it.

"You gotta go, Lydia. This isn't a good time!" Vic was shouting, and she was crying. "Oh, Vic, PLEASE! Let me come in. Just for a minute!"

"NO! I'm busy. I'll call you later." Vic lied. She knew it. I knew it.

"Not later, Vic. PLEASE! I need to apologize to you." Lydia hadn't listened to me, or if she had, she ignored it. She thought she loved Vic. She thought he loved her. She was mistaken. She was addicted to Vic, and his shenanigans. But Vic had moved on to Abby now, and Lydia didn't stand a chance.

I slipped out of the bathroom and into my room as the arguing at the front door finally came to an end. I had stalled long enough to hear the front door shut. I could hear Vic in the kitchen, and the squeal of tires out front. I prayed Lydia wouldn't end up in an accident. I stayed in my room, hoping Vic would leave. When I heard the front door open and shut again, and then silence, I breathed a sigh of relief. I didn't want to confront Vic any more than I had to. I dressed and called Mom.

"Hi, TL. How's your day?" Mom asked cheerfully.

"You have no idea," I sighed.

"Uh, oh," she said.

"Yeah," I moaned.

"What's happened now?" Mom's voice was taking on an agitated tone.

"Same old stuff, Mom. Vic. A new gal. A jealous old girlfriend who is caught in his web and doesn't understand. It's heartbreaking."

"It is. It makes me sad. Can I tell you some things I've been learning?" Mom asked.

"Please do. I could use some sound advice, although I have had an interesting conversation already this morning in the park. I'll tell you about it sometime. Right now, I'm just gonna sit and listen to you for a bit, and hopefully regain some sense of peace around here. I don't need to tell you how disruptive all this can be. I don't like it one bit."

"I'm so sorry, TL. And yes, I want to hear about your park conversation, too. There is a lot that I'm learning, and I'm seeing some changes in your dad because of it. I don't expect a miracle, or maybe I do. But I'm going to trust that God will work on him as I let Him work in me. I'm healing, I can feel it. But I know there are many wounds that need to be dealt with. And as I do that on my walks, asking for God's healing in those places, He shows me my brokenness. But the enemy is still relentless—he will bring things back up to me again. I have to keep remembering that it has been dealt with—that I have laid it at the feet of Jesus, and the enemy needs to take it up with God now. I have to not think about it. We have to allow God to change us, heal us, deep at the root level."

"I know. But how do we do that, Mom?"

"I'm learning that we have to understand who we are, that we were created in God's image, and follow Him. We have to pray, TL. Lots! And ask the guidance of the Holy Spirit to help us break old patterns that keep us from loving ourselves and being willing to put up with so much garbage from other people. If we just run away and ignore things, we aren't being truthful with ourselves or with others. Jesus didn't avoid things. He dealt with them. We have to live a real life, and stop pretending everything is okay. We are the Temple of the Living God, and we need to take good care of ourselves. It can feel wrong, but it's where living the abundant life Christ promises us begins. There comes a time where we need to know who we are in Christ, and refuse to be controlled by others any more. It may seem like we are hurting the other person when we do this, but that's not true. We can continue to love them, we just no longer let them control us."

"I'm listening, Mom. But this is a lot to take in. I hate to admit it, but I've been hiding in my room, waiting for Vic to leave. Talk about running away from things."

"I'm just getting a hold on this, too, TL. I'm no expert, but I'm willing to learn. We need to be teachable. And you are."

"Thanks for thinking so, Mom."

"I want to live close in relationship to God, TL. But if I'm hiding from your dad, how can I do that? The better I know me, the better I can know God. I've read that most people don't really know themselves. How sad is that? I was one of them. I lived how others thought best...mostly, your dad. But no more. I know I'm sounding a little feisty, even saying that, but maybe the pendulum has to swing just as far the other way, and then settle in a healthy middle?"

"Maybe so, Mom," I said.

"This healthiness comes by spending time with God, TL. He can reveal things to us. God knows what's impacted every day of our lives. It's pretty amazing! I know we talked about this before, but I didn't even know there was a difference between what I was thinking and what I was feeling about things. I didn't take the time to slow down and examine a lot of things. I do now, and it's helping. Even if it's something that's small. I stop, and ask myself—What do I think about this? What do I feel about this?— instead of ignoring it all in an unhealthy way and giving Satan control in those areas. Jesus has all the power, unless I give that power to the enemy."

"That's a true and interesting thought," I commented.

"Whatever God shows me, I tear down those lies, telling those things to leave me in Jesus' name. I lay those memories at the feet of Jesus. God is in the business of tearing down strongholds. After I've settled my thoughts and emotions about something, and asked God to heal and clean out any infection that's there, I then ask Him to pour His healing balm into that place in me--I breathe in His Holy Spirit. I don't want those things to grow into something even bigger and more damaging later on. God is in the business of healing us. When we follow through on His promises, those hurtful things become His responsibility. God has all the power. The enemy is weak in comparison. I don't need to dwell on damaging things anymore. I can more easily dwell on the Truth in God's Word instead. He says His yoke is easy and His burden his light."

"Yes. We have talked about some of this. But it's good to hear again. Where are you finding all this out? What exactly is a stronghold?" I asked Mom.

"I'm reading books, looking online, talking to people. And PRAYING! It's a combination of God teaching me through the Bible, and God speaking through other sources. Then I put it into practice and see if it works. It's not overnight, it takes time and effort. But I believe it's paying off. Strongholds are lies we've been living in, and then ruminating on them for years sometimes. Replacing those old lies and hurts with Truth and goodness from our heavenly Father is tearing them down. We can't really heal without Jesus helping us do these things. He is the Healer! We have to follow what God tells us and keep at it! We need to trust that God is working all things out for good to those that love Him. Even when we feel physically sick, sometimes even that is God telling us that changes are needed. We should pay attention!"

"You mean like when I have that knot in the pit of my stomach?" I asked.

"Yes. Exactly. Sometimes things in our bodies show up before our minds know what's going on. We have to be able to know ourselves, physically and emotionally. God gave us our feelings for a good reason. It all works together in our relationship with Him. If we shut down our feelings, and ignore our bodies, how can we even get close to God? We have to be real about stuff, because God is real! His love is real! And He's the foundation we build our lives on. When that foundation gets cracked, what oozes out through the cracks isn't pretty," Mom laughed.

"That sounds gross!" I laughed, too.

"Relationships get pretty ugly at times, don't they?" Mom commented.

"They sure do," I answered.

"God knows us through and through. We aren't hiding anything from Him, so we have to stop hiding from ourselves, too. We don't have to please everyone. Being less than perfect is okay, because Jesus is perfect. He will take care of the places we don't do so well. We can bring our broken selves to Him and rest in Him."

"How do we rest there, Mom? It sounds good, but I'm not quite sure I understand it."

"Even that rest takes practice, TL. I know that sounds sort of backward, because how are we to rest if we have to practice it? How can I explain this to you? There's a lot of pressure around us to do well. But ultimately, God is the only One we really need to please. That sounds harder than it is. God just wants us to spend time with Him. That's our main job. The Fruit that comes out of that time will be the best fruit ever because it's produced by the Holy Spirit. That's a whole lot easier. We just have to stay attached to the Vine, Jesus. And He will do the work."

"Okay. Stay close with God, and let Him work in me," I said.

"Yes, TL. The practice is, we practice getting quiet with God and allowing Him to heal and teach us. We can't wait until the people around us change to do this. We have to start now. There are a lot of people who have no desire to change, or even think they need to change. But all our relationships, especially the harder ones, will be more balanced when our life is focused on God."

"Mom, this is good stuff. I'm going to be processing this... I'm sorry to interrupt, but I need to go now. Can we talk again soon? I'm proud of all that you are discovering. I know your life hasn't been easy. But you've always set a good example for me, even in the worst of times. I'm not sure when or how this Vic situation will end, but right now I do know one thing, I have to work on myself like you are. So, thank you."

"You're welcome, TL. I love you. Take care of yourself. I hope I haven't overwhelmed you with all this. I'm working through it all, and talking it out with you helps me, too. The doctor has given you permission to exercise physically, but I caution you to be good to yourself on the inside, too. Don't let your brother abuse you because of your kind heart. I'm going to keep studying and practicing this, and we'll talk soon."

"Okay. And I'll be careful, Mom. Thanks. Love you. Bye."

"Bye."

29

The days in New Mexico pass by so quickly. With Bobby back at the fire station, I'm able to do some exploring on my own. It feels good to be free of all the tension back in California. Not talking to Vic seems best right now. I'm glad his calls and texts have stopped. He's probably found someone else to focus on for his needs.

Sitting outside the RV this morning, I wonder what the day will hold? I'm not really looking for a job yet. What's really on my heart is to pay a visit to Great-Aunt Martha. I know Bobby's mom is not an easy person, just like my dad, but I think visiting her might reveal some things. I haven't really spent time with her in years. I think I'll give her a call here in a bit. For now, I'm going to continue reading my Bible. Mom has encouraged me to start to see myself as God sees me. If she's finding healing in this way, also discovering who she is and what her needs are, I think I should do the same.

It's interesting reading through Matthew, and how Jesus is so deserted and treated harshly before His crucifixion. He stays so quiet when they accuse Him of false charges. I notice that the time He does answer them is when they are speaking the truth about Him, like here in Matthew 26, around verse 62. The high priest said to Jesus, "Well, aren't you going to answer these charges? What do you have to say for yourself? But Jesus remained silent." That's interesting. I'd want to defend myself against their lies. Jesus knew who He was, and who He wasn't. He wasn't wasting His breath on their foolishness. But when they got to the truth, He spoke right up. Here in verse 63 when the high priest said to Him, "I demand in the name of the living God that you tell us whether you are the Messiah, the Son of God." Jesus immediately answered, "Yes, it is as you say. And in the future you will see me, the Son of Man, sitting at God's right hand in the place of power and coming back on the clouds of heaven."

Jesus gave them an answer, and probably more than they expected. He told the truth, but did that make them mad! The high priest then tore his clothing to show his horror, and shouted, "Blasphemy!" among other things. The truth really riled the high priest up. It seems like he was more comfortable with the lies. Maybe we all are at times. Maybe that's why Mom said we need to be real. I wonder if Martha will be real with me? I think I'll give her a call.

"Hello?"

"Hi, Aunt Martha. This is Tracy Lynn."

"Oh, hi! I heard you got here. How are you doing? I haven't talked to your dad in quite a while. You know how it can be with relatives who live far apart. Will was always a fiery nephew. He had a good strong mind of his own. Your Grandpa Joe used to say he took after his own dad, Bart. Could be! I was just getting myself something to eat here. Will you be coming by? I'd love to see you. It's been so long, I don't..."

Interrupting feels uncomfortable, but if I don't, I think Martha will go on for a long time without pause. She asked me how I was doing and didn't take a moment to listen to what my answer would be.

"Aunt Martha, I'd really like to come and see you. Are you available in a bit?"

"Oh sure. Come on by. I have some sewing projects I'm working on, but I don't mind taking a break from that. It's nothing that needs to be done right away. I used to sew clothes for my kids, but of course Bobby wouldn't be caught dead in anything I'd make for him today. He's quite busy with the fire department. I don't know how he keeps that schedule, it seems rather odd to me. Working days, and then not working days. Why can't they just work regular shifts like the rest of the world. I've talked..."

"OKAY THEN! We can talk about all that when I see you. I have a couple of things to do, and then I'll be over."

"Oh. Oh sure. Okay. I'll wait for you to get here."

"Okay, bye!"

"Bye-bye."

Hanging up, I'm already exhausted and I haven't even visited my great aunt yet. I can see this will be challenging. I'm not sure what kind of family information I'll get out of her, but from this first phone call, she seems very willing to talk.

"Lord, help me!" *I say out loud. I feel a tightness in my chest. Mom says I should pay attention to those things. So, what is this, God? Am I okay? Is it physical, or emotional? I think from hearing Aunt Martha go on and on this morning it's probably emotional. Help me be strong, Lord. Help me get to things quickly with her, and not let her go on with negative talk about Bobby, or anything really. Bobby is a good guy. I hope this is worth it.*

Showering in the RV park showers, and then finishing a few other things, I'm ready to go. It's a short drive over to Martha's. Her neighborhood is nice, although it looks very different from California. The wind isn't too bad today, so the Organ Mountains are crisp and clear. The last couple of days the wind did pick up, and I could barely see them. With a knock on the door, Martha appears.

"Hi, Tracy Lynn. Come on in!" *Martha is enthusiastic.*

"Thanks."

Martha's place is small, but nice. Ushering me into her living room, she takes a seat in what is obviously her chair. Her sewing basket sits beside it, and I see her machine over in the corner. I hear a bird singing in the kitchen. It doesn't sound large. I haven't visited many people with birds, but those that have them sure seem to love them.

"That's Whitey in the kitchen. He's my buddy. He's welcoming you. We don't get many visitors so he probably wonders what's going on. Would you like to see him? Come with me."

Martha is quickly back on her feet and heading into the kitchen. Without a choice, I follow behind, knowing this visit could be challenging.

"Whitey, we have a visitor! This is TL, he's Bobby's second cousin. He's just moved here. Are you hungry? I'll get you your special treat. Take it easy, it's okay. TL won't hurt you."

Turning to me, I can tell Martha is fully enthralled with her bird. I know I'll need to wait, but I'm hoping this won't be an hour-long bird visit.

"Whitey was a baby bird that was injured. I rescued him. He had a broken leg, and the vet didn't think he would make it. He said that to keep him alive I would need to feed him every 20 minutes for six weeks. So I did. And look! Here he is, years later, doing so well! He will fly and sit on my shoulder, and in my hair, and we just have the best of times...don't we, Whitey?"

I manage to get in a "Uh-huh," in before Martha continues.

"Some people don't like birds. They are actually afraid of them. I don't know why. They are not out to harm anyone. Maybe it comes from that old horror movie about birds back in the 60's. You're probably too young to remember it. It was quite the sensation in its day. Now, when I watch it, I can see the movies have so much more quality. Have you heard of it? Doesn't matter, there are better movies to watch today. There you go, Whitey, settle down in your cage now. I have company."

"Aunt Martha?"

Turning to me, it seems at last there is a break in the action and I might be able to get something accomplished after all. Maybe she is just an old lady who gets lonely?

"I'd like to ask you some questions about our family history."

"Oh boy. Family...there's a complicated subject. What is it you want to know? Are there skeletons? You bet. But doesn't every family have some? I don't think..."

"Aunt Martha, can I talk with you about your Great Grandma, Minnie, who died in the Sanitorium?"

"You want to go that far back? Oh my...that's a story in itself. You know she had eight children at home when they carted her off to that place up in the mountains. Eight children! Can you imagine? Her poor husband, James, he had his hands full. He had to depend on my mom, Lucy, for help there. She was the oldest of the siblings. And she stayed at home with those kids until she was at least 25. Then I think she'd had enough, so she up and married my dad, Bart. I can tell you, that wasn't the best relationship. My mom was pitiful. So weak. I was determined not to repeat that pattern. When I married Harry, bless his soul, now gone almost three years...I miss that man. But I knew I wouldn't live like my mom did. Harry needed to know he was not going to be telling me what to do. We were a partnership, equal. Even though that wasn't popular in my day like it is now. Your generation has it right, women have rights!"

By this time, back in the living room, Martha is deep into her stories, and I might as well just be all ears. Once in a while, I try to interject a word to get her off on a different tract that I'm more interested in. It seems to be working.

"Aunt Martha, what about my Grandma Betty? What would you say she is like?"

"Oh, you didn't know her well, did you? She was such a weak woman. Sort of like my brother, Joe. Both of them, God bless them, but really, TL? Neither one of them had a full back bone between them! I think Joe saw how our mom was, and he was such a momma's boy. He took after her, and married Betty because she was a woman just like our mom. Ahh, they were a sweet couple, I guess. Never did ever hear them fight with one another. I didn't really like Betty. For a sister-in-law, I guess she was okay. But..."

I'm starting to get a picture of my family history the longer Martha talks. Who needs history books, when someone like Martha has it all in her head and is so willing to share it?

"What can you tell me about my dad, Will? Any thoughts on him?"

Martha looks at me. I think she's wondering if I'm serious. For a second, she pauses, but then can't help herself dive into just how she sees my dad.

"Will is a man I admire. He is strong. I don't see much of him in you Tracy Lynn. You're on the quiet side. Not Will, he will tell you how it is, and he keeps your mom in line, too."

I sort of reel back at the brutal honesty that just spilled out into the room. I need to be able to withstand this to get the full picture, but I'm really not liking where all this is going.

"Now your brother, Vic, although he's younger than you...from what I hear that young guy knows his mind. I've talked to your dad. You're more

like your mom, TL, so much like her. We can't be like that in this world. This world will chew us up and spit us out if we don't go for it first. Vic knows that! Your dad says you hang back more. I know he wouldn't want you lazing around. He'd want you out getting a job. Are you looking? What do you have in mind?"

Swallowing my pride, I answer... "I'm thinking of opening a little taco shop. There are..."

"TACO SHOP!? TL, do you know how many Mexican food places we have around here? You'll never make it! You should go to one of the other restaurants, and just get a job there as a cook or something. I know you can cook. But striking out on your own is too risky. You'll be belly-up within six months! It's a proven..."

"Aunt Martha. I have to end our time together today. I have an appointment I need to get to, but thanks for letting me come over." Walking quickly to the front door, I know that this last hour and a half has not been good for my mental or physical health. I can feel my heart beating rapidly, and my mind is swirling with so many thoughts I can't sort through them. I feel the need to escape! This is how I felt back in California!

"Come back soon, Tracy Lynn. I should have you and Bobby over for dinner. Maybe you can bring some chicken when you come."

"Okay. I'll talk to Bobby about it. Thanks!"

It feels good to be back in my hot car. The sun has heated it up, but I could sit there and sweat and be happier than I was in that house. That woman is CRAZY! Oh, I better be nice. NO! That was crazy! That was a very one-sided, uncaring, conversation. I don't think she had any interest in me at all, other than to just spew whatever came into her head next. And I thought my dad was bad! He's a pussy-cat compared to Aunt Martha! It will feel so good to get back to the RV and chill until Bobby gets home. We will certainly have some things to talk about tonight!

30

After getting off the phone with Mom, and telling her about Lydia, I left the house. I wanted to have the day to think about many of the things we talked about without interruption from Vic or his antics. I pretty much avoided him and let him do his thing. But after a few more weeks, things got even worse. When coming home from work, I saw the firetrucks in front of our place. Vic was standing on the front lawn talking rapidly to the fire chief, or so it seemed. He looked like the fireman in charge. I parked across the street and made my way over. I had no idea what had happened. The house still stood, but there were firemen still inside and things looked pretty messy.

"What's going on Vic? I practically yelled as I came across the street. Vic turned and looked at me with eyes that shot right through me. The fire chief, too, looked my way. I suddenly felt like the suspicious one, for whatever reason, I wasn't sure yet.

"THERE YOU ARE!! That's my brother. He did this! He left the stove on when he went to work this morning, and now look what's happened."

"What's happened, Vic? Sir? Can someone fill me in?" I asked, feeling the tension rise quickly as I got closer to the two of them.

Reaching out to shake my hand, the fire chief filled me in. "We have had to extinguish a fire that started in the kitchen. It seems to have come from the stove. Your brother told me that you cooked this morning, and you were prone to leaving it on in the past."

Looking at Vic, I was beyond mad. I could hardly look him in the face. I knew, and he had to know, that this wasn't my fault. I hadn't even cooked that morning. He was asleep when I left, and he probably got up to make some breakfast after I went to work.

"Vic, I didn't make anything this morning on the stove. Did you?" I knew my voice was harsh, but I couldn't help it. I felt like we were kids again, trying to place the blame on each other so we could escape the consequences of what had happened.

"Seriously," Vic said. "This is NOT my fault. You know how you always forget to turn the stove off. I've been gone most the day. This is not my doing. Wait until you see the damage it's done. The landlord's going to be furious!"

"Gentlemen," the fire chief said, both of us turning in his direction then. "I don't know who is at fault here, that's not my responsibility to place blame. All we know is that a fire was started by the stove, and it has been put out. I will fill out the paper work, and you can settle this with your landlord and each other."

I thought Lydia was the last straw, but that wasn't personal. This was. I knew, beyond a shadow of a doubt, that my time with Vic was ending. After almost eight months of sharing this place together, we would get this kitchen repaired and I would hit the road to somewhere. Vic was unable to admit any blame in any relationship, and in any situation, and I had had it. Once the firemen left that day, and we went back into our stinky, smoky, burned-up stove and area around it, Vic and I barely spoke. Oh, he tried, but all my buttons had been pushed too many times. I was "out of order," and unwilling to be his scapegoat any longer. I wouldn't tell Vic I was leaving, but I was planning to head out of town as soon as I could. Sadly, it would take a number of months to make that happen. The kitchen repairs, I paid for. Vic didn't have the money. The blame for the kitchen, I left with Vic, although he never admitted to any of it.

I hadn't talked to Mom in a few weeks, and I didn't want to call her about this. She would be beside herself. I knew it would eventually come out, and when it did, I felt worse for her than I did for myself.

"TL, I don't know what to say about your brother," Mom said, when I finally called her. "It's not about the fire, those things happen. It's the way he handles life. I would hope that I taught him better than that. How can he totally put the blame on you? I believe you when you said you didn't even cook that morning. You would own up to this..."

"I would, Mom. Seriously. If I had cooked that morning, I might question my own sanity, that I might have done this. But I KNOW I didn't even touch the stove that morning. Vic probably made something, and then went back to listening to his music like he is known to do. From what I could gather, he got a call later from Abby, and he went out the door without looking back. I heard him on the phone with her a couple of days later, and it sounded like the timing was right. He didn't know I was listening to him. I'm not talking with him, Mom. I can't right now. And I'm making plans to leave. Maybe I'll calm down...maybe. But for now, I just can't hardly be in the same room with him. Like you said, it's not about the fire. Those things do happen. It's that he can't see the truth. I think he believes his own lies! And there's no convincing him otherwise.

It's just not worth it."

"I understand," Mom said. Then she was quiet.

"Mom, I'm sorry to be such a downer. I do have some good news to report! I have met a wonderful new friend. Her name is Isla, spelled I-S-L-A. With a long 'I' sound. She is sweet. We met at the ball game the other night. She was getting a hot dog in front of me, and when we were both over at the condiments stand, we started up a conversation. It turned out that our seats were close to each other, so we switched where we were to sit together and enjoy the rest of the game. She lives not too far from here. It's so nice to have her to talk to. I don't know if it will be more than a friendship, but for now, it's going well."

"That's so good to hear, TL. You need a bright spot in your life," Mom said.

"I do, and she's it. And, she's a Christian. I know that will make you happy," I added.

"It does. Where does she go to church?" Mom asked.

"At the non-denominational place over on Pete Street. I have attended with her a couple of times now. I like it better than where I was going, I think. The sermons have been encouraging. And, I'm reading my Bible more. I'm really trying to get myself healthy, like we talked about."

"All good news. It makes my heart feel better to hear these things," Mom said with a spark of joy.

"Any new info you have to share before we hang up?" I asked.

"Uh, yes. Always. This is a process, and it continues," Mom answered. "I was online the other day and was fascinated by this one therapist talking about not reacting, but responding, disengage and walk away. It reminds me of what you're going to do with Vic. You have to show the narcissist that you're not tolerating their behavior. That's setting a boundary. This is hard though, isn't it?"

"It is, but it's possible, and I have to believe it will help," I answered. "What else, Mom?"

"He said what happens is that when the narcissist is confronted, they react and try to control and manipulate the situation. Then the co-dependent person will cower and regret speaking out. They feel it's not worth the fight."

"Oh, I get that," I said.

"I know, me, too. But he went on to say that there doesn't need to be a fight if the narcissist would simply say they were sorry. But that rarely happens."

"Yeah. Vic is not one to apologize. I don't even think he realizes when he has overstepped where he should be in most situations. Hey, Mom, I've kinda had an idea since the fire. Maybe it was the 'heat' of the situation that put this hot place into my thinking," I laughed. "We have family in New Mexico. Maybe I should give that area a try?"

"Well, that doesn't sound so far-fetched. We do have family there, and I know you and your cousin Bobby used to get along well. Maybe you could connect with him?"

"That's a good idea. He's still out there, huh?" I asked.

"As far as I know. Last time your dad talked to Aunt Martha, she mentioned him. So I wouldn't think he's moved away."

"Okay. I'll think about that some. It's a nice distance away from here. That would be good."

"If you do leave, I don't want you to worry about Vic. He's going to be just fine. He will act like he misses you but from what I've read, it's just that he has no one to take his frustrations out on. If you play into his pity party at the talk of you leaving, he's just acting sad to gain back control and make you feel less-than. I'm not just talking about Vic here, this is how narcissists are. I hate thinking of my son this way, but I want to be real, too. As much as we want to take them back after their bad behavior, it makes them feel very powerful. During their silent treatment toward co-dependents, they know the co-dependent one is waiting for them. The narcissist might even be out having a great time, in the meantime. In fact, sometimes they create conflicts so they can go out and do what they please—this triggers abandonment wounds in the co-dependents."

"We all have issues, don't we?" I said, with a bit of sarcasm from the old days. I was trying not to do that.

"We do. And sometimes it can feel almost impossible to get away from a narcissist, because the co-dependent's self-esteem gets so low. They wonder who else would want them? Sometimes the only way to detach from them is to have no contact, and to completely block the narcissist from being able to reach you. Sometimes your brain just needs this time, TL. Maybe you will be able to have a relationship later in life with Vic. But for now, I believe you need to get away and rest emotionally and spiritually. Get a better perspective on life, and where God is taking you in it. I would hate to see all this lead into some sort of depression, or confusion. We know those things are not of God."

"Well, I'm not going to tell Vic I'm leaving, when I do. I can't deal with what that would look like. I will let you know, Mom. And I'll probably stop and see you on the trip there if I do absolutely decide to go to New Mexico."

"That would be nice. I need to go now, Tracy Lynn. I'm meeting up with a friend in a bit."

"I appreciate the time you spend working with me through this, too, Mom. It really is a big help. I haven't spent the time you have researching all this. Maybe that won't really come until I'm out of here. Time will tell."

"Be well, my son. Talk with you soon!"

"Bye, Mom. Enjoy the time with your friend."

31

"Hello, Isla, how have you been?" I'm glad she answered on the second ring. It makes my call feel welcomed.

"Tracy Lynn, it's so good to hear your voice. How was your drive, and the visit with your parents?"

"It was good, for the most part. I miss you. I'm sorry we didn't have a chance to say good-bye in person before I left."

"You have to do what you have to do. How's your cousin, Bobby?"

"Bobby is great! Such a nice guy. We had an interesting hike into the mountains together, and I just got back from visiting with his mom, my Great-Aunt Martha."

"Oh, how was that?"

"Well, I'd rather talk about other things first. Does that tell you anything?"

"It does. But let's get right to the meat of things. That is why you left for New Mexico, isn't it?"

"It is. I appreciate how you're not afraid to discuss the hard stuff, Isla. I'm only sorry we didn't have longer together before I left."

"Me, too, Tracy Lynn. But God has a plan in all things."

"He does, and being here is part of that, I believe. Visiting with Martha today was more eye-opening than ever. She had all the classic signs of narcissism, and then some. I was exhausted just after a short visit. Why is it with some you feel the conversation could go on forever, and you are energized by it, and with others it sucks the energy right out of you and you're ready to be done?"

"That's what makes the world go around, I guess," Isla responds. "What was Martha like?"

"She was a lot like my dad, but different, too. How can I describe her?...She didn't really have any interest in who I was, only her own life.

Oh, and her bird. She is really into her bird. Which is fine, but... Oh, I don't want to complain, Isla."

"You're okay, Tracy Lynn, you can talk to me about anything. It's good to get it out."

"Remember one of those last sermons we heard at church about what defiles a person? I think it was in Matthew?"

"Yes, Matthew 15, Jesus was talking."

"Yes. Well, after being with Martha, I'm thinking about that sermon. How the words we speak come from the heart, and that's what defiles us. Not what we eat. What we speak shows our heart. It's scary to think of that. It makes me want to be more careful about what I say."

"Are you saying that Martha's words were scary?"

"Sort of. They just didn't show any concern, any care, just opinions, and then..."

"Then, what?"

"It was hard to hear her slander relatives, including me. I'm weak in her sight, just like my mom. She respects those like my dad, and others, who she views as strong. But I disagree with her."

"Tracy Lynn, you are a man that impresses me by your kind heart. And any weakness you may feel can be made strong by Jesus. God is teaching you right now how to walk more closely with Him. Don't let Martha's words make you feel bad."

"I know...there I am again. Allowing the narcissist to define me instead of God. I read that a narcissist uses words as a weapon to demean others. That sounds like Vic. They humiliate people by their words and families are deeply affected by what they say. When these negative words keep going through my mind, I have to stop them from playing. I'm still learning these things, and trying to put them into practice. Mom said being away could give me a better perspective. I surely hope so. And I can still check what's real with healthy people like you."

"I'm here for you, Tracy Lynn."

"I know you are, and I appreciate you, and miss you. But I also know the love and approval in my life needs to ultimately come from God...not my dad, and not other unhealthy relatives like Martha and Vic. I'm not going to escape narcissism by living here in New Mexico. I already know that. I'm going to escape it by finding healing within myself. One video said that the more dysfunctional a family is, the more we expect perfect relationships. Isn't that something? One thing leads to another."

"It is. I would like to think that you and I could have a perfect relationship, but that's not even true. There is no one perfect except for our Savior, Jesus Christ. We must always look to Him for perfection."

"I'm so glad to have met you, Isla. You bring my focus back to God, always. I don't know what I would do without you and my mom right now, as I work through this."

"And I'm glad I met you, too, Tracy Lynn. God has blessed me with knowing a gentle man like you. I miss you around here. But I'm glad you have made the move away from Vic. We'll wait and see what happens now."

"I see Bobby pulling in. So I need to go now. Sorry we can't talk longer, but we'll talk soon. Take care."

"You, too. Talk to you soon. Bye."

Bobby is taking a few minutes to get inside, talking with the neighbor. He seems to get along well with everyone.

"Hey there! It's good to be home," Bobby says eventually coming through the door.

"Good to see you! How's the fire business?"

"Interesting as usual. We never know what a day will hold. That's what I love about this job. How was your visit with my mom today? Or should I even ask?"

"Oh, Bobby, man, I want to be careful what words I use here."

"TL, I already know what my mom is like. You're not going to say anything that will shock me."

"I did find some good information about our family history. Let's start there... Lucy was the oldest, and she did end up caring for the rest of the kids after Minnie died there in the sanatorium. What a houseful James got left with. Sounds like Lucy and Bart had the typical narcissist/co-dependent relationship. But I was particularly intrigued by Joe and Betty, my dad's parents. They sounded like the nicest couple. Sorry to say, Martha didn't have a lot of good to say about them. She viewed them as weak. I'm thinking my dad gave them a run for their money as a kid. He must have been a chip off the old block of his grandpa, Bart. I wish I could have known my grandparents more. That cancer has run through our family and taken too many people so young."

"Yes, it has. It robs us of people we would like to have a lot more time with. Maybe that's something that affected people in our family, too? Emotionally? First the TB way back, and then cancer through the years."

"Maybe so. How could it not, I guess?"

"What else did you learn from my mom?"

"She loves her bird."

"That she does. I think more than me sometimes," Bobby quips.

"And, she didn't want to take after her mom, Lucy. She viewed her as weak, so I'm sorry to say, I think your dad, Harry, must have had a time of it."

"Oh, he did, TL. He surely did. Enough of all that for now. I have learned one thing, that negative talk isn't good for us. How about we stop and balance out the negative with the positive! Let's go get some good food!" Bobby laughs as he says it, adding, *"If you're hungry, I'm buying dinner. It's time to celebrate you being here, and there's this cool old place*

in the town of Mesilla I'd like to take you to. It's a bit fancy, but you don't have to get too gussied up. It will remind you a bit of San Francisco inside."

"Great. Let me get changed, and we'll go."

32

Isla was definitely a bright spot in my life those last months in California. It was good to be around someone I could really talk with. She was as shocked about the fire incident as I was, but she refrained from bashing Vic. She was so good about that, always looking at people as God saw them. I had a harder time. I was so mad at Vic! I knew I needed to get over it for my own sake. Isla was helping me with that. When the kitchen got fixed, I tried to forget about it and rid my mind of the anger I felt. Forgiveness was needed, but I was struggling to let it go completely.

Vic was still hanging out with Abby, and eventually Lydia seemed to have gone her own way. I was happy for her. She was never going to find with Vic what she was looking for. The divorce with Mandy was progressing, and Vic didn't seem to really care. Whatever sparkled most for him in the moment had his attention. He was getting a few offers for work, but he was stalling as much as he could. Unemployment was keeping him afloat, and that satisfied him for the time being. Then, he got a call he couldn't refuse. It was just across town, and they had a full-time position in sales. Vic was definitely gifted in that arena. He could talk a good talk. He took the job. It got easier around home with him out all day. He came home tired, and that worked better.

"Hey, TL," Vic said coming through the door one Friday night, "I was wondering what you thought about having a little group over tomorrow night?"

I was talking to Vic again, but not a lot. And with this, he took me by surprise. He was asking my permission? Was Vic wanting to cooperate more now? Was he softening? I tried not to care about Vic, but I did. So, like I was prone to do, I answered, albeit cautiously, "I don't mind. Who were you thinking about?"

"Just some new friends from work, and Abby of course. Why don't you invite your friend, Isla? I've barely gotten to know her."

"That sounds good. She might like to come." Isla hadn't spent much time around Vic so far. I was glad for that.

"Okay. Let's run to the store later and get some ribs and stuff. I'll pay. I'll be getting a paycheck soon."

"Uh. Okay." Again, I was cautious. This was sounding like someone I'd like to hang out with. Where did the real Vic go?

Saturday night, after everyone arrived, I was pleased with Vic's colleagues. Billy was about 40, and a single dad. Marcy worked in Human Resources, and came with her husband, Dan. They seemed like a nice couple. Eddie was a little younger, probably late 20's, and he brought beer. But he didn't over drink. We grilled the ribs out back, and everyone brought stuff to share. The evening seemed normal, and Vic was actually behaving himself. He laughed a lot with his co-workers and was treating Abby with respect. Even Isla was impressed and seemed to see a lot more good in Vic than I had been describing to her. Actually, I was thankful. Maybe this new job was good for him. It seemed to be bringing out the best. I liked this change. I decided that evening I should take another look at my brother, bring my protective walls down, and give him another chance. Once everyone had gone home, I ran Isla back to her place, and returned to find Vic sitting in the living room listening to his music. It wasn't too late, so I took a seat on the couch across from him and we listened to his music for 20 minutes or so before much was said. It felt good to just hang out like normal brothers would do.

"Vic, that was a nice group from work. I especially like Dan, Marcy's husband. He seemed like a super nice guy."

Vic looked over at me and didn't say anything. I should have prepared myself in that moment for what was to come, but I didn't. Once again, Vic caught me with my defenses down.

"You did, huh?"

"Sure. He said he's been in California for about ten years, having grown up in Maryland. I like the way he supported Marcy in her job change and move, what a great way to..."

"I don't know!" Vic said with more force than seemed appropriate.

"Don't know what, Vic?" I should have thrown my walls up in that moment, but I didn't.

"I don't know what you see in the guy. He's a namby-pamby. Did you see the way he got Marcy her plate of food! What is she, some sort of invalid or something? She could get it herself. She's got him so whipped, he can barely speak for himself."

"Vic!"

"It's true. You don't see what I see, TL. You're always so blind to what's really going on. And you and Isla, what was that all about?"

"What do you mean?" I was sitting on the edge of the couch by now, brow furrowed, and heart beating faster by the moment. Vic was turning into a monster right before my eyes.

"Oh, TL. What an idiot you are!"

"I beg your pardon?" Although I wasn't begging, and didn't care about his pardon, but that's the way it came out.

"Isla's got your number. She's all sweet and caring. What a bunch of malarkey. And she calls herself a Christian? She's a hypocrite! She's playing you for all you're worth."

"I've had enough Vic. Stop right there. You don't..."

"You need to open your eyes, TL, and see what's happening around you. You let these people take you in and fill your head full of what you want to hear. I can see through them all. They are all false fronts to an empty store."

By this time, I was standing, to not only exit soon, but to let Vic know I was not going to succumb to his vicious nature any more. With what I'd been reading, and from what I'd been talking to Mom about, I was learning who I was, and that his behavior was not to be tolerated.

"Vic, I don't know what got into you after the BBQ, but you need to get a grip. I enjoyed your co- workers. I won't even call them your friends anymore. And as far as Isla goes, she is exactly who she portrays herself to be. She is one of the kindest women I have ever met, and if anyone is being a hypocrite, it's you!"

Vic's laughter in that moment was nothing short of evil. It sent chills up my spine, and the look on his face was void of emotion when he spoke.

"Look at you...all in love or something. Now I know why you haven't even been talking to me lately. Your whole life is revolving around Isla. I don't seem to even matter to you anymore..."

"Look here..." I said.

"No, you look here, TL. We share this house. We are brothers. I deserve some respect from you--some conversation when you come and go. You've barely said a word to me lately. I thought maybe if I had a few friends over, you would warm up to me. And you have, but to what end I ask myself now? You like all of them and could care less about your own brother."

"I...the reason..." I stalled...not saying what I wanted to, that I was mad about the fire situation. I knew that would blow the roof off the house.

"You what? You have good reason for not talking to me, like I've done something wrong? It seems I never do anything right in your book. Isla, oh, she's all so perfect. Isn't blood thicker than water? We share this house..."

"Vic, look, I'm done with this conversation," I said. When you're ready to talk sense, I'm available. Until then, I'm going to bed. I'd say thanks for the BBQ, but at this point, I don't owe you any thanks. I don't know what you were up to tonight, and maybe I don't really care. You're going to find yourself to be a lonely old man one day, and probably still you'll be blaming it on everyone else. When you can start to see who you really are, maybe there's a chance for a real relationship in your life."

"I don't see lonely in my future, but you might," Vic snarled.

"We'll see my brother, we'll see. I don't know how much longer I can put up with..."

Vic interrupted, "Oh really. You planning on going somewhere? Don't forget we have a lease here. You signed it. And you gotta stick with it."

"Is that a threat, Vic? PLEASE! I am a man of integrity. I know what's expected of me. But I also know..."

"You BETTER!" Vic interjected.

"I'm done tonight, Vic. Really done."

"Whatever..." Vic responded.

Walking to my room, I felt sick. That was not at all how I expected the evening to end, and I wasn't sure how I had even let it happen. I got sucked in once again. A little light from Vic into our dark relationship, and I was hooked like a gullible fish going after fake bait. Why did I keep going back for more hoping Vic would turn some sort of corner and be the Jekyll instead of the Hyde, or whichever one was the nice guy? I knew I wasn't perfect, but it seemed at least I tried to be nice. Vic didn't seem to feel the need. If it was in his head, he let it out his mouth when it suited him. I always felt I wanted Vic to need me as his brother, to even want me, but I was seeing that was only getting me in deeper as time went on. When would I ever learn? What would it take? Vic always made me feel inadequate, like I never measured up to being the kind of brother he wanted. I fell for it every time. I tried so hard to make up for my lack in his eyes. Where had his love for me been? Where had his care for me been? I'd allowed this...I was seeing that I was as much a part of it as Vic was. If I didn't play into his schemes, he'd have to play with someone else. I'd always hoped he would change, but then I was realizing he's simply not capable of being anything other than what he is—especially without God. If I had a hard enough time finding my own healthy boundaries, while in a relationship with God and healthy people, how in the world would he ever find his way out of the darkness without God? He seemed to only be able to operate this life on his terms, and I was ready to give him my termination notice!

Collapsing on my bed, I couldn't have felt any worse. I wanted to pack my bags and leave that very night. But I knew I couldn't. My job awaited me on Monday, and I wasn't one to run out on the lease. It was for a year, and I would count down the days until the rental agreement could be placed solely in Vic's name, and I'd be gone.

Waking the next morning, I was glad to be joining Isla at her church.

33

"I'm going to run over to the box and get the mail, and then we'll go to dinner.".

"Sure. Sounds good Bobby."

It feels so good to not be on guard with Bobby. He's so easy going. Coming back through the door, Bobby hands me a letter.

"Hey, this is for you," he says.

My heart jumps in my chest. There's no return address, but the writing I know. Vic has decided phone calls and texts aren't the answer, I guess. I don't think I want to read it now, so I stick it in my pocket.

"Let's head on out. I can read this later."

"Sounds good to me," Bobby says, understanding from the look on my face it's probably nothing very good. "I'll drive! Mesilla might be a good town to think about opening up your taco place."

"Oh, cool."

Driving along, Bobby fills me in on the town of Mesilla.

"The reason why I think this might be a good location for you, TL, is that Mesilla is old, but a lot of people come here because of the history. It's even been named one of the top ten small towns in the country to visit. You'd have plenty of customers."

"That's a plus!"

"There a bunch of stores and galleries, and a ton of restaurants and cafés. They all seem to keep busy. There's a plaza right in the center of the town, so most things are within walking distance of one another. Now, I'm a bit of a history buff, so I hope you don't mind me telling you a bit about it before we get there?"

"I love to learn, so go ahead."

"Well, we've all heard of Billy the Kid, right?" Bobby asks, smiling in my direction.

"Of course!"

"Guess what? Billy was seen in Mesilla a lot, in the bars and dances. In 1881, he was tried in the building on the corner of the plaza. He was given the death sentence by hanging."

"For what crime?"

"For the murder of the Sheriff."

"Oh. Guess justice was swift in those days?"

"It was, TL. And if we think that the Republicans and Democrats go at it now, back in the late 1800's, politics sometimes caused bloodshed here. Real blood! The two parties came head to head on the plaza one day, and it was called the bloody 'Battle of the Bands.' Nine people died, and a lot were wounded. That would really make the news today, wouldn't it?

"I'd say so!"

"Things really changed for Mesilla," Bobby continues, *"when they didn't allow the Railroad to come through their town. Kinda sad, really. The people of Las Cruces decided they would okay it and look what has happened. Mesilla remained just a small village. Only 2,000 people live in Mesilla. Las Cruces has a population of...I don't know...almost 100,000 people."*

Bobby went on with his history report, *"Mesilla was part of Mexico, but in the mid 1800's, it was purchased by the United States for 10 million dollars—Mesilla, and other land in this area. That made it so there was a reliable route for the Stage Line. Back then, Mesilla had a population of 3,000, and Las Cruces and El Paso were just small towns with a couple hundred people. In 1861, Mesilla, was the capital of New Mexico. I'm sorry, you probably don't really care about all this. I told you I was a history buff."*

"Hey, go on. I need to know all I can if this is to be the future home of my taco place. Who knows what questions I might get asked, and I need to know the answers. Or, I can phone a friend...or a cousin."

Bobby and I laugh at that. Bobby laughs easily and is always considerate. And, he is truly taking an interest in what interests me. What a cool guy he is.

Pulling into town, I see the plaza. It's good sized, and there is a church at one end, and a gazebo in the center.

"They built homes close together around this plaza back in the day to protect against the Indians," Bobby says, pointing to the plaza. *"There are still a lot of direct descendants of the early settlers here in Mesilla. One interesting thing that happened here with that church,"* Bobby says, pointing again... *"the first church was built there in 1855, but the present church was built in the early 1900's. It was actually built around the old adobe church, and when it was finished, the old church was taken apart and carried out the front door."*

"You're kidding me! Wow!"

"This is still a very religious community, lots of Catholics. And that gazebo there is a national monument," Bobby adds.

"Why would they make a gazebo a national monument?"

"I learned it's because of the historical significance of this town in the state and even the nation. This was once the largest U.S. town between San Antonio and San Diego. It was the railroad decision that changed all that."

Parking and getting out, Bobby is still filled with historical facts about this unique town. I'm all ears, knowing nothing about it, and very little about New Mexico. Bobby is changing that quickly. He's being quite the tour guide.

"This is where we'll be having dinner, TL. Funny thing, Mesilla means 'little table.' So, let's go on in and get us a table. I'm hungry!"

"Me, too! Thanks for all the info. I feel a little more at home here already."

34

Slipping into the seat next to Isla at church, I breathed a sigh of relief. Vic was asleep when I left. Just being away from him and here close to Isla, feeling the peace in the church, began to ease the fiasco of the night before. Isla turned to me, but the look on her face quickly changed from one of calm to concern. She could see that I was visibly shaken. The last she knew the evening had been a success and Vic was actually a reasonable guy. I wondered if she would believe me when I told her what happened? I just shook my head as the worship music started and indicated we should try to put our focus on God.

By the time the pastor began to speak, I was all ears. And it seemed God was there, in him, speaking to me, helping me sort through what was sane and what was not. Sometimes I wondered if Vic would cause me to lose my mind. He had me on such a roller coaster of emotions. I wanted to trust my brother, I wanted to have a relationship with him. But I was truly beginning to realize that might never be possible...that he was not capable of having a healthy relationship with me, or with anyone, for that matter. I kept hoping, but I wondered why I even still had hope? It was probably because I believed that God could heal anything, physical or emotional. But then again, didn't the person need to be open and willing to God's intervention? I would suppose so.

I remember the pastor talking about the greatest gift we can give ourselves is to be living in a loving union with God. And how every instruction He gives us in His Holy Book, when/if we will really follow them, will bring us physical and emotional health. Oh, that sounded so good. He encouraged us to pray for courage. Well, I knew I needed that. Moving out and away from Vic was not going to be easy. It sounded easy. Just pack and go, but I was such a practical guy. I would need to make sure the bills would be paid once I left. I would need to give proper notice at

144

my job. I would need to NOT tell Vic what I was doing. And I wondered how much I should even say to Isla? I hadn't known her that long. It wasn't until after church that day that I knew I could confide fully in her. She listened to all I had to say, and she was so understanding of the difficult situation I lived in with Vic. She was not surprised that things had turned sour once the evening was over. What I began to realize is that most people have narcissists in their lives. It's just that so many are not aware of what the problem is. Isla was aware. She was a smart woman, and a praying woman. She was truly a blessing that God had brought into my life...and all because of a hot dog at the ball game. At lunch later that day, Isla showed me her true colors, and they were beautiful.

"TL, I'm so sorry about what happened with Vic," she said. "You are such a nice guy, and you don't deserve to be treated this way. It sounds like Vic put on a good show while we were all there. The reason why he set up that evening, we may never know, but we do know how it ended. I'm glad I got to see your brother as I did, but I totally believe you when you tell me what happened later. I have had my own problems along these lines. I have had to learn some things about being on the co-dependent side of relationships. It sounds like you are having to take that same course in life. I think you and I get along so well together because we understand each other, and we are both on the 'Oh, how can I help you?' side of things. Vic is on the 'What can I get from you?' side. I am very comfortable with you, TL. But I have been in friendships that weren't like this at all. I have been wounded by certain people in my life...so I get it. Thankfully, I would call what we have here a nice friendship."

"Isla, thank you. Thank you for listening and understanding. Too many love us for what we will do for them. The ones who love us for who we are, are few and far between. You are one of the few. The pastor said this morning that learning how to pray and worship is easy, but pulling out ingrained habits at the root is very hard. Vic is an ingrained habit. I keep going back for more—even with this...I know me. I want to forgive and forget."

"I understand," Isla agreed. "I have done the same and am still tempted to. We need to forgive, of course, but not forget that someone has been mean. I believe forgiving is Biblical, so that's good. But making ourselves available for more abuse doesn't seem to be what God would have us do. The Word asks us to be as innocent as doves but as wise as serpents."

"Yes. I like that. It's an interesting contrast," I said.

Isla added, "And being a part of God's family now, as believers in Jesus Christ, there can be a glorious future for us, both on this earth and in Heaven eternal. We don't have to be stuck in our old habits forever. That is the *be wise* part. There is healing available."

"I like the sounds of that, Isla. Keep talking!" I said.

"Our first priority in life is to Jesus. Matthew 10:37 talks about loving our father or mother, son or daughter, more than we love God. If we do, we are not worthy of being His, it says. We are to take up our cross and follow Jesus, and not cling to this life, but give it up for His sake. I realized a while back that sometimes I was playing god in another person's life. I worried too much, thinking I could fix them, help them, change them. But I'm not God. I'm only an instrument that God can use to help another. They have to realize their true need is Jesus, not us. I needed to understand that and stop worrying so much and start praying more. Worry doesn't add a day to anyone's life. It's useless. Prayer adds so much more to each day, and to each life. How has your relationship with Vic affected your relationship with God, TL?"

"Well, I have to be honest with you, it is very distracting. I want to pray. I need to pray and read the Bible even more because of this chaos. But it also makes it very hard to focus. Vic gets my mind spinning in circles, and I'm trying to figure out ways to work things out with him. I know what I need to do...take my focus off him and put it on God instead, but it's so hard. You are right about playing god. I think I've done that, too."

"It sounds like you do need to put some space between you and your brother. I hate to say it, because I love spending time with you. But when you talk of going somewhere else, I understand. I have had people in my life that I've had to put some space between them and me. We can get so wrapped up in their chaos, we can't seem to find our peace in Jesus. Even Jesus, when the crowds got large, and the chaos was surrounding Him, went up into the hills to pray by Himself. He was such a good example of drawing near to His Father in Heaven. Matthew 6:33 says we are to seek His Kingdom above all else. And you can continue to pray for Vic, always. I have many people that I pray for, that I no longer choose to spend time with. We can't stay doing the same things and expect different results."

"You sound a lot like my mom," I said. "You are both very wise women. I can see God helping me through this. I know to some it sounds easy to escape such a troublesome relationship, but it's not. I am a very loyal person. I will stick with a person till the end...but I'm realizing that might not always be what God is asking me to do, otherwise it might be the end of me!"

"TL, in Mark 11, I find it interesting how when Jesus arrived in Jerusalem, he went by the Temple, but it was late in the day. I wonder what he was noticing? He didn't do anything. But then next morning, He went back to the Temple, and that's when He turned over the money changer's tables and kicked out the merchants and customers. He told them all that His Father's House was a place of prayer. So many times we think that Jesus was so loving and kind, and He was. But He was also very realistic and confident. He was always about pleasing His Father first, and not the people around Him. He knew right from wrong, and He didn't blur the lines. As co-dependents, so many times we blur the lines. We want to see the good, and we want to overlook the bad. That's a very good trait, but it's also a dangerous one. We have to stand up for ourselves, like you did even with Vic last night, and say *Enough*. We have to kick out the wrong and keep our Temple pure and a place for prayer. If what is going on with you and Vic pulls you away from God, pay attention, and ask God what needs to change so that you can remain close to Him, and not be confused by the ways of the enemy."

"We have never had such a long, deep conversation about all of this, Isla," I said. "I truly know you are sent by God. Thank you for your brutal honesty. I need to be realistic. I need to see what's happening. I need to pray and follow God."

"TL, you won't always know that what you're doing is right" Isla responded. "You will question, and it's hard when it's a family member. God knows that. But stay prayerful and search for God's peace. Do what it seems He is asking you to do, one day at a time. It can be very sad to say goodbye to some, but it will be necessary. We can grieve those losses, and then we can move on and heal. I read once that being able to detach from the things and the people of this world is what will bring us our inner peace—this will lead us into a more loving attachment to God. When we can turn off the chaos, we can draw nearer to God. God wants us in relationships, of course...but healthy ones."

"Wow. That's powerful, Isla," I said. "I want to walk more closely with God. But I'm having a hard time right now."

"It will come, TL," Isla encouraged me. "I see the desire in you. Keep at it, one small step at a time. It's not easy to yield totally to Jesus. Sometimes, many times, we hold onto the garbage rather than allowing God to transform our lives. Changing can be painful, but it can also bring so much renewed joy and energy."

The rest of the day, Isla and I spent walking in the park, and enjoying each other's company. We knew as much as we would have liked our relationship to progress, it might not be the right timing for it. It was more important that I sorted things out, personally, during this season of my life. But we also knew that with God, He could have a plan somewhere in our future with one another. Walking hand in hand, we were both willing to take it all one day at a time.

Yes, Isla was truly a gift.

35

"This place is amazing, Bobby."

"I know. There is so much history just in this one building. What if we could travel all over the U.S. and learn all the cool facts about our country? I've always wanted to visit the east coast, which would be really different from this area. I'd love to do the Freedom Trail in Boston, and see where Paul Revere lived. And also travel to Philadelphia and learn more about the signing of the Declaration of Independence. There were 56 people who signed it, and to know each one of their backgrounds. How fascinating would that be?"

"We should do that together some day—travel out there and feast on the history of our nation. But first, I'll need to sell lots of tacos!"

"And I'll need to put out a lot of fires!" Bobby says.

Laughing with Bobby and dreaming together is fun! Enjoying our dinner, Bobby is in his element as he tells me more about this restaurant.

"The interior of the Double Eagle Restaurant we're in is from the mid 1800's. It's one of the oldest places on this plaza. Both historical and architectural facts put it on the National Register of Historic Places. Right in this town is where the ending of the Mexican American War was, and the Gadsden Purchase was signed, which was the one I told you about earlier for 10 million dollars. Lots happening in this little town so many years ago."

"And the food is delicious, too. Let's not forget that!"

More laughter ensues, as Bobby continues with the fun facts.

"Judge Roy Bean, who was the famous Texas Hanging Judge, got his start in this town. He stole the town's money, and kept it in the only safe in town, the one at the bar. Then he headed for Texas. This building was once a cotton warehouse, too. It was abandoned for some years."

"Really? This beautiful place? That's hard to imagine."

"Yes," Bobby answers, and then continues, "A rich guy from New Mexico bought it and turned it into a restaurant. I'm so glad he did. He also brought all the gold, crystal and art in here. He named the restaurant after money...the famed twenty-dollar gold piece of the 1880's. Obviously, this place wasn't air-conditioned back in the day. That was another owner in the 1980's. And those gates we walked through out front...they are from the Civil War."

"Bobby, between this great dinner and your knowledge about Mesilla, it makes for a great evening. I love the historical stuff you know. How do you remember it all?"

"I'm glad we share a love of history, TL. We're going to get along just fine! I don't know why, but these things just stick in my head once I read or hear about them. Oh, and there's more Billy the Kid stuff in here. There's a letter from Billy to the Territorial Governor, Lew Wallace, in a frame on the patio over there. He was asking for clemency, but his plea was refused."

Walking out, Bobby is leading me to the room that has a stained-glass ceiling that was salvaged from a San Francisco hotel after the Great Quake of 1906. It does have a California feel to it. Then, Bobby has us stop at a framed post as he tells me, "Billy the Kid carved his name and his girlfriend's name here. He didn't do it in this spot, but in another place in this county."

"I don't know that I would want to have known Billy the Kid—or be in this town when he was here. Maybe I would have gone to his trial though."

"Wouldn't it be interesting to be able to travel back in time, and watch these things happen," Bobby says. "But maybe not be seen, so we could be totally safe from harm, TL?"

"Oh, yeah. That would be cool."

"We can come back here again, more in the day time, if you're interested in scouting out some possible places for your tacos? It's getting kind of late tonight to do that, so maybe we should head back."

"I'm fine with that. It's been a blast hanging out here with you. Most people wouldn't know all the facts you do about this place. I certainly wouldn't. As much as I like history, I could never remember it when test time came—my history grades showed that."

Riding back to Bobby's RV, it feels good to sit quiet for a bit and just take in the sunset. New Mexico sure has some beautiful ones. I know I need to talk to Bobby still about his mom. I hate to bring it up, but I don't know if I'll sleep well without talking to him first.

"Bobby, I hate to wreck a good thing, but can I talk to you about my visit with your mom a bit more?"

"Oh, sure, TL. You're not gonna shock me with anything. I've known her my whole life!" Bobby laughs. I laugh, too, hesitating, but then knowing he can handle it.

"First of all, that was really a great dinner! Thanks! Much appreciated."

"It was awesome being able to take you there. I'm glad you liked it," Bobby responds.

"I really did. And now I'm sorry to be the bearer of tough news...but your mom is tough, Bobby."

"I'm laughing," Bobby says, *"but I know it's really not a funny matter. Yes, she is. She doesn't really invest herself in the person she's talking to...she is much more concentrated on herself, But go ahead, TL. What was your time with her like?"*

"She is concentrated on herself, and the bird."

"Ahhh, yes, the bird." Bobby laughs again. *"He has been her companion the last few years. Maybe it's a good thing! She talks to it instead of calling me so much."*

"Let's hope he lives a long time then!" We both laugh at that.

"Here's to Whitey!" Bobby chimes in.

"What I did find interesting was all the information your mom had about our family, going back to Minnie in the Sanatorium."

"She is the keeper of many family secrets, shall we say? That's good though, right? You came looking to see what makes us who we are. She may have some answers for you, if anyone does. Tell me, what did she have to say? I don't really want to ask her because, sadly, I don't care all that much and it's too exhausting to be with her most times."

"It is, but I'm glad I did. I'm here to find healing, and I believe that involves knowing who I am, to begin with. Between our hike into the Organ Mountains, and talking with her, those are some steps into the past that can lead into a healthier future, I hope."

"Here's to that," Bobby says, raising an invisible glass in his hand. *"Here, here!"*

36

I'm was so grateful for Isla during this time. Between her and my mom, they were some of my only sources of sanity. I was keeping a watch at work to see when and how I would give my notice. It was hard to give up the income and head into the unknown. But maybe New Mexico would hold an untold number of surprises if I did decide to go that way. I thought maybe I could start something new in my life, and in my relationships. Although it was beginning to look like leaving Isla behind would be a sad part of the picture.

I really tried avoiding Vic following his last outburst. He pretty much did the same, but I think he knew he had pushed me to my limits. Not that he really cared, but he did need me to pay half the rent, so he probably wanted to be a little bit careful. One Saturday, I planned on spending the day with Isla. We were going to take the train to Jack London Square out of Martinez. It was a nice ride along the Bay, and fun to walk around looking at the shops. I called Mom that morning before leaving. Vic had gone out for something. He didn't talk to me before he left.

"Hi, Mom. How're things in Chino?"

"Oh, good, TL. Hope your week was good at work."

"It was okay. I'm looking for a time to give my notice. I'm seriously thinking of going to Las Cruces now," I answered.

"You are, huh? Good for you. I back you all the way," Mom said.

"I haven't told you what happened recently, and I don't really know if I should go into it all. I mean, it didn't last long, but times like that can wipe me out with Vic."

"You can always talk to me, TL," Mom replied with genuine concern. "I know it's been a little while since we've talked."

"I know I can talk to you. But I should be able to handle these things..." I stopped there.

"One of the most important things is to deal with the reality of it, TL. Bring it into the light. For far too long I have shoved stuff down deep inside just hoping everything would work out. The problem with that is that things don't change when we don't face them. Now, I'm not telling you that you need to stay there with Vic. I'm more talking about myself with your dad. Job, in the Bible, really talked about his losses, his pain. He cried out to God and got real with God."

"But sometimes I feel like I'm whining when I keep bringing this stuff to God. Maybe God gets tired of it and doesn't want to hear it anymore," I said, with a bit of doom and gloom to my voice.

"TL, God never gets tired when His children come to Him for help, advice, healing, etc... When we bring those hurts to God, I truly believe He is glad. The enemy wants us to keep things in the dark and away from God where they can fester. I believe God says, 'Yes. Tell me all about it. Open up that *can of worms* and we'll make a way through it together.' He helps us sort out our thoughts and emotions and heals them. Never think you're tiring God. He can take it. And He wants to."

"That makes sense, Mom. Thanks," I said with a bit more lighthearted tone.

"You know, TL, sometimes as young children, it's best to not fully feel the painful stuff in life. I even think sometimes when we lose someone we love very much, God puts a protective fog around our heart. He knows we can't handle all that pain at once, so He shields us from feeling it all in the beginning. Slowly, as time goes by, we can deal with different layers of the pain. And we should. As things arise in our lives, our adult lives, we shouldn't ignore it. We need to be willing to walk it out with God as adults. Not that God doesn't help the little children, we know how much He loves little children and is grieved when they are harmed. But as adults, it's time to think and act like an adult."

"Yeah, that sounds right," I said.

"As adults we can't deny, minimalize or put all the blame on other people. Even what's going on with Vic, and between your dad and me, we are partly to blame for all of this. Our co-dependent side feeds their narcissistic side, and until we realize that, we'll all keep riding the same merry-go-round. God wants us to get off the ride and walk on our own two legs into a healthier way of doing life."

"We get accustomed to going around and around, don't we, Mom? In the beginning, I didn't even see what was happening. I just figured it's how life was with Vic, and with Dad," I added.

"We have to follow God into healthiness in all our relationships," Mom said. "We have to learn what it's like to be in a give and take relationship. What it really looks like. We have to get off the ride long enough to stop spinning in our own minds and experience the peace that comes first and foremost with God. Sitting, and talking, with Him. I hope you are developing those habits, TL. I know I didn't at your age, and I wish I had. Old habits die hard, but they can die when we give them to God."

"I'm working on it Mom. That may be one of the good things that comes out of this time of living with Vic again. And I believe Isla is a help for me in that, too."

"Oh, how is your new friend?" Mom asked.

"She's great. We're going to take a little train ride over to Jack London Square today."

"That sounds wonderful." Mom truly sounded pleased for me.

"She gets me, too, Mom. I think she understands more of this narcissism thing than I do. I'm starting to realize we all deal with this in one form or another. We are all on the spectrum, aren't we? I think you told me that a while back. And we have to find a healthy balance between being selfish and selfless."

"Yes. I feel like there is a constant readjustment to do that. The pendulum wants to swing too far one way, and then too far the other!" Mom laughed. "You don't have to spend long amounts of time with God, TL. It's more just doing it with regularity that matters most. Keeping God in your thoughts, asking His guidance as you go through your day. Building that relationship."

"That's hard when it seems like I'm talking to air, Mom." I laughed at this.

She chuckled a little with me. "I know. But little by little, you're going to start to hear His gentle whisper more and more. It comes with time, and closeness." Mom's voice felt gentle to me in that moment.

"Thanks, Mom. I always appreciate talking with you. I don't mean to rush off, but I do need to go pick up Isla now. I hope you have a good day."

"Oh, please go and enjoy yourselves. Tell her I said, 'Hello'."

"I will. Bye for now."

"Bye."

The drive over to Isla's wasn't far, but it gave me some time to think about my conversation with Mom. I wanted to learn to be with God more, to hear His voice. I began to speak to Him, asking Him about the day ahead. I still couldn't say as I heard anything from His end, but I was willing to give it time.

Ringing Isla's doorbell, I heard the chimes from inside. It sounded like church bells, and it reminded me of her heart for God. She wasn't preachy, but she had a light in her eyes that not many had. As I waited, I thanked God for bringing us together.

Opening the door, Isla said with a smile, "Hi, TL! I'm just about ready. Come on in!" She reached out to take my hand and usher me in.

"Hi. No hurry. We have plenty of time to catch the train," I responded, appreciating her warm interaction with me.

"Oh, good! I didn't know for sure what the schedule was. I've never done this before, and I'm looking forward to it." Her personality lit up the room.

"There are many trains back and forth, so if we miss one, we can catch the next. It's a nice little train station there in Martinez. And parking isn't usually a problem."

It wasn't long, and we were on our way, getting there at just the right time to catch the next train about ten minutes later. I offered up a prayer of thanks to God, remembering what Mom had said about it not being long amounts of time spent, but regularity. I wanted to start to remember God throughout the day.

The ride along the Bay was pleasant. The water contained all kinds of interesting things from posts still left that once held piers, to bridges and boats. There were factories along the way, and homeless people with their tents. Isla and I talked about this and that. She was a good conversationalist and interested in most things. When we got to Jack London Square, there were craft booths, so we walked around, and had some bits of food here and there. The sky was so blue, and the cool breeze coming off the Bay made for a perfect morning—not too hot, not too cold.

"Say, Isla, have you ever taken the ferry over to the city? It's really a nice ride."

"I haven't. I know a lot of people commute with it. I've never actually been on the Bay in a boat," she said.

"Let's go check it out. I think we just get our tickets on board. It looks like some people are lining up over there."

"Sure. I'm up for it," Isla said cheerfully.

As we waited in line for the ferry, my heart was at peace. I wanted to experience more relationships like this—ones where there was no competition, no tense atmosphere, and a genuine concern from both parties toward the other person. Isla was a good, safe person to be with. I offered up another "Thank you" to my Father in Heaven as we boarded the ship. It was fun being with Isla, and she made it easy to practice being connected with God.

37

The rest of the ride home after dinner with Bobby, I feel at ease. He's a good listener, and not quick to judge even though we are talking about his mom. He knows where I'm coming from and seems willing to be a part of it.

"Your mom seems familiar with the generations in the past, so that's good. And it was sort of what was expected. Like I told you already, she said Lucy was the oldest in the family of eight kids that got left behind when Minnie died in the Sanatorium. So, the bulk of helping with all the kids did land on her. Her dad, James, was probably working hard to put food on the table. I don't know what Minnie and her husband, James, were like, your mom didn't go into that. It's probably too far back, since she died in about 1918. But Lucy seemed to have the co-dependent, help-everyone-in-sight, personality traits. That worked well with taking care of the family, but probably not so well in choosing Bart for her husband, or even in raising your mom. Lucy fell right into the trap of narcissism with Bart, and he passed that on to your mom, from the sounds of it. I sure wish I knew if it was genetic, learned, or maybe even a demon! Maybe it's a bit of all three! I talked to a lady once, and she said it could be a spirit. I don't know a lot about that."

"Maybe," Bobby says. "I wonder if anyone can pin that down, since all our lives are so different."

"Yeah. And your mom said that Lucy was well...what did I tell you earlier? Weak? And when it came to Joe, your mom's brother, and his wife Betty, who were my grandparents, they were two sweet people who found each other. Barely a harsh word between them. What a novel idea that would be? It's said only the good die young...maybe that's why cancer took them both before they grew very old?"

"Who knows. My mom is still here. She'll probably live to 100, so you

may be right about that!"

Bobby is laughing again. *I know he loves his mom, but she can be exasperating for him.*

"I don't know that I got all my questions answered about our family history, and even what happened in the Sanatorium situation, but maybe there's not a lot else there? What I probably really need to do is take all this, shake it up, pour it out, and find the missing pieces of my own life. Who am I? What blood lines are affecting me? Where do I go from here? I once heard that the great news of Jesus is that our family of origin doesn't have to determine what the future holds. I don't know if you believe in Jesus or not, Bobby, but there is great Hope in being in the family of God and not just belonging to our biological families."

"Sounds like a good thing to me. I haven't really given God a lot of thought. But maybe I should one day."

"Honestly, Bobby, going through this with Vic, and discovering the dysfunction that's surrounded me so much of my life, I don't know how I would really do it without some sort of guidance from God. My mom has been a big help in encouraging me to get to know God. This world can sure distract us from that. But I really believe Jesus is needed to not only survive this life, but to thrive in it. I don't want what my dad has dumped on me, and my brother, too, to wreck the life I've been given. I want to live fully, and out from under their oppression. I want to be all that I was created to be. And if that means even opening up a taco place against all their 'expert advice,' then I should do that. If it fails, at least I tried."

"I'm in total agreement about that. My mom doesn't understand the schedule I work with the fire department. She thinks I should be in an office somewhere working 9-5, but I love my job. I wouldn't want to be doing anything else. She's also probably afraid of me getting hurt, but she doesn't say that. She just complains about my schedule."

"We need to ask ourselves what it is we want? What were we made to do? And how do we feel about things? Everyone will have their opinion, but we're all given one life to live. The choices should be ours, and not our parents. We have to find what we need to do to find fulfillment. If you work a 9-5 in some office for 40 years and get your gold watch, will you be satisfied at the end of it?"

"Probably not. I know it works for some, and that's what makes the world go round." Bobby adds, "I like fighting fires."

"I heard a young boy tell his dad, 'I'm going to wear cleats to work when I grow up.' He was about seven at the time. It was amazing to see him do exactly that in his twenties. Maybe he was prophetic? I don't know much about that. But his dad and I got the biggest kick out of watching him wear his cleats onto the baseball diamond and getting paid for doing what he loved to do."

"That's what we all should be doing...what we love!" Bobby says with

enthusiasm.

Pulling into the RV park, I realize in that moment that I still haven't read the letter from Vic. I feel it in my back pocket and pull it out going through the door. Sitting down while Bobby gets himself something to drink, I read:

Hey Bro,
Lots going on here. I'm finding a new roommate ASAP. I don't think you're coming back, even though you left some stuff here. It's in the closet for now. That was a bad way to do things. I don't deserve this. I talked to Mom. She's on your side, as usual. I don't understand what's going on. Things are hard for me now. I had to renew the lease just in my name since it's a new year. Not sure why you had to leave so fast. You make things hard on me.
Vic

When I sigh deeply, Bobby turns from the sink to look at me. I shoot him a glance that causes him to ask what's going on.

"It's this note from my brother. He's playing the martyr, life is hard on him, I put him in this position, Mom's on my side...yada, yada... Seriously? I really think I'm done, Bobby. There is a part in me that keeps hoping, after time has passed, that we can still be friends. But the more time that goes by, and the more I see his true colors, the less I'm thinking that's possible. And how sad is that? I want my little brother in my life. But any light that I thought might be left at the end of a long dark tunnel seems to be snuffed out by this note. I wanted to blow on it, bring out any spark that's left there, but it seems beyond my doing at this point."

"I think you captured it right there, TL. 'Beyond your doing.' You can't change your brother; I can't change my mom. But we can go on and live our lives apart from them. It seems selfish, and wrong. I don't know. I don't have the perfect answers. But I do know what keeps me sane."

"Yeah. Sanity. They are toxic people, aren't they? Not good for us. If they would only 'play nice.' But they won't. Vic didn't need to send me this. He didn't even ask me how I was doing? No taking any responsibility for his actions. It's all my fault...just like the fire."

"Fire? You know that perks my ears."

"Yeah. We had a fire at our place. Vic left the stove on. He put the blame on me. Never did fess up. Just couldn't handle that something was his fault. That was probably what really sent me over the edge, although I stayed a while longer with him. My thick head takes a while to catch up with the cruelness that is going on around me. Vic can be...no, he is, cruel."

"Hmmm." Bobby sighs deeply now. "I say we call it a night."

"I agree. Thanks for listening. Sorry, I don't want to be a downer for you. You're nice enough to let me stay here."

"You're not a downer. You're helping to make some things clear for me, too."

Turning in, it feels good to be so far from Vic. It is time to start a new life. As I drift off to sleep, I'm hoping this note will be the end of our communication, at least for a while. I've been willing to text a bit with him, but I think that should even end. If I'm going to heal and move forward, I've got to let him go. Barring a miracle, Vic is stuck, and will stay stuck. I have to get him off my mind and heal into my future. It's a choice I need to make. I know no one can make it for me. With God's help, all the garbage he's dumped on me for so many years can be cleaned out and I can start fresh here in New Mexico. I need to choose to think right about this now, just like I chose to walk away from what wasn't healthy. If I let my thoughts drag me down, I'm no better off here than I was there. Distance won't work if my mind is still ensnared. Wow, I need to pray...

"God, thank you for bringing me here. Thank you for showing me the way of escape and starting new here. Thanks for Bobby, and my mom, and Isla. My past doesn't have to destroy me, as long as I look to You for my future. I feel the tug to go back and repeat the same patterns over and over, even if only in my mind. I don't believe that is what You are telling me to do. You want me to forgive Vic, and all he's done so I don't have to carry that garbage with me the rest of my life. You want me to forgive my dad, and his ways of being so he won't have any power to affect me from this point on. I agree with You, God, and I forgive them, and anyone else who has not been healthy in my life, anyone I harbor unforgiveness toward, I want to forgive them here and now. Please help them and bless them. I want to leave what they have done to me with You, and let You deal with it. You are a just God. I trust You. You can love them and me perfectly. You know what's best for them, and for me. If I have hurt others, I ask for Your forgiveness for that. I don't want any of this junk to be an anchor that drags me down into the depths. I want to rise up and keep my focus on You. Help me to do that. I'm not very good at hearing You yet, but I'm wanting to. Maybe You could speak a little louder until my hearing gets better. Show me the way I need to go from here. Thank You, in Jesus' name. Amen."

38

It couldn't have been a more beautiful day to ride across the Bay into the city. Going under the Bay Bridge, looking at the skyline of San Francisco, felt freeing. To be out on the water with someone as kind as Isla, made for a perfect day. We docked at the Ferry building, and walked around the venders there, trying a sample of some freshly cooked pasta. It only wet our appetite for a larger meal, so we walked up to California Street to one of the oldest restaurants in the city, Tadich Grill. After being seated in a cozy nook, and feasting on sourdough bread, Isla and I got to know one another better.

"Where did you grow up, Isla? I'm a California boy, myself," I said.

"Well, I didn't start out an Oakland A's fan. I only became one after moving here from Pittsburgh. That's where I grew up, until I came out here to college. It was hard to change loyalties, but I wanted to root for the home team since I can go to the games here. I'm so glad we chose to go to the same game that day. I've always been a sports fan," she said.

"Not all women get as excited about baseball as you do! I could see your love of the game when I first met you. You really understand a lot about it. Probably more than I do," I commented.

"I do like it, but I'm no expert. I know people who can quote stats and history like nobody's business. That's not me. But I do enjoy it all," Isla said.

"Have you been back to Pittsburgh to see a game recently?" I asked.

"Yes. Just a couple of months ago, in fact. Right before I met you. I still cheer them on when I'm back home, and when they play the A's...I can't help it, I have to root for my Pirates. I try to keep it down low, though," Isla laughed.

"With the A's, it's probably okay that you root loudly. But certainly not at a Raiders game. It can get crazy there," I said.

"I have heard. I've never actually been to a Raiders game. I'll always been a Steelers fan. Just can't help that one. And I know there is a rivalry between those two teams, so I best stay home when the Steelers are in town!"

"I agree," I said.

"Last time I was in Pittsburgh," Isla continued, "I enjoyed a tour of the PNC Park. What an experience that was! We started with our guide talking to us as we looked out onto the field, and then we went into this special room that held lots of memorabilia. They had pics of the very first World Series game played between Pittsburgh and Boston in 1903. They played nine games in the series then, first one to five wins! I think...if I remember right, Boston won. They were called the Americans then."

"I have no idea, so I'll take your word for it. What else did you see?" I asked.

"They have an amazing picture of the winning home run being hit in game seven of the 1960 World Series—an old black and white photo that even captures the ball in the air. Think of the way photography has changed since then."

"I know, Isla, we don't even carry cameras or video cameras any more. Just our phones, for the most part. I remember my parents saying they had to lug around half the VCR to take home movies. And they thought it was the greatest!" I laughed at that, as did she.

Isla continued, "They had pics of the first All Minority starting lineup ever, on the wall in this room. And it wasn't planned, it was just who the manager thought would play the best ball that day in 1971. Baseball sure changed after the Jackie Robinson days, didn't it? So good."

"Yes. And didn't Roberto Clemente play for the Pirates?" I asked.

"Yes. He did. How sad that he died in that plane crash at only 38. He was helping to deliver food to earthquake victims in Nicaragua in 1972. He left a wife and three children. They had a framed jersey of his in the memorabilia room."

"That's nice the way they are honoring him," I said. "What was next on the tour?"

"From there we went all throughout the stadium, to the locker room, batting cage, press box, and even into the dug out and onto the field. We were told not to step onto the grass though."

"Wow, what a treat, to see all that. Wish I could go see behind the scenes at the A's game. Not even sure they have tours like that," I said.

"I don't know...this was a surprise for me. I can't believe they let the public into some of those areas. It was such fun to walk the halls where the Pirates walk. And there was this one saying on the wall that struck me, I took a picture of it. Let me bring it up here on my phone..."

While waiting, I was so impressed with Isla's enthusiasm for baseball. I wondered if she grew up with brothers. She told me later that she had.

"Here it is," she said. "The wall had these words on them, 'Honor the Past. Own the Present. Create the Future.' I really liked that."

"Let me think about that...hmmm. I like that, too. It's wise advice. I don't mean to interrupt our fun conversation with 'junk', shall we say. But those are things that I need to work on. Living with my brother, I'm discovering that I need to be aware of the past, live in the present, and see a future that doesn't have other people's shadow dimming where I'm walking. If you know what I mean?"

"I do, TL. I think we all can take something from that quote on the wall. That's probably why I took a picture of it. Do you think we can get more bread? I really like the sourdough!" Isla laughed.

I asked our waiter, and he promptly brought some, along with our lunch. The conversation that day was easy and fun, and by the time we made our way back over on the ferry to Jack London Square, it felt like we knew one another so much better. Not just about sports, but everything, from Isla growing up with brothers, her college days in California, the relationship she has with her parents, which was a good one. She said her mom is like her best friend, although she misses spending time with her since she is still in the Pittsburgh area. Her dad is a postal carrier, and is just about to retire, so her parents hope to get to California more often then. Isla became a Christian during her high school days. A friend of hers introduced her to Christ, and they started attending church together. Then Isla's parents started going, and her whole family, even her brothers, have become Christians. The more I got to know Isla, the more I wanted to be with her. But my heart was torn. The more I thought about New Mexico, the more it seemed like the place I needed to be. I brought it up to Isla on the ferry trip back across the bay.

"I've enjoyed this day so much. Thank you for spending it with me, Isla."

"It's been a pleasure, Tracy Lynn. Thanks for inviting me," she said.

"I have to tell you something...I'm very torn right now." I stopped there, not sure if I should tell her.

"What about? Have I said something that has confused you?" she asked.

"Well, yes, and no. Nothing you said has confused me, but everything we've shared today makes the decision I need to make harder."

"Oh no, I'm sorry. What is it?" she asked, very concerned.

"It's nothing wrong. The day has been so right, and that is what makes it hard. I know that my time with Vic needs to come to an end. You and I have talked about that some. I'm considering when I should leave my job...and move...to New Mexico." I could see the expression on Isla's face change. A sudden look of sadness passed over her, and then she turned away for a moment. She wasn't surprised...but I could tell this was affecting her, too. New Mexico was a long way...not like moving over to the Sierras or something. By the time she turned back my way, her look was serious but compassionate.

"Tracy Lynn, I have to tell you, I've enjoyed this day immensely. It does sadden me to hear that you might be moving so far away, but I understand. Sometimes we have to do things that aren't easy but make sense. When I came out here to go to college, leaving my parents behind, especially my mom because we were so close, was one of the hardest things I've ever had to do. And then when I found a job here after college, that was hard again. My mom took the news well; she understood, even though she wanted me to move home. She knew the opportunity I was offered here was the best place for me. So I have lived far away from the people I most want to be around. And now, meeting you, I feel a real connection with you. You're honest...and real, and kind. But I want the best for you. And living with Vic is not healthy, it seems, so you have to make decisions that will work during this time of your life. It doesn't mean we can't remain friends. I hope you will want to. And we can trust God for what comes after that. Sometimes you have to let go to take hold."

"Isla, you make this easier and harder, all at the same time. You say, 'Yes, go,' and my heart says, 'No, stay.' I hope you're right. And maybe...maybe things will change somewhere down the road. Of course I want to remain in each other's lives. Certainly! And maybe you can come to New Mexico for a visit?"

"I would really like that, Tracy Lynn. I've never been there," she answered, with a little more peace now settling on her beautiful face.

The train ride back to Martinez was a bit quieter, but there was an understanding between us that we both felt. It had been such a good day. I hoped God had something good in mind for Isla and me somewhere down the road.

39

The weeks in New Mexico seem to be going by quickly. I know it's getting close to time to start my life here, permanently, if I'm going to stay on longer with Bobby. He isn't even hinting about me moving out. But I have been helping with the rent and expenses. The money left from my savings has worked well, as long as I budget it.

Taking a drive over to Mesilla, I can see that Bobby is probably right. It is a good area to look for a place where I can start in with making tacos. They won't be what the locals are used to, being that it's an original chicken taco recipe, but I'm hoping when they taste them, they will love them!

Arriving back in the town square, I park and walk around. When we were here before, I didn't make it into the gift shop where Billy the Kid was once on trial, so I think I'll go in there and just have a look around. There is such rich history here, with even this building being built in early Mesilla years. This pamphlet says it was a store in the 1850's. It's a pretty cool place. It says it was after the Civil War that it was used as the county courthouse and jail until the later 1800's. Billy the Kid was tried and sentenced to hang here. But he escaped! Wow! A sheriff later killed him. I wonder how hard it was to escape jail in those days?

Walking down the street, there's a fudge shop, which I always have a hard time passing up. And there's other shops and restaurants. Around one corner and down the street a ways, I see a little shop with a "For Rent" sign out front. Peering through the windows, I'm amazed. It looks like what would work perfectly for a small taco stand, so to speak. It even has a wide enough sidewalk out front for some small tables and chairs. I will give this number on the sign a call and see what I can get arranged. It seems too good to be true. But if God truly did bring me here for this time in my life, and for a new beginning, why wouldn't He provide the perfect place for my chicken tacos!

The phone is ringing, and my heart is pounding...I'm not quite sure what to say to whomever answers on the other end. I've never done anything like this before. But when a man says "Hello," the rest, as it seems in Mesilla, is history.

"Juan Franco here! How can I help you?"

"Hello. What a cool name you have. I'm Tracy Lynn, also known as TL, and I'm calling about your shop in Mesilla. I got your number from the sign in the window."

"Ahh, TL...is it okay if I call you that?" he asks.

"Sure. All my friends do."

"I hope to call you amigo," he says with just a twinge of an accent. I wonder if he is one of the locals whose family never left this area? "Are you interested in renting my shop there in town?"

"I believe so...I'm not very experienced in all this, Juan, so I don't quite know where to start. But I'm hoping to serve some tacos and other foods there, and wondering...well actually, any advice you can give me will be appreciated."

"It's not all that hard. I don't mind stepping you through it," he says confidently, with even more of an accent this time. Everything he is telling me sounds perfect. The size of the shop, the kitchen facilities, the tables stored in the back for outside seating. He's even sharing a few recipes with me.

"May I ask, why are you no longer doing business here?" I hated to ask, but it seemed important to know.

"Ahh, amigo, it is only because I have moved on to a larger restaurant over in Las Cruces. I have a growing family, and I needed more income than I could make at this spot. But let me tell you, you will do well there. Lots of people come to Mesilla to shop and eat."

As he says, "Mesilla," I love hearing his spin on that word. We would want to pronounce it in English with the "L's" being heard. Of course, in Spanish, the "L's" are silent.

After a lengthy conversation, Juan Franco and I finish, and I'm left sitting in the square, feeling a new sense of freedom. I want to give Mom a call and see what she thinks.

With the phone ringing, I watch as the people walk by, and the birds soar high above.

Mom answers, "Hi, Tracy Lynn. How are you today?"

"So good, Mom. So good."

"That's wonderful. It sounds like you have news for me?" she asks.

"I do. I know you won't be surprised when I tell you how God has provided for me here. I have located the perfect little place to serve my tacos to the community. It seems too good to be true."

"Well, our God does work miracles. I like the sounds of this. I've been *wondering about you and praying for you there. I know moving and starting over can be difficult."*

"Yes. But it's feeling more possible. I met the coolest guy. Get this, his name is Juan Franco. Doesn't that just sound like a character in a book?"

"It surely does. Who is he and how did you meet him?"

"I called the number in the window of the vacant shop. It was his restaurant. He's going to help me get everything set up. It's like God is handing me this opportunity on a silver platter. Now all I have to do is fill it with tacos!"

Mom laughs at that, and I can tell by the sound of her voice that she is truly happy for me. She turns to Dad to share the news. I can't hear what he's saying, and Mom doesn't repeat it into the phone. That is probably wise of her. He probably made a sarcastic remark, and she knows I need all the encouragement I can get.

After filling Mom in on all the details, I drive back over to the RV. Bobby should be home soon, and he will be excited to hear the news. He told me he will be one of my first customers.

Coming through the door, Bobby lays his stuff down, and sees me with a big smile on my face.

"Hey, TL, you look like the cat that swallowed the canary!" he says.

"You might say that! How would you like to be eating some of my soon-to-be-famous chicken tacos?"

"You found a place?" he asks excitedly.

"Yes. And the guy who was there before me is such a big help. It shouldn't take too long before the doors will be open. I do need to find someone to work with me. If you have anyone in mind, let me know."

"I sure will. This calls for a celebration! Let's go on over to that place by the theater and get a bite to eat. You're buying!" Bobby quips.

"I'm in! It's my turn!"

On the drive to dinner, I'm able to fill Bobby in on all the details and how cool Juan Franco has been. By the time the evening ends, we've even contacted a friend of Bobby's who is out of work right now. He's willing to start with me for very little, and work into the business if it takes off.

As I fall asleep, I feel such a sense of satisfaction. After being here for almost a month now, I'm happy to know this may truly be my future home. I want to give Isla a call in the morning. It has been good to stay in contact with her, but for neither one of us to have expectations of the other that we can't fulfill. It's hard to be away from her, but she lives way too close to Vic at the moment. I need space, and she understands that.

40

The times with Vic weren't improving. Abby was gone, another bad ending to their relationship. He seemed to always just use each new girlfriend until something better came along. But now, even though Vic would have loved to have had another woman in his life, it didn't seem to be happening for him. His frustration level was rising, and the atmosphere at home increased in intensity. Thankfully, Vic was working and came home tired, so he didn't stay up late. For me, I mainly tried to stay out of his way, and spend time with Isla. One Sunday after church, we had an interesting conversation at brunch.

"TL, you look tired today. Are you okay?" she asked me at the table.

I pushed my food around the plate and kept quiet at first. Isla was always so upbeat, I hated to be the downer when we were together.

"I don't know, Isla. I hate to say too much. It's such a nice morning, and the sermon was powerful. Maybe we should talk about that instead of my continuous problems. Vic isn't going to change. I'm beginning to face that. I always have hope, but it does seem to be dwindling."

"What spoke to you most about the sermon today, then?" Isla asked. Not pushing the Vic subject as she waited for me to respond.

After a few bites, and collecting my thoughts, I did want to talk with her about the sermon.

"Isla, this world can be so harsh. People aren't nice sometimes. I mean, when I'm with you, the world seems brighter." Isla smiled at that. "You are patient, and you listen to me. You ask me questions. You genuinely care about other people. I hope I do the same for you."

"Thank you for saying that, and yes, you do," Isla responded humbly.

"Well, it's true what I'm saying about you. You are a rare jewel. I'm sorry that I will probably need to be leaving California. And I appreciate that you still want to spend time with me while I'm here."

"Of course I do. I've learned that even if we only have a short time with someone, it can touch us in many ways, and sometimes for the rest of our lives. I was with a person recently, just for two days, who you would think would have little impact on people. She was so quiet, so reserved, but there was just something about her that was unique. While everyone around her was louder and more opinionated, she remained quiet and peaceful. When I did get a chance to talk one-on-one with her, even just for a short bit, it was like...well in your words, a 'rare jewel.' We went right to the heart of things. It really showed me that it's not the length of time we spend with someone, or even that a lot needs to be said, to leave an impression on another person's life. In fact, the louder interactions sometimes make us want to just get away. But if we can get quiet, still, and move more slowly, really making each word count, it can be more powerful...very lasting and wonderful. This woman will have forever touched my life in a good way, even if I never see her again. I'm thankful."

"See, there you go, Isla, you look at things in such a different way. I like it. I'm truly going to miss you," I said.

"And I will miss you, too. But I do have a bit of good news," Isla said gleefully. "What is that?" I asked, with a tinge of hope in what seemed glum at the moment.

"My company is opening up an office in El Paso. They just announced it on Friday, and...and..." Isla stalled there.

"AND! Don't leave me waiting here!" I said while chuckling.

"There may be times that I will need to take a business trip to El Paso and check on things. They haven't said for sure yet. But I'm sure hoping. I mean, it's not that far from Las Cruces is it?"

"No. Not at all. Even though it's in Texas, it's only about an hour or so from Las Cruces. And believe me, if you end up working in El Paso, and I'm in New Mexico, I WILL make a point to get to there and see you! You can count on that."

"Maybe by then you will have your taco shop, and I can try these tacos you keep telling me about. Where did you get the recipe, anyway?" Isla asked.

"I have an uncle who makes them, and he shared it with me. It's not complicated, but it sure is good!"

"I'm ready and waiting. But it does seem that we have veered off track a bit. Weren't we going to talk about this morning's sermon? I love talking over what the pastor has shared. I know he puts many hours into teaching us. It's only right that we go over our notes when he is finished," Isla added.

"It is. And here's what struck me, if you don't mind me giving my opinion first?" I asked.

"Of course not. Go right ahead. I'm just going to sit and listen while I enjoy my meal."

I began to tell Isla what I noticed as the pastor went through some Scripture in Mark—"Jesus was always being attacked by someone. They were always questioning Him, trying to trap Him, wanting Him to flub up with His answers to them so He could be arrested, or even killed. I noticed that even with all the good that Jesus did with everyone He came in contact with, the love seemed very one way. Even the disciples, at times, were only out for what they could get, asking if they could sit next to Jesus in His Kingdom." I then asked Isla, "Where were you? What I mean is, where were the people who really cared? Who really listened? Who really wanted what was best for Jesus instead of themselves?"

"Well, I don't know how I would have been in Biblical days, Tracy Lynn. Please don't put me onto some pedestal that I will easily slip off of."

"I know what you're saying. But I do have to tell you, when Pastor Dan started talking about the woman who came in with the jar of expensive perfume, and she poured it on Jesus, and she wiped her tears off His feet with her hair, I thought of you."

"That's a huge compliment, but I will give all the praise and glory to God if that is what you see in me," Isla said, with a look in her eyes that spoke of how she truly meant that.

"It just seems like Jesus met with such opposition, with such cruelty," I added. "Oh man, maybe narcissists were rampant even in Jesus' day? Who would have thought? Everyone wanted to prove how right they were. Jesus didn't have to prove anything. He knew who He was. I heard the other day, someone said, 'Don't give up being you, because you will lose your freedom.' Jesus never lost His freedom. He understood who He was, and He walked as the Son of God all the way to the Cross, and rose again..."

"Amen!" Isla interjected.

I nodded in agreement and was so glad she was with me on this. I continued on, "I've been thinking more lately about seeing the log in our own eye, it humbles me. It helps me not be so quick to try and remove the splinter out of someone else's. Even with Vic, I know it's not all on him. I've played into this, not really knowing who I am. Giving up being me... My mom has done the same with my dad. Jesus never, ever played into it. He stood His ground, He spoke the truth, boldly, and He also loved everyone through it all. What a perfect example of being a healthy individual. I mean, we can't expect anything less from the Son of God, but we should take a lesson from it and learn from it each day we live."

"I like your thinking, Tracy Lynn. I really do. What else did you get from this morning?" Isla asked as she continued eating her meal.

"That there are some, few and far between, who were kind. But kindness was shown to Jesus by the woman, I think it was Mary, who didn't think about the cost, but who did what she could to comfort Jesus...to love on Him. I think she was sent there by God to encourage

Jesus as His time was drawing near. He knew what was coming. Most seemed oblivious to it. She may not have known, but she still truly cared about Him. Think about it, she walked into a room, probably full of men, eating dinner, and risked their rebuke to tend to Jesus. How awesome is that?"

"It's amazing," Isla answered. "And Jesus, in turn, was so kind to her, telling them not to berate her for what she was doing. He soaked in the expensive perfume, probably thankful for that compassion in such a compassionless journey toward Jerusalem and His death on the Cross. I've heard that ignoring conflict is not being a peacemaker. It is those who are able to address conflict in a loving yet firm way that is best. True peace does not come from pretending that what is wrong is right. To call it what it is will bring persecution. Jesus knew that. He faced it every day. But He set such a good example for us, and how we are to walk out our faith and be in our relationships, good and bad, and not ignoring things. He also truly looked at those who surrounded Him as being made in the image of His Father. No one was less in His eyes. Not even Judas. Jesus called Judas His friend when he betrayed Him with a kiss. Can you imagine?"

"Honestly. No," I stated matter of factly.

"But Jesus did. He always said what He needed to say. No more, no less. He would let others know if what they were saying wasn't true and right, desiring that they understood Him. Sometimes He did that by telling them the truth. Sometimes He just wouldn't even try to defend himself from their lies," Isla said.

"Sadly, most didn't seem to understand Him," I added. "I'm seeing more and more that there were many narcissists surrounding Jesus. A narcissist will provoke others with lies, stating things as they see it from their own unreality, and they want to draw us into an argument. Vic does that a lot. Jesus never fell for it; He knew what was real. Sadly, sometimes as co-dependents, we get caught up and confused when a narcissist spins things. It's better to walk away in those moments and pray. When Vic is mean, it affects my thinking, and it seems I can even feel it physically in my heart. Maybe that's another reason why Jesus went off by himself so often to pray to His Father. It was important that He stayed on the right path."

"I know. But I wonder how we would have been back then? We shouldn't judge them too harshly until we have walked in their 'sandals.'" Isla laughed, taking another bite of her omelet. "What I practice when I'm listening to someone is to put what I'm thinking about up in a cupboard, getting it out of my head, and really try to *hear* the person talking. I have my own ideas, my own agenda, but I know it needs to sit on a shelf for the moment. I should not only listen, but really *hear* what someone else is saying, even if I need to repeat their words back to them so I can fully understand where they're coming from. Both for their sake and mine."

"If people had done that with Jesus, they might have actually been more supportive of Him," I commented. "Didn't He ask His disciples what people were saying about who He was? Well, if people would have listened and really heard Him, they would have known He was the Son of God."

"Possibly. They might have even asked Him to tell them more...you know it was all good. And the Bible says that there would be a ton more books if everything Jesus said and did had been written down. We're only getting a small glimpse of it, I think."

"I think you're right," I said.

"When people talk, they want to be heard, and they want you to remember what they're saying. If those around Jesus had truly remembered what He was telling them, they wouldn't have been so shocked that He died on the Cross. They would have understood that in just three days, He'd be back!" Isla said this with oomph!

"We can't read anyone else's mind, and we shouldn't even try. I mean, I try to figure Vic out, and it's nearly impossible. Why? Because I think he thinks like I think, and he doesn't. When, and if, we ever do get to the bottom of some of the things he's saying and doing, I'm usually very surprised how far off I was from his thought process! It really shows me how minds can work so differently."

"Well, you know, Tracy Lynn, most women want those that care about them to be able to read their minds!" She laughed at that.

"I guess they do! But PLEASE, don't expect that from me, okay? I'm not good at it at all!" I laughed then, too.

"Okay. I'll try not to. I've read that expectations only hold water when they are actually agreed upon. So I hope we can keep that in mind in all our communicating with one another." Isla said.

"One thing we have actually agreed upon is that if you come out to El Paso, we WILL get together!" I said.

"AGREED!" Isla responded with more laughter.

"I have thoroughly enjoyed this time together, Isla, but I think I need to get you home, if you don't mind. I have some things to take care of before work tomorrow."

"I understand and agree. You have things to take care of, and it's time you take me home. See how easy that is!" Isla giggled after repeating my words back to me.

Our time together had been so warm and genuine, it was hard to say good-bye at her door.

41

"Good morning, Isla," I say cheerfully, after hearing her groggy voice on the other end. "Sorry to call you so early. Did I wake you?"

"Well, you did. But that's okay. From the sound of your voice, it will be worth the early alarm."

"I surely hope so! How are you doing? I miss you!"

"It's going well, and I miss you, too. But tell me, what's up? You sound excited!"

"Well, I am! After being here in Las Cruces for only a month, it looks like I have secured a place to open my new taco shop! It's over in Mesilla, not far from where I'm staying with Bobby. It's a great little town, with lots of tourists and history. When you come...and notice I say 'when' and not 'if,' because I want to think positively about your company needing to send you out this way, I will be able to serve you my very own tacos. On me!"

"Hey, I'm SO happy for you! That is the greatest news. I didn't think it would take you long there to get things going. But what do I know about the restaurant business?"

"Maybe more than I do," I laugh. "But this guy, Juan Franco, I like saying both his names together, is being so good to me. He's going to help me with all the licensing, and he will show me the ropes. He even has some regulars there in Mesilla, and he's going to spread the word that I'll be open for business soon."

"Sounds like it can't get much better than that!" Isla says, sounding more awake now.

"I'm sorry I haven't been calling you as much these last couple of weeks. I've been doing a lot of soul searching. I'm wanting to get healthier before I get busier. It's been kind of good to disconnect from everything in California for a bit. But please don't think I haven't been thinking about

you."

"*TL, I trust that what you're doing is what you need to do. I knew I would hear from you when the time was right. And I have been busy with these new acquisitions my company is making. Not only in El Paso, but two other cities, one in Arizona and one in Colorado.*"

"*Oh, wow! I hope they send you here and not there.*" *I know I have a bit of a worrisome tone.*

"*Now, TL, don't you be concerned. I'm going to do my best to make sure that when someone needs to be in El Paso, it will be me. I have a certain amount of pull here.*"

"*Okay. I feel better,*"

"*You don't have to worry. We share a very special friendship, and I'm here for you, no matter what,*" *Isla says with such confidence.*

"*You always make me feel so good, Isla. Your reassurance helps. Vic has made me question people's loyalty. Even when I had that trouble with my heart, he flaked on me. Other people did in my life, too. I need to find some healing there, and I need to pay more attention to who I am spending time with. Those difficult relationships, I see now, have affected how I respond to other people in life. I don't trust like I could. I should have surrounded myself with people more...well, trustworthy. These hurts have caused me to close parts of my heart off, and I don't want to do that anymore. I want to live my own life, the way God designed me to. I can't live my dad's life, or Vic's, or anyone's. I have to live mine. And even if they think I'm crazy for doing this, it doesn't matter. I will sink or swim, with God.*"

"*I like your focus, TL. God has a plan, and we can trust Him. Small changes in our life can keep us on the path that we are meant to be on. I know the changes you have made recently aren't small...quitting your job, moving away, starting a new business now. But you're doing it, one step at a time. Good for you!*"

"*Thanks, Isla. Thank you for being a healthy person in my life. You don't know how much I appreciate you. I am learning. I'm a bit scared, but I will do this, even in my fear. With the way I see the doors opening for me, the helping hand from Juan Franco, and the perfect little place there in Mesilla, I know I need to keep putting one foot in front of the other and see what happens.*"

"*Yes. Do that. And right now, I need to get up and get ready for work. I'll look forward to hearing how this all goes, TL. Pray your way through it, and I will be praying for you.*"

"*Thank you. Bye for now.*"

"*Bye, my friend,*" *Isla says in such a tender way.*

Hanging up after talking with Isla, I already miss hearing her voice, but I also feel so full inside. That knot in the pit of my stomach is becoming a thing of the past. I wondered if it would ever go away? It seems with leaving that it finally has. Bobby is so sane, and so is Isla. They always encourage me and give me good feedback. It helps me know that I don't have to be around people who are like that. I've met too many who are probably on the narcissistic side of things. Maybe by me understanding my own insecurities and co-dependent tendencies, I can choose more wisely as time goes on. I will look for more people like Bobby and Isla,, and less like Vic.

When the phone rings, I'm surprised when Dad's name pops up. My stomach jumps, my heart starts beating, and I wonder if I should even answer it? By the time I decide, it's already going to voicemail. Maybe that's better. I'll just listen to Dad from a distance, and not have to respond. I wait a few moments, and then dial my voicemail.

"TL, this is your dad. Your mom told me what you're doing. Call me. We need to talk."

That's all he says, but it's not good. I can tell. He's wanting to give me his truckload of advice. Do I call him now, or give it some time? I think I'll wait and do a bit more investigating about narcissism in preparation for talking with him. This is going to be battle with my dad, and I feel sorry for my mom. She is going to have to listen to it a lot more than I am.

Bringing up more info on narcissism, it says here that a third party is needed for a lot of these discussions. Well, I'm not going to sit with Dad and a counselor at this point. I don't think it's the time for that. I want to change, but I'm pretty sure he's not even thinking in that direction. But one thing I don't want to do is put Mom in the middle. Although, she is getting stronger as she's learning, too. Her self-esteem is growing, a little bit faster than mine is. But by taking this stance with the restaurant, no matter what criticism I hear from Dad, it will stretch me and make me stronger. It will help me move into my own future, with or without his consent. For so much of my life I depended on Dad's view on things. I didn't know anything different. I saw Mom do it, and I followed suit. But he could be so harsh, and still can be. He wants me to live his life, and I need to live mine.

This says that a narcissist is toxic and seductive, and even disguised. But maybe we just don't have a clue about that until someone turns on a light? I don't think I did, or I never would have moved in with Vic in the first place. Maybe narcissism appears more as a shadow than total darkness, so we just learn to live in it. But Vic lives in an unreal world, the world he creates. He drew me into that until I think I really started to lose myself. He could make me feel really stuck at times, by his treatment toward me. And how sad that he had me hiding in my room so much of the time...as a grown man. He saw himself up on a pedestal, and I left him there, while he worshipped himself. How sick is that? But then, I don't think trying to call him down from his lofty perch was possible either. Vic would have to want to change, so would Dad. In the midst of it all, I now know I was unable to see who I was, what I was good at, and what I could do. This restaurant is one way for me to do that. They have not ventured down this path, so they really don't have much they can offer me concerning this. I'm glad for that. Oh, Dad will give me his business advice, and some of it can be good. But I will sift through it, carefully, cautiously. And as far as Vic...I don't know. I don't think I need to be talking to him any time soon, especially after that last note from him. That pretty much tells me where he's at in his thinking.

What is this saying here? When we hit bottom, we start to make changes. True, dat! I didn't recognize that I was not me, that I was engulfed in Dad's world, and then getting sucked into Vic's. I need to know who I am, and with Mom and Isla's encouragement to walk this out with Jesus, I can feel it working. I can't do this on my own. I don't have the strength in me to fight this. I remember Jesus saying somewhere in the Bible that the spirit is willing, but the flesh is weak. I get that. But God is so strong. I will make a point to learn more and more how to depend on Him. The more I do this here, the better I will be able to deal with Dad and Vic. I don't want to never see them again. But when I do see them, or talk to them on the phone, I don't want to go back into their darkness anymore...walk around in their shadow. I want to stand in the light...the light of God. If they aren't willing to be in that light with me, then I will hang up the phone, or walk away. Wow, it sounds good to even be able to think that will be possible. I know I need to do more work, but this says here again that acknowledging is a big first step into changing. I acknowledge my weakness, and that I need You, God. Please help me!

It's settling into my bones that I need to know these things, see these things, so I don't have to fear these things. I've been living my life like a scaredy cat! No more, I want to roar like a LION! I no longer need to defend myself or prove myself to any of the narcissists in my life. Even when I call Dad back, I need to remember this. "Yeah, Dad, okay, I hear you, but..." He may not be able to really see me or hear me, but that doesn't have to change who I am, or the path I am on. And God has brought me Isla, and has given me Mom, to talk all this through with...and Bobby. I am not alone in this. If Dad doesn't respect who I am, then I won't be talking to Him about it...any of it. He will probably never come over into thinking anything about my life is a good idea unless it matches up with his way of doing things. If I don't expect that he will, I won't be disappointed when I don't get it. I will be me. He can be him.

For the first time in my life, I'm feeling more grateful, more optimistic, more able, to fulfill my life's dreams. I will call Dad back, one day soon. But if it doesn't go well, then it will be a long while before I talk to him again.

Right now, I need to start making restaurant plans. I'm excited!

42

For the next couple of weeks, I couldn't stop thinking about that Sunday brunch with Isla. Even though we spoke many times since then, there was something on that day that really touched me. I tried not to get too drawn into a relationship with her past our friendship, because I knew it wasn't fair to her, or to me. I was moving on soon, and we would both need to live our separate lives. Oh, but it was so hard.

When Isla's birthday was a week away, I still wanted to make sure it would be special for her. She didn't want the attention, but I wouldn't take "No" for an answer. She would be treated as she deserved. As I made plans to be in the city for her special day, I think even she was looking forward to the celebration. Thankfully, her birthday landed on a Saturday, and she had shared with me what her favorite kind of date looked like. I made the preparations and picked her up early. She seemed excited!

"Good morning, Tracy Lynn," she said upon opening the door. "You look strikingly handsome today for such a casual day in the park."

"Isla, there is nothing casual about today. Happy Birthday to you!! And from this point on, I will have the pleasure of treating you to a day in the city, picnic lunch, and music in the park, just as you desire it. I would like to spend bucket loads of money on you, but since I don't have but a cupful, I'm thankful your taste in what's fun fits right into what I can give you."

"Tracy Lynn, just being with you today, and being remembered by you like this, is enough for me. Anything beyond that is just the cherry on top," Isla said, with true sincerity in her voice.

"Shall we go?" I said, taking her hand, and leading her to the car, opening her door for her with the utmost of chivalry, as she sweetly laughed at my playfulness.

It was a beautiful sunny day. The fog in the city was rolling back out to the ocean earlier than normal, and we were both grateful. We drove to a small park outside of all the congestion, having arrived in good time to get a place on the lawn not far from the bandstand. Spreading out the blanket, I told Isla to just take a seat. I would be serving her today. It was hard for her to allow this, but I reminded her that it was her day, and she should accept it all with gladness, telling her it is sometimes harder to receive than it is to give, but it's very important. By not accepting the goodness offered to us by another, we may be robbing them of their blessings. That was something my mom had always impressed upon me, and really for the first time, I could see it clearly. By Isla allowing me to serve her in this way, the joy in my heart knew no limits. To see her smile, to know this was her chosen way of spending the day, and that I could be a part of making her birthday special for her, satisfied my soul deeply.

We started the day with chocolate croissants, her favorite, and I poured us both a steaming mug of hot coffee. I'd borrowed the thermos from Vic without asking. But we weren't talking much these days, and I figured he would never notice it was gone.

The morning air still had a chill to it, and I could tell Isla was shivering some. I had thought ahead, being that this was San Francisco, and pulled out a blanket to wrap around her shoulders. Our beach chairs were placed close to one another, so when she offered me a part of her blanket, I accepted. It seemed so right to be here together. We watched as others arrived and set up their places of comfort. Everyone seemed to come very prepared. I was glad we were no exception.

By the time the concert began at 11:00, the lawn was full, and the sun was warming up the day. Isla laid the blanket to the side, and then she looked at me, and took my hand as the concert began. I didn't hear the music begin on stage because suddenly the beat of my heart was so much louder...it was a song of hope and joy that I hadn't experienced before. It took me by surprise. Isla seemed to be engrossed in what was being played from the stage. She seemed to not know the impact her touch was having on me in that moment, and I was glad. While I was soaking her in, I wanted her to soak in the music she so much enjoyed.

When the band announced it was time for intermission, I told Isla it was time for her birthday feast. She, of course, wanted to help me with the preparations, but I would have none of it. I loved to hear the sound of her oohs, and ahhs as I pulled out the assortment of the things she loved. It had been hard to get it out of her, but she did tell me some of her favorites. Deli meats and cheeses on sourdough bread, sweet pickles, black olives, BBQ chips, potato salad. I knew there would be more food than the two of us could eat, but I didn't mind. This was her day.

When the band began again, we were ready for the second half, having enjoyed each bite. Isla didn't know, but I had more surprises waiting for her inside the ice chest. Once again as the music started, Isla took my hand in hers. And once again, my heart thrilled to her touch...I knew I was in trouble. This woman was affecting me in ways that I had secretly hoped would not happen. I couldn't stay, I had to go, and this would make leaving so much harder. Maybe if she didn't feel as I did, it would make it better somehow? I would not tell her what I was thinking, what I was feeling. I would ignore these things and do what needed to be done. I tried my best to focus on the band, while all the time barely hearing a single song they played that day.

When the concert ended, the applause was loud, and an encore was called for. The musicians seemed pleased to oblige and I was thankful for more time there with Isla. When they finally took their last bow, and all those around us started to pack up, I asked Isla if we could just sit a while. The sun had moved in the sky to a place just behind a large tree, and our seats in the shade made for a perfect temperature. As most the crowd left, and things quieted down around us, I wanted to bring out Isla's birthday surprise. Her eyes lit up when she saw the small, round, chocolate mousse cake with delicate icing and her name written on the top. I pulled out a candle, and when lit, I looked into Isla's eyes and sang Happy Birthday to her as best I could. I don't think she minded that my pitch wasn't perfect. I truly think she was thankful that I would care for her in that way.

When her birthday song ended, and I got us a couple of plates, she laughed at me as I pulled out a second small cake for myself.

"Tracy Lynn, you are too much!" she said, laughing heartily. "And honestly, I'm glad to eat this whole cake myself! I don't indulge much in sweets, but on my birthday, I like to give myself the freedom to do it, not counting the calories."

"I have heard, and I think you can quote me on this, calories DO NOT count on a person's birthday."

"I believe you," Isla said, laughing all the more.

As we enjoyed our cake, and the very last of the concert goers left the park, we were quiet for a bit. Isla sat with her eyes closed when her cake was done, and I didn't want to disturb her thoughts. I waited for her to speak.

"Thank you," she said, looking at me, and stretching out her hand toward mine.

I didn't say anything in that moment. I just took her hand and laid my other hand over the top of hers. We sat that way for a while, but then I knew I had to gently pull back. She didn't seem to notice, or to mind, but I did. I could have held her hand for all of eternity. I just knew I couldn't. I had to go.

43

Setting the tables out on the sidewalk, I take a look around. Being early morning, there aren't many people strolling the streets yet. I can still hardly believe this dream is coming true. The first months of being in the restaurant business weren't easy, but with Juan Franco's help, and the friend Bobby connected me to, it is working out as the months go on now. Long hours, and some stress, is paying off. Each day, more people make their way here, and seem to be enjoying the food.

"We have an order from the tortilla company arriving today, TL," Chuck calls to me from the doorway."

"Thanks, Chuck. I'll be here. Go ahead to your dentist appointment. Don't worry, I just appreciate all you've been doing here. I wish I could pay you more, but hopefully in time, that will come."

"Hey, don't worry about it. I get plenty to eat here, and it's covering my rent. I know our customer count is growing, and I'm with you all the way. I enjoy working here with you," Chuck says, with a wave of his hand as he walks to his car.

Bobby really helped me out by introducing me to Chuck. He didn't have any restaurant experience, but neither did I. We've been figuring it out as we go, and Juan Franco can answer any questions we have. Dad still isn't easy to talk to about all of this. When I called him back, it was so difficult— it's best I pretty much stay off the phone with him. I don't think he'll be coming out this way any time soon. Poor Mom! Sometimes she still struggles so much with him. She's trying her best, but he's so difficult. I know she won't leave him. She loves him. But it breaks my heart. I wish she could come out for a visit, but I don't think she will without Dad.

"Hey, TL! How's business?" It's Mason from the shop next door, placing his sign out front.

"Hey...doing all right. How about for you?"

"*Can't complain,*" *Mason answers.*

"*It's going to be a little cooler today, so I'm putting out all the tables. The people love it when they can sit outside.*"

"*They do,*" *Mason agrees.* "*And when they are done there, send them my way.*"

"*Will do. And you do the same. Have a good one!*"

It's been a good first six months here in New Mexico and living with Bobby is still working well. He does his thing, and I do mine. Bobby likes to come by for tacos, too. It's always on the house for him. He doesn't like it, but it's the least I can do after he took me in. He's been so helpful. I think I'll give Mom a call before things get busy. I haven't talked to her for a while.

Answering, her voice sounds tired. "*Hi there, Tracy Lynn, I thought you'd be working today? Everything okay?*"

"*Sure, Mom. It's great, actually. I'm just waiting on a delivery of some fresh tortillas and was thinking about you. Thought I'd take a seat at my own tables and see how everything's going. Sorry, I've been busy and can't call as often. You sound tired.*"

"*Oh, I understand. Restaurant work is not for wimps!*" *Mom laughs a bit at that.* "*I'm a little tired.*"

"*Why are you tired, Mom? Didn't you sleep well? Is it Dad?*"

"*No. It's not your dad this time...uhh, well...I don't know if now is the time...I don't want to worry you...*" *Mom says, with her voice trailing off.*

"*MOM! What!?*"

"*I've been to the doctor, and the news wasn't so good. It's not as bad as it could be, but it's not good either.*"

"*I'm listening, Mom.*"

"*I had some blood tests done and the results showed...Leukemia. But...but...*"

"*Mom. What? What does that mean, exactly!? I mean, I know it's cancer, but just how bad is it?*"

"*Let me explain. From what the doctor has told me, I have CLL. There are many different types of Leukemia, and this is a type that old people get. Usually older than me, like in their 70's. Since I'm mid- sixties, it's not as common. The good news is, sometimes treatment isn't even needed. The disease just runs along with the person. Mine is a little worse than that so I will need to have some things done.*"

"*What were your symptoms? Are you able to get around?*"

"*Oh, sure. I have some tiredness, but mostly...I don't know, I've just felt out of it. Weird. A little light headed. I had one person tell me to put some sea salt on my tongue. Just a pinch of it. It actually helped. But even still, I didn't feel bad all the time, just every so often. Finally, I had to get it checked, though.*"

"*Sea salt, huh? I wonder what that did?*"

"I don't know. I really don't understand, but I'm getting a better idea of what is happening now. When they did a blood test on me, my White Blood Cells were high. They are supposed to be 10-11, or so, mine were at 40. A follow-up blood test showed they had risen to over a hundred. What happens then is that it causes a clog up in my system, and then other organs start to suffer. The medication they give me will bring my levels back to normal."

"How harsh is it, Mom? Will you lose your hair?"

"The doctor said with these newer drugs, they aren't as hard on the patient, so I should keep my hair. I will need a total of six infusions, about every three weeks, depending on how my body responds to everything. It will make me feel sick, but they have good drugs for that now, too, from what the doctor says."

"Oh, Mom. I can't believe this. Do you want me to fly home? I want to see you!"

"No, no, no, no...that is not necessary. I'm doing okay. And I have to tell you, your dad...this has really shaken him up. I don't know, Tracy Lynn, but God does work through these things. He has been gentler with me, and he even went to church with me. If this is what it takes to save that man's soul, then so be it!" Mom says, emphatically. "God can bring the good from the bad!"

"You've always said that, Mom. I would hope that Dad would take good care of you."

"He's getting better. He is. Keep praying for him."

"And you, Mom! I will be praying for you!"

"Of course, Tracy Lynn. Pray for me. But I don't want to keep you much longer, I know you probably have a busy day ahead. And please, don't worry. I know you will, but still..."

"I will try not to, Mom. But I will keep in close contact through this. You will get tired of hearing from me. Have you...have you told Vic yet?"

"Not as yet, but I will soon. Have you talked with your brother at all?"

"I have been keeping my distance. After his last note to me, by mail, it's better that way. Is he doing okay? You know I never stop caring about him."

"I believe so. I think he has a new girlfriend. Her name is Amanda. At least that's what he's told me, but he's pretty quiet about it all," Mom explains.

"Okay. Well, you get some rest. And we will talk soon. I really love you, Mom."

"I love you, too. Bye."

"Bye."

I can barely move, it's good there's no one here yet. I need to sit a bit and absorb what Mom just told me. Leukemia? That word alone scares the bejeebers out of me!

44

After gently letting go of Isla's hand, I said, "Happy Birthday. I hope you have enjoyed your day."

"Oh, I have. Very much. This has been just perfect. I will miss you when you go. But I will always remember this day. I'm so very glad we met. I hate to even ask this, but do you have any idea?"

"Idea?" I asked, but really knowing what she was getting at.

"Yes, idea when you will go to New Mexico?"

I sighed deeply, not wanting to answer. I spoke slowly, "Isla, I gave my two-week notice yesterday."

I could see Isla's eyes tear up as she looked up into the sky, not wanting me to notice. My eyes filled also, and I had to look away. This was not the way I wanted her birthday to go, not in this moment. It felt suddenly that I had put my own dark cloud on the day, and I surely didn't mean to. But Isla, being who she was, surprised me when she looked back my way, wiping away the tear that had escaped.

"I understand, and I agree," she said. "You need to do this Tracy Lynn, so that you can be all that God created you to be. Your birthday celebration for me today was so wonderful, how could I not want what would be most wonderful for you? I cherish your friendship, and I know this won't be the end for us. When two lives intersect like ours have, it's for all time, even though we will no longer live in close proximity to one another. I will always have you in my heart, and in my prayers, and I will be coming out to New Mexico to see you when time allows."

I had no words in that moment. The woman I'd always dreamed of sat there next to me, and I was leaving. Suddenly, I felt anger in my heart. Isla could feel the shift, and she looked at me waiting for me to say something. I remained quiet. She waited longer, still looking at me, and then looking away. Her patience in that moment only made me love her more...love her? Did I love this woman? In that moment, in that anger, I knew I did. Finally, I was able to speak.

"Isla, this is harder for me than I even want to admit. It scares me, it makes me angry about what I have to do because I haven't been as healthy as I need to be. I've let others run my life. I've let Vic affect me in ways that I shouldn't have. I could put all the blame on Vic. And honestly, I want to. But I won't. When I cried out to God, 'When will it stop?' and He clearly said, 'When you do,' I knew...this wasn't about Vic, my dad, any past friends or any other relationships I have had. This is about me, and who I am. How I see myself. Until I get my relationship with God right, I can't have a right relationship with anyone else. Not really. Not even with you, as wonderful as you are. It wouldn't be fair to you. You're one of the healthiest, most stable people I know, Isla. Truly, you are."

"Tracy Lynn, I have my stuff, too." Isla said quickly, not wanting to interrupt.

"I know, you're not perfect. And the minute I think you are only proves I have more work to do on myself. I can't place unrealistic expectations on you, or anyone. That would be greedy of me, depleting what you are, what you have, to satisfy my needs. I would never want to do that to you. I need to have the fullness of God in me, allowing Him to make me whole. When Jesus healed the woman with the issue of blood, He told her your faith has made you whole. I need to be whole like that, to be healed like that, so I don't depend on you or anyone to make up for what I'm lacking. If I'm not healthy, then I'll even cling to people like Vic, hoping they will love me...and narcissist are not capable of loving in a healthy way because they don't even know what that looks like. They don't know how to love sincerely and honestly."

"You're making sense, Tracy Lynn," Isla said with a heart full of compassion.

"When I fill my soul with the things of God, instead of the things of this world, then I know I can handle the things that come across my path, the people I meet, in the best way possible. My mom talks about being rooted in Christ. I'm not even one hundred percent sure what that is, but she tells me if I keep praying, and I keep reading the Bible, this will happen for me—that I need to plant myself in God's garden, and let my roots, my thoughts, my desires, my life, grow out of His pure, good, soil."

"Wow, I like that," Isla commented with raised brows.

"I do, too, Isla, but I want to not only like it...as they say on social media." We both laughed at that. "I want to learn how to live it. That's a lot tougher. Mom says that she's learning if we crave acceptance from being loved, we will either learn to get that love from the people around us, or from God. Of course, we know the best choice in that. But we so quickly go to people first, don't we? I could hold onto you now, Isla, so easily. I'm sorry, I hate to admit this..."

"It's okay, Tracy Lynn, you go right ahead and say what you need to say."

"I hate to be so vulnerable in this moment, but maybe it's needed," I said.

"I believe it is," Isla agreed with a nod of her head and a gentle smile.

"I don't want to cling to you because you are so...well, you are exceptional. And I want to be thoughtful of you. I want you to have the very best God has for you in a relationship. And I'm not that person...not yet at least. But I'm working toward it. I'm trying. I have to be willing to say no to my desires, so I can say yes to God right now and the healing He has for me. And honestly, this is one of my biggest challenges...with you in my life. I'm ready to throw it all away and be...well, more serious in my relationship with you. You're everything I've been searching for in a woman. But I have to believe God brought us together so I could be made whole, not so that I could use you to make me whole. Actually, what comes to me just now is that you are such a great motivation for me. You make me want to be spiritually and emotionally healthy more than ever, because I would never want to hurt you. God sure knows what He's doing. Vic showed me where I am lacking...you are showing me who I want to be. So, thank you."

"You are much too kind, Tracy Lynn, but I'm glad you're sharing all this with me today. We have to walk in this Truth every day, even when we don't feel it. I struggle on many days, but I've walked with Jesus long enough to know that He never changes. He is the same yesterday, today, and forever. I need to cling to Him, to His promises, even when I want to cling to so many other things...like you."

"You're so sweet. You get it, Isla. That's right. And I can't cling to you right now either. I have to cling to Jesus, if I'm ever to be right for you."

Isla nodded at that, not saying anything more. I didn't know if she knew that I loved her that day. I didn't know if she loved me. But I did know that we were communicating with one another on such a deep level, and it felt right and good.

45

Leukemia? I'm frozen here in this chair. I know I told Mom I wouldn't worry, but I already am. I'm glad there are no customers yet this morning. My legs feel weak. God, please help my mom...please help me...

"Hello. Do you mind if I use your chair here for a few minutes?"

My eyes are closed. Looking up now, I see where the question is coming from. A woman is standing in front of me. I don't know how long she's been there. I hope she doesn't think I was sleeping on the job...so to speak.

"Uh, the chair?" *I almost don't know what to say, my mind is so absorbed with Mom's condition.*

"Yes. I can see that you're not really open yet, but my friend is still next door and I was wondering if I could wait here for her and rest a bit. She's more of a shopper than I am."

"Uh, sure. Not a problem." *I'm starting to come to my senses...* "We aren't open, but we will be soon."

"Oh, I won't take up your table space. And in fact, my friend and I would love to come back when you are open and try some of your tacos. The store owner next to you said they are very good."

Ahh, Mason. He was helping me out, just like he said he would. "I'm glad he directed you this way. Go ahead and have a seat. Don't be in a hurry."

"Thank you. I need to ask you, if you don't mind..." *she says.*

"Yes, is there something else I can help you with?"

"Ummm, no. Not really. But I got the sense when I walked up that you were troubled about something. Is there anything I can pray about for you? I don't mean to barge into your personal business..."

I find myself looking into some of the kindest eyes I think I have ever experienced—this woman with golden brown skin and a white halo of hair looks like an angel.

"Pray for me? That's interesting...the timing, I mean."

"The timing?" she responds while taking a seat.

"Yes. Can I tell you about it?" I feel this need to tell her everything, and I don't even know her.

"You sure can," she responds.

"I just talked with my mom in California. I'm from there..."

"So am I. Go ahead, I don't mean to interrupt."

"Well, she just told me she has Leukemia. And I'm really struggling with it, although she made it sound like it wasn't super serious. But just that word...if you know what I mean."

"I do," the white-haired lady responds. "Cancer can be a scary business. Without an eternal Hope, where would any of us be in times like this?"

"Eternal Hope?" came of out my mouth almost as a knee-jerk response. Has God really sent this woman here in this moment to talk about Heaven...and to pray for me?

"Yes," she says, then she stops. She's looking at me in sort of a waiting mode. Am I supposed to say something? Is she some sort of missionary?

Gently she speaks up then, saying, "I'm so sorry to hear about your Mom. I truly hope she will be okay."

"Me, too." I'm a bit stumped for words at the moment. I'm trying to file through Mom's news in my brain, and I'm also wondering what might be happening here with this woman?

"Receiving this news is shattering. Thank you for your kindness in allowing me to sit here," she says. The white-haired woman stops there again. It seems she is very patient with all this. My mind is racing, but I'm starting to feed off her calmness, and I can feel things in me start to slow down some.

"Can I get you something to drink? I'm the owner of this place, and I'd like to treat you to a little refreshment."

"That would be very nice. Just some ice water works. I know it's going to be cooler around here today, but I know it's important to keep hydrated in the desert."

"It is. I'll be right back."

Returning with the water and offering it to her, I feel led to take a seat again. I know I should be doing some things, but she has me intrigued. "Do you mind if I sit with you a bit?"

"Not at all. And thank you for the water. You have a nice place here. Have you been in business long? By the way, I'm Rosie."

"Tracy Lynn. Most call me TL."

"Do you mind if I call you, TL?" Rosie asks.

"That's fine. I like your name. Do you like gardening? I bet you get asked questions like that a lot."

"I do like gardening. It's my favorite past time, other than spending

time with my Father."
   Rosie can tell I'm puzzled. She is probably close to 70, how old must her father be? She gently laughs while answering my quizzical look. "Yes, He is ancient, but He is better known as the Ancient of Days."
   "Oh...oh, oh. I'm sorry. You lost me there for a minute. Are you a missionary or something? I'm not used to most people offering to pray and talking about their Father like you do."
   "No, TL. But I do love Jesus, and I do spread His Good News wherever and whenever I can. Do you know Jesus as your Savior?"
   "Yes, I do. But I have to say, I don't know if I could ever be quite as bold as you are with my faith. I'm more the silent type when it comes to speaking to strangers about God."
   Rosie smiles at this. She has me shaking my head. Who is she?
   "TL, faith can be a very personal thing, but it also spills out more easily the closer we get in our relationship with Jesus. When Jesus is flowing freely through every part of our being, it becomes easier to share Him with others. And when we become more sensitive to the Holy Spirit in our lives, He will guide us...even on vacation." Rosie seems to say all this as if she was talking about the weather.
   "I'm not so familiar with the Holy Spirit."
   "Many are not, but He is a great gift from our Father in Heaven, and He lives in us. Daily, we can listen to Him, and be led by Him. It really helps us. I believe He is Who brought me to you today," Rosie says.
   This raises my eyebrows. "Really?"
   "Yes. God can work like that. Our Father knows about your mom. He is caring for her, and He is caring for you at the same time through this," Rosie says in an assuring tone. "I don't want to keep you much longer, but I would like to pray for you before your work day begins, if that is okay?"
   "I think that would be good for me. I have a long day ahead, and I know my head is going to be filled with Mom thoughts....and worries."
   "That's not surprising. Let's pray," Rosie begins, "Father in Heaven, thank You for bringing me to TL today. I know You are watching over him and caring for him as he is far away from his mom right now. I pray for TL to know Your peace in these difficult times. I pray Your blessing, not only on his business here, but on all his life. TL loves his mom and is concerned with this cancer scare. You are not a God of fear, but of confidence. Perfect love casts out fear. You know the beginning from the end. Place Your healing hand on...What is your mom's name?"
   "Evon."
   "Place Your healing hand on Evon, and help her through this time in her life... Is your mom a believer?"
   "Yes. She is. And my dad, Will, went to church with her when this was found out, which is pretty much unheard of."
   "Father, thank you for what You're doing in Will's life through this.

We pray Evon can be Your bright light to all those she comes into contact with. We know that none of this will be wasted. You will bring the good from the bad to those who love You. Help me remember to pray for TL as I finish vacation here and return to California. We look forward to meeting again one day in Heaven when all these earthly troubles are finally put behind us. In Jesus' powerful name we pray, Amen." Looking up at me when she is done, she is seemingly asking if there was anything else she might do for me. What a kind lady!

"Thank you. I've never been prayed for on the street like this before, or really, in many places. I hope one day to be as bold in my faith as you are in yours. I really do need to get to work now. But please come back. Lunch is on me today."

"I thank you, but my friend and I would be honored to eat here later and pay you for our meal," Rosie says.

"It's up to you. But I'll be here, and I hope to see you when I get the tacos going."

Walking inside, I feel so relieved. The way that I feel now is so different compared to how I felt after getting off the phone with Mom earlier. I'm shaking my head. That was very interesting, and very nice. Looking out the window, I see Rosie walking off. I surely hope she will be back to eat. But if not, I will never forget her kindness and perfect timing after talking with Mom.

46

Finishing our time together in the city, Isla said, "Tracy Lynn, Jesus anchors us in these storms. I've been through my own. We all will go through them, at some point in our lives, and we all have choices to make. Will those storms destroy us, or make us stronger? That's the question. So many say Jesus is for the weak. The more I think about this, the more I want to ask anyone who says that, 'Show me one person who doesn't need some sort of help in their life?' I mean, really, we all have pain we are needing to dull. What are our choices? Alcohol? Drugs? Shopping? Cleaning? Travelling? Sex? TV? Video games? Food? Work? We have to take our pick with what gets us through this life. When we pick Jesus, He lifts us up and out of the muddy pits. Everything else eventually pulls us under like quicksand. I pick Jesus! And it sounds like you are, too."

"I am. I want to. I'm learning to," I answered.

"And I'm with you. Again I want to thank you for a most wonderful day. You have made my birthday one to remember. Whatever happens, Tracy Lynn, we will be there for one another. And one day, I'd like to meet your mom, too. She sounds like my kind of lady!"

"She is, and you will. Let me get this stuff gathered up, and then I want to show you something."

As the sun started to set, I drove Isla up to Twin Peaks, and we watched the lights of the city turn on. I knew I had a very good friend beside me, a friend that I loved deeply, and my heart was full. While Isla stood looking at the city below us, I looked up at the stars now starting to appear in Heaven above us. I prayed silently, "Make me whole, Lord Jesus, and if this is the woman You have for me, prepare me to be the man I need to be for her. Help me to be patient in that. It's so hard, but I want it to be so right."

The next morning, I tried to get to church with Isla, but things just didn't work out. My car was having some problems, and I knew I should start preparing for New Mexico. It would need to be road worthy for the trip. I had contacted Bobby, and he was all for me coming. I wasn't certain of the day I would leave, but I knew I only had two more weeks on my job.

Getting something to eat in the kitchen, I hadn't seen Vic for a few days. We had been in and out at different times, and that was good. I wanted to get his thermos washed and put away before he gave me any lip about that. Just as I was placing it back in the cupboard, I heard a noise behind me. I could feel in my bones that this was not going to be good. Maybe it was the grunt, or the sound of his footsteps coming up behind me. Maybe I just knew my brother at that point, and no day with him seemed to be good lately.

"Whatcha got there, TL, ole buddy?" Vic said with a snarl to his voice.

"What do you mean?" I responded, closing the cupboard and walking back to the sink.

"My thermos. The one I bought. You've been using it." He said as more of a statement than a question.

I turned in his direction. He was taking a seat at the table, fiddling with the stack of mail that was left from yesterday.

"I did. I borrowed it for yesterday's picnic. Got it washed and put back. It's all good to go for you now." I hated that I was tip-toeing around him again. I needed to stand up for myself. This was ridiculous. But did I really want an all-out war again? Over a thermos?

"Hmmm. Really? Seriously, Bro? I don't go borrowing your stuff. You used that for a pic-a-nick with Isla?" *Picnic* was said with a sarcastic tone that I didn't much appreciate.

"Yes. I did. Isla and I had a great day yesterday, concert in the park and lunch. You don't ha..."

Vic interrupted loudly at that point. "I don't LIKE Isla. She's uppity. Who does she think she is anyway? I barely see her. Is she too good to come by here after inviting her to my party? Are you calling her your girlfriend? And if you are, what kind of girlfriend is that, that never comes to visit after being a guest in my home?"

"Vic, stop it. Isla is not uppity. She is one of the..."

"Not uppity?" Vic interrupted. "Okay then, stuffy? Boring? You choose the word."

"I won't choose any word you're using. You barely know her. Stop judging her like that. I don't..."

"Judging her? She's judging me, by not coming over. That's why I barely know her. She's your girlfriend, right?"

"Vic, I don't know how to really...I mean, I don't have to answer that right now. Isla is a very special friend of mine. We had a nice birthday celebration yesterday, and I would..."

"You would what? Want me to support you in that? Really? You borrow my thermos for a girl I barely know, and who won't come around...or maybe you don't want to bring her here? Are you ashamed of me? Your brother?"

I sat down at the table hoping we could resolve this, although in hindsight, I should have known better. Vic flung the mail off the table onto the floor, and pounded his fist, shocking me with his force. What was happening to my brother? This was getting way out of control. If I hadn't already given my notice, I would have the very next day. I wasn't about to tell Vic about it either.

"She's got that flaming red hair. Who dates a girl with red hair like that?" Vic said, arms flailing with emotion. "You know she probably has a temper. She's probably Irish, and all Irish people are known for their tempers."

I remember thinking, really Vic? Who's the one with the temper? But I just tried to defend Isla at that moment. "Her hair is beautiful," I said defensively. He was getting to me, though, and I knew it. "And what if she is Irish? We're German. Would you have her judge us for that?"

"Irish is different. They do that silly dancing...what's it called? Clog dancing, or something. Does she do that?"

"Vic, I don't even know if she's Irish, and if she is, I don't know about the dancing. All I know is that she and I get along very well. She's kind, and patient, and loving..."

"Oh, now you're saying you're in love with her? Come on, there are other fish in the sea. Why would you settle for her so quickly?" Vic was starting to get up now, and I didn't know if we were almost done, or if he was just getting started.

"I'm not a player like you, Vic. I like to be faithful to the women I..."

"PLAYER!?! Is that how you see me? Is it my fault that the women I date all seem to be incapable of being faithful to me? They all turn into such flakes, and whining...I can't tell you how frustrated I'm getting with this whole dating scene. And you." Vic glared at me when he said that.

"Me? Hmmm. I see. Listen. I've got some things I need to take care of. I think this conversation is finished. When you have something good to say...about anybody, including Isla, maybe we can talk again."

"There you go! Wanting to walk out like you always do! I don't know why I even get into these discussions with you. You never hear a word I say. And it always turns into my fault when we do talk."

"Vic, if we could talk without all the judging and negativity, maybe it would work better. But you tear down everything that is good." I wanted to go on, but I knew I was stepping all over Vic's egg shells, and this was going downhill fast. I did feel somewhat stronger in the battle rather than totally avoiding it. I wasn't letting him run the show completely.

"Negative? You're always the one complaining." Vic wasn't going to let this go. "I'm just trying to get through a day. You have no idea how stressful my job is. The people I work with are imbeciles. I tell you, if a one of them could put two thoughts in a row, it would be a miracle. And the manager, he's the worst one of them all. The other day he calls me into his office, says I didn't do my paperwork right on this one job. Really? He was the person who trained me. If I'm doing it wrong, it's his fault. I'm just doing it exactly the way he told me to. I don't think he liked me saying that, but I was right. And no one else does it as fast as I do. I watch them; they are slower than a snail. I have all I can do to work with these people, they..."

"Vic, listen. I have some things I need to take care of today. I can't..."

"Yeah, why aren't you in your church with your girlfriend this morning?" Vic said in a namby-pamby sort of way. "I don't know why you go to that church; it's full of hypocrites. I ran into a guy the other day who says he goes there. He was trying to talk to me about all that Jesus stuff. That's good for you and Mom, if you want, but Dad and I don't need any of that junk. If you two need a crutch, then you go for it. I don't want anything to do with it. I told that guy, too. Oh, he tried to be nice...what a fool. I cut that conversation off as quickly as I could. I think he said his name was Adam something...started with an 'M," Miler or Meeber? He..."

"Oh really? Adam Meeser. That's the pastor, Vic. You were rude to the pastor of the church?" I was just shaking my head at this point. Pastor Adam is an amazing man of God. I highly respected him.

"Your pastor, huh? Looks like God sent His top man to reach me. He knows I've got His number."

"Whose number, Vic? Surely you're not saying that about God?" I could scarcely contain myself at this point.

"God, if there is one, knows He's got you all bamboozled. The Bible is just a book written by a bunch of guys who want to sell you on being like them."

"VIC, have you ever READ it? Pick it up sometime. It might..."

"Uh, NO! You and Mom go ahead. I've got better things to be doing with my time. And you can tell your Pastor Adam that."

"I'm done here, Vic."

I could hear Vic's voice fading as I walked to the back of the house, gathered my things, and left. I was exhausted, and the day had just gotten started. How could one day be so wonderful, and the next so horrific...for just the morning to already be such a disaster. Vic really needed mental help. I wondered if anything could ever really change him though. God was right when I'd heard His words. This will only change when I do. Two more weeks on the job, and then soon after, I will be gone. I hoped the car repair wouldn't be expensive. The money I'd been saving was only going to go so far.

47

It feels so good to get up and go into work in a place that I call my own. Chuck is always so helpful. He never fails to show up and do all he can. After being open for nine months, it's starting to be routine, but I'm not taking it for granted. Each day I'm thanking God for what He is doing here. I'm also thanking Him that this week Isla will be in town. I've really been missing her, and I'm anxious to share with her, in person, the healing I've been experiencing. The distance from Vic has helped me clear out my head and figure out my relationship with God in a new way. Those old arguments are a thing of the past. I don't have time to deal with such nonsense anymore. I don't know why I ever did. There was no talking to Vic, especially once he got going. I can breathe again, and now with Isla coming, everything seems right. With the delay in opening their office in El Paso, this is the first opportunity she's had to fly out here. Chuck has a friend willing to help him for two days while Isla is in town. I'm so glad! I will get to go to El Paso and see her, and maybe bring her here to see the place. I've called it TL's Tacos. Not so original, but it works.

It was so nice to see Rosie and her friend come back later in the day and get to talk a bit more. I wanted to treat them to lunch, and was so glad when they let me. Rosie was definitely an encouragement to me right when I needed it. I don't know that I will ever see her again, but I will never forget her. Mom's diagnosis was such a shock to me. When I look back, it seems God heard my cry for help, and he sent Rosie to me. I'm seeing God more up close and personal now. It seems almost daily I can sense His interaction in what's going on around me. Mom is right, daily time spent reading my Bible, and praying, develops that relationship. Even Rosie's talk about the Holy Spirit is making more sense to me now. I'm learning what it is to be feeling Him leading me in different ways throughout each day. Yes, I'm looking forward to sharing so much with Isla. But right now,

I need to give Mom a call. She's into her chemo, and keeping in close contact with her is good.

"Hi, Mom. How're things?"

"Doing very well. I love hearing from you, but please don't be worried. I'm getting through each treatment, with barely a hiccup." *Mom's voice sounds so much better today.*

"I know you are, Mom, but it helps me focus on work here when I know you're okay there. Oh, and Mom, Isla is coming this week! She's finally able to fly out here for business. I've really missed her. We talk pretty often, but it's not the same as being with her."

"I'm so happy for you. WILL, Isla is flying out to visit TL!" *Mom sharing this news with Dad shocks me a bit. We usually just keep our conversation between the two of us. When Mom comes back on, she says,* "Dad says to tell you he is happy for you."

"Uh, Mom? What? Dad's happy for me?"

"TL, your Dad has something he'd like to tell you. He's waving his hand at me... Is it okay with you if I give him the phone?" *Mom waits for my answer.*

I'm stalling. This is usually not good. I want to say "No." But I don't...

"If you think so, Mom. I've got kind of a busy day and I don't need to be pulled in a bad direction."

"I think you're gonna want to hear this, TL," *Mom says.*

"Okay. If you say so. Put Dad on."

"Hey there, Son. How're things in New Mexico?" *Dad's voice sounds strange.*

"Fine, Dad. Doing well. How are you?"

"Well, I didn't want your mom to tell you the news. I felt it was important that you and I talk." *Dad stops there, and I wasn't sure where this was going.*

"Okay. Go ahead." *I knew I wasn't being super friendly, but I learned to be very cautious with Dad.*

"TL, your mom's illness has opened my eyes to some things...things I've needed to see...well, for most of my life."

"Oh."

"Yes. You see, Son, I've realized that I have some apologizing to do, and some of it needs to start with you."

"With me?"

"Yes. I've not encouraged you along your life's path, and I'm sorry for that. I've been holding you back, wanting you to live in my shadow, do what I think you should, and that's not right," *Dad says.*

"Uh. I don't know what to say, Dad."

"TL, I know your mom and you have been the churchgoers in our family. Sadly, I've pulled Vic to my way of thinking all these years. All this time I thought you and your mom were idiots...but you were the smarter *ones. And when I could get you or your mom riled up about this, I would think to myself, 'Look at you, you call yourself a Christian?' But when your mom was diagnosed, it really shook my world. I started seeing her in a new way and realized how much I hadn't appreciated the woman I married. I didn't know what to do to make it up to her, other than maybe go to church with her a time or two. I knew that would make her happy. Seeing her not feeling well, I don't know...it was bothering me in a big way."*

"That's interesting to hear, Dad."

"Yeah. So I went with her one Sunday thinking that might do it. But the next Sunday was a particularly hard day for her. She really wanted to go but wasn't able to drive herself. She wasn't feeling up to it. I figured going one more time wouldn't be all that bad. The first time hadn't killed me. That Sunday the preacher said some things that really struck home with me. He said atheists think Christians just believe what they are told. But I started to wonder about what I was believing that I had been told. Was it true? I didn't understand what he was saying, but part of me wanted to know more. That really surprised me. He caught my attention even more when he said that by believing all that the world contains was formed by itself would be like thinking a car put itself together without the factory. You know how I love and understand cars. I wondered if God was trying to get MY attention. And then he talked about something really amazing. The guys who were with Jesus went to their death, not because of what someone had told them, but because they were eyewitnesses to His resurrection. They saw it with their own eyes and were willing to die telling others about it. That's some pretty serious stuff!"

"Yes, it is, Dad."

"At the end, the preacher wanted to know if anyone wanted to be prayed for. I didn't. But my heart was beating so fast, I thought maybe I needed prayer. I thought maybe I was having a heart attack. TL, I didn't know what was happening. What I wanted to do was just get your mom to the car and get back home. But what I did was go toward the front of the church. I didn't know what I was doing, but I told your mom I would be right back. There was this man standing there, silver grey hair, about my age. I figured maybe he would be safe to explain this to. Maybe he would understand my predicament...if you can call it that—maybe I was having a heart attack."

"Did he? And were you?"

"Did he understand my predicament?" Dad asks.

"Yeah."

"He did, and so much more. And it wasn't a heart attack...although, in a way it was, because it changed my heart bigtime. When I explained to him that I wasn't sure why I was there, other than maybe something was wrong with me, and I only came this morning to be with my sick wife. He

looked at me with a very different expression than I expected, and he asked me some questions about your mom. I told him about the Leukemia. Then I start like confessing...it was so bizarre. I told him that I really wasn't a very nice guy, but she had put up with me all these years and I was here trying to make it up to her. And then he said the strangest thing. He said, 'That's not what she wants.' I was like, 'WHAT? You're telling me I don't need to be here with my wife?' But, TL, that wasn't what he was saying. Of course, being with her was important. But he said what she really wants from me is so much more than that. I said, 'Whoa, I'm in way over my head then. This is the best I can do, just being here. What am I supposed to do, start waiting on her hand and foot?'"

"And what did he say to that, Dad?"

"He looked me straight in the eyes and he said, 'No. What she really wants is to have you in Heaven with her.' Then I was really shocked! Was he saying your Mom was dying, and I was supposed to die, too? What did he mean by that? I almost turned and walked away at that point, and he knew it. He reached out his hand and placed it on my shoulder, and TL, it was the most comforting gesture. I don't know how to explain it...there was a peace that flowed through his hand into me that I've never experienced before. I suddenly didn't want to leave, I wanted to understand what he was saying."

"Did you ask him?"

"I didn't, because what he did then was he asked me if he could pray for me. I didn't know what that would be like, but for some strange reason I knew I wanted him to. So I nodded, 'yes.' What happened then was...well, it was the weirdest thing. He started talking like he knew my thoughts. He started saying things that I hadn't thought about for years. He started to tell those things that had hurt me, things I was angry about, to get out of my life. He mentioned things about you and your brother, and then when he started talking about your mom, I couldn't help it TL, I started bawling like a baby. You would have been embarrassed to be with me."

"I don't think so, Dad. I'm glad you let him pray for you."

"Thanks, TL."

"What happened then?"

"He asked me if I knew Jesus? I told him I never wanted to before. He asked me if I wanted to now? I told him I did—that even shocked me. He talked about repenting. I wasn't sure what he meant, but he explained it very well when I asked him. Then he had me repeat some things after him about my sins, and Jesus' forgiveness. He had me forgiving people who had hurt me through the years. Now this whole time, I can barely believe I'm doing this. But somewhere in me, I knew I wanted to. I was realizing that I always had, but I'd rejected it because of my own stubborn, I-can-do-it myself attitude. When Sam, that was this guy's name, was done praying for me, I felt so different. I felt relief, like a huge weight was being

lifted off me. It seemed I was free of that mean old man I'd always been. I wanted to be nicer now. My whole life had felt like such a struggle, and suddenly, it seemed the struggle was over."

"Wow, Dad. That's amazing!"

"Your Mom came up to be with us at the end, and she had tears in her eyes. I was glad I wasn't the only one crying. I have to tell you, I felt a bit weak in my knees. I didn't know if I could keep standing at one point. TL, I'm not here to tell you that I'm a perfect man now. The exact opposite...I know I'm so far from perfect. But I have Jesus now to help me be a better husband, and dad."

"Oh, Dad. I can't tell you how happy that makes me. You're bringing tears to my eyes."

"I realize, TL, that when Sam told me your mom wanted me in Heaven with her, this is what he meant. Not that she's dying, or that she wants me to die. What she wants is for both of us to really live our lives in a way that when we do leave this earth, we will be going to the same place. I always figured there was something after this life, but I also thought there is no way for me to get there. I knew I wasn't being who I was supposed to be. I heard the critical words coming out of my mouth toward you and so many others, and especially your mom, but I didn't really care. I thought I had every right to say them. It didn't make me feel good, but it did make me feel powerful. But after I went and talked to Sam, and I felt so weak there with him, I have a new kind of strength now. I know it sounds crazy."

"No, it doesn't, Dad. Really."

"Okay. Good. I'm okay with not being in control anymore, TL. I'm okay being weak because I found a different kind of power. Sam said the Holy Spirit lives in me now. I needed to surrender to God, wave the white flag, because honestly, I was getting very tired living like I was. I felt so alone. I knew somewhere in the back of my mind that I was the one pushing everyone away from me. But I never wanted to admit it, I just wanted to look at it like it was everyone else's fault. I think your mom's illness pushed me to a point where I just couldn't do it on my own anymore. Holding a grudge against the world, trying to hurt everyone else, only hurt me more. And I ended up with this huge hole inside, and nothing to fill it with—not even a six pack at the end of the day could dent it. Honestly, I saw your mom happier while she was sick, than I was while I was well and drinking. Instead of the cancer being the worst thing that could happen to us, TL, it may be the best thing because now I realize I was the sick one that needed healing. Just in saying that to you now, I think I was using taking her to church as an excuse to go myself. I think I've always known the answer was there, but I was too afraid to go and find it. I'm sorry your mom got sick, but I'm realizing just in this moment how grateful I am for how it has changed things in my life...and I hope, in all our relationships. TL, I'm sorry for being so mean, and not listening to you. I hope we can start new

today. I want to. I hope you do, too."

"Oh, Dad. I do. I can't tell you how much I appreciate all that you're saying, and I'm so happy for you and Mom. And I'm thankful that if Mom has to be sick, that something this good can come out of it. I only hope and pray that Vic will be part of this change in our family, too."

"I'm with you there. I'm sorry for the things I've done that have pushed him away from God. It's not easy, TL. Vic and I are so much the same— very stubborn, very proud. I don't know much about miracles, but for God to get ahold of me like this, it gives me hope that He can do the same for Vic one day. It's taken me 68 years to get here. We may have to be patient."

"We will pray, Dad."

"Yes. We will. Hey, I've taken enough of your time. I'm gonna put your mom back on the phone, and then I know you need to get to work. I hope we can come out to New Mexico and have some of your tacos in the future...when your Mom is feeling more up to it."

"That would be awesome, Dad. I would love that! Actually, tell Mom I'll need to talk to her another time. I really do need to get things going around here."

"Okay, we understand. We'll talk soon. I love you, Son."

"I love you, too, Dad. Bye."

"Bye."

48

Secretly, as I was preparing to get out of town, I tried to make it look like nothing was happening. Slowly, I was packing certain things and getting rid of other stuff. I tried to keep the door to my room shut. If Vic got wind of my plans, the last two weeks or so would have been even worse.

I planned on taking Isla out to dinner after my last Friday at work. We were going to drive over to Sausalito and eat at an Italian restaurant there. It was going to be a bitter sweet dinner, knowing that, very soon, we wouldn't be able to spend as much time together. But when Friday came, Vic was in crisis mode, and I just couldn't leave him. He called me at work, telling me he really needed me to take him to Brentwood for an appointment...his car was not reliable, and he couldn't miss it. I wondered why he hadn't thought of that before? I felt so bad calling Isla and cancelling on her. She was understanding, but she encouraged me in the decisions I was making about leaving. She could see that the distance was needed. I was still too much in Vic's shadow of control, and having a hard time refusing him when he whined about how hard things were for him. Isla was being patient, but I knew it was wearing on her, too. I was realizing I was not ready to be in a more serious relationship with her. I think she saw that, too. Sadly, as much as I didn't want to, I knew I had to get away to clear my head.

On the drive over to Brentwood, I didn't say much to Vic—probably because I was in a bad mood. I wanted to be having dinner with Isla. Vic was only concerned about his appointment and didn't seem to notice my silence. He was lost in his own world and telling me about work while complaining about the traffic. When we finally got to where he needed to be, I got slammed again with his selfishness. It wasn't an appointment with a doctor, an accountant, or even to get a haircut...he needed to see a girl. I'd passed up Isla for that! Why hadn't I asked Vic where we were going?

I let out with, "VIC! You're kidding me, right? I thought this was important!" I was not being quiet anymore.

"This IS important," he responded. "I really needed to get over and see Janice tonight. She's the best thing that's come along in a long time."

"Well, YOU made ME miss the best thing that will probably ever come along in my life," I answered with anger. "Vic, I just...you...you know what, I can't blame you. This is me. This is me not seeing you for who you really are, a selfish brother who doesn't give a rip about me or anyone else. I'm dropping you off here, and you can find your own way home."

"You can't do that to me!" Vic yelled.

"Watch me!" I yelled back, pulling away from the curb as soon as he was out the door, causing the door to slam shut on its own.

I knew by that time it was too late to set things right with Isla. She'd made other plans with a girlfriend, and by all rights, she should have. I knew it was probably better that I go home at that point and get some time by myself with God. I definitely needed to get my plan worked out. Things weren't going to change with Vic, not with me here. Maybe when I left he would change, but I seriously doubted that, too.

Walking in the front door, I flopped on the couch. I was exhausted from it all, and the knot in my stomach was turning into the size of a bowling ball. I took a look around, and knew I wasn't going to miss any of it—not the music, not the nonsense, not the chaos. I'd held on as long as I could. I just needed to figure out the right time to leave, with Vic out of the house...

When the phone rang that evening, I didn't answer it. I didn't even look to see who was calling. I just let it ring in my pocket. I knew it wasn't Isla, so it wasn't important to me in that moment. What I needed to do was get my head right with God.

I went to my room, got my Bible, and flopped back onto the couch again. At least with Vic out for the evening, or however long, I could focus. I hoped God would show me something that would help. "Please, Lord," I prayed, "I'm a mess tonight. What could have been a wonderful evening was once again ruined. And this time, I'm done blaming it on my brother. I'm blaming this one on me. I'm taking full responsibility for my actions in this. I'd like to blame it all on Vic, but he doesn't even know what he's doing. I want to hold myself more accountable for this. I cancelled my plans with a wonderful woman because I don't have healthy boundaries. I want to not care, but I care too much. I need to detach here. Can You please get this through to me! Where have I lost my own sense of worth?"

Suddenly, God brought a memory to me from when I was about 14 with a friend, Riley. It shocked me at first. I hadn't thought about that for so long. I wondered if God was really answering my cry for help? Mom told me how I could take a look at these things, and find God's healing there. I figured I had nothing to lose, so I went through the steps she told me about while remembering how Riley was taking stuff out of my locker at school. He thought he was being funny. I was very irritated, but I didn't really want to confront him about it. I just picked it up and put it back each time he did it. One day, he got a couple other guys in on it, and they were very mean. Riley sort of meant it in good fun. The other guys didn't. We got into a brawl, and we all got sent to see the principal. Of course, no one would fess up to anything, and I wasn't going to point the finger. So, I took the punishment with the rest of them. Thankfully, it ended the "locker torture," but I never forgot the injustice of it.

I asked God that night if I needed to see something in this that was causing me to be like I was with Vic? I asked myself what I *thought* about that incident?... I thought it was mean, violent, invasive, crazy. I asked myself how it made me *feel*?... Embarrassed, abused, sad, angry. I told those things to get out of me, in Jesus' name. Then Mom said, ask God for His healing, so I prayed, "God, pour Your healing balm into this wound in my soul. Fill me with Your Holy Spirit. Cleanse the infection that has irritated me all these years. Heal this wound completely and restore in me what went missing from this abuse. Renew my mind, showing me how much You love me even when the world treats me harshly. You died on the Cross for me, to save me. Renew my mind in this area. I don't want to have a victim mentality anymore. I don't want Satan or anyone else to have control in this area any more. I want to see my worth in Your eyes, not the enemy's...not in these boys. Thank You, in Jesus' name. Amen."

Mom told me after she'd been doing this a while, she wondered if it was really effective? When she tried to go to one of those old places in her mind again, she found that the bridge was gone. I asked her what she meant by that? She said when she thought about the incident, she could still see it there in the distance, but her thoughts weren't able to travel to it anymore. She believed the Living Water of God had washed the bridge out between where she was now and where the wound once was. God had given her mind a new route to travel...a new healthier focus on things that were true and right, pure and admirable, excellent and worthy of praise like in Philippians 4. She said if she wanted to, she could probably rebuild the bridges, but that would be a crazy thing to do. She just let her mind move away from it, and travel along the new path.

Allowing the boys to get away with being mean, and now allowing Vic to do the same, with barely a consequence wasn't right. It's how my mind was wired, who I thought I was, but no longer. It was costing me more than time spent in the principal's office—it was costing me precious time spent with Isla, and my own sanity. I pulled the phone from my pocket. I saw the call earlier was from Vic. I didn't listen to the voicemail, instead I pulled up some info on narcissism. I really hated even looking at it right then, but I needed to stop whining about missing Isla and figure out my best course of action.

I listened to how a narcissist was more than happy with a phony relationship, and how their love is based on the level they can derive use from you. They want a relationship on their playing field. I thought of the new gal that I just dropped Vic off to see...what was her name? Janice? The poor woman. Once again, she probably wouldn't have a clue. I heard another expert on narcissism saying to work hard to make yourself safe and build other social networks. Well, I'm trying, but...and then I said out loud, "NO BUTS! I have to change, Vic won't!"

One video suggested thinking more and feeling less, because with a narcissist we end up feeling too much. I sure do! What else is here? One article said, "Find a safe place and see reality!" Yes. That's the plan. It also addressed the question, "What do we do about the guilt when we go no-contact?" That was something good for me to read. I did need to put up a shield against the shame and guilt that Vic would want me to feel. I knew I had to become emotionally stronger because from what I was hearing, false guilt is not based on reality. That's something I would need to remember. This warned me, when I read it, about it taking at least a year to know if the narcissist has changed, and to not be drawn back in too soon. This wasn't going to be any quick fix, if ever, with Vic. I could change. He may not.

When, "Make space to find peace again," popped up, I liked that. It was confirming what I thought needed to happen. I wondered if I even really knew Vic when I heard, "The narcissist can't be around people who see them as they are. They are phony people because nothing they reflect is real." He sure didn't like it when I called him on things. That's why I avoided it so much! I just let him get away with most daily things, until big things blew up in my face! Sadly, the more I heard and read, the more I knew I was just sick enough to understand it...but maybe still well enough to escape it.

I still wondered why people are narcissists? Are people born that way? There was information about that, too, saying the bottom line is, it's demonic. I'd heard that a couple of times. It went on to say a narcissist's main purpose is to destroy people, especially those who believe in Jesus. It also said the demon destroys the person it is working through by destroying every relationship they have—and they don't even know why! And that these demonized people are envious and jealous of people who have freedom in Christ. I guess it made sense, especially if this was true, that the ultimate covert narcissist is Satan. This was dark spiritual stuff.

So many sites were saying drugs and alcohol are involved in this a lot of the time, too. Narcissists don't want to think about the way that they make others feel. And a narcissistic person has to be in agreement before they can be healed of this. I didn't think I could get Vic to even talk about it.

It looked to me like prayer was needed to be a big part of the healing, on both sides! I wondered how people do any of this without God? Before real healing can happen, maybe we need to hit rock bottom? I felt about there, ready for some healing. I'm not so sure Vic even thought it was necessary. But isn't that what I had just read?

Turning in that night, I remember reading Psalm 39:1-4. *I said to myself, "I will watch what I do and not sin in what I say. I will hold my tongue when the ungodly are around me." But as I stood there in silence— not even speaking of good things— the turmoil within me grew worse. The more I thought about it, the hotter I got, igniting a fire of words: "LORD, remind me how brief my time on earth will be. Remind me that my days are numbered—how fleeting my life is."*

I fell asleep knowing that time was a wasting, and I needed to trust God for this next step. I was not able to absorb it all just yet, but it would come in time. I would need to keep learning and growing...and praying. Most of this would probably need to be repeated over and over in my mind until it sunk it, but I was willing to do the work.

49

My heart is beating out of my chest. Isla is in town, and I can't wait to see her. It seems like forever, even though it's only been nine months. I have so much I want to talk with her about. But mainly, I just want to be with her...to share this area with her...to serve her some chicken tacos!

Pulling up, I can see her standing out in front of the hotel. Her smile already lights up my world. I can't just open the door and let her in. That would be so wrong. I keep the doors locked as she tries to open it after I stop. She gives me a strange look. Hopping out, I run around to her side of the car and grab her in my arms, giving her the biggest hug ever! She seems open and receptive to it...laughing and smiling with me and hugging me back. It feels so good to be together again.

Pulling away, I look directly into her beautiful face as the New Mexico sun glistens off her beautiful red hair.

"Isla, I can't tell you how happy I am to see you again!"

"You don't have to, because I feel exactly the same way. I thought this trip would never come about. But finally, it has!" she says with great joy.

"There is so much I want to share with you, but I don't want to overwhelm you. So instead of making this all business, and no pleasure, we're going to make this a pleasure day. No tacos yet. I'm taking you to an amazing place that Bobby and I went to a while back. When he showed me this area, out in the middle of the desert, I couldn't believe it."

"What is it?" Isla asks, wide-eyed.

"I don't want to say. I want it to be a surprise."

"Okay. Let's go then! You can unlock the door for me now!" She says jokingly.

Opening her door, I take her hand and guide her into her seat. Not that she needs it, but I long to feel her hand in mine again. I remember her birthday well, and how I wanted to hold her hand for all of eternity. I've missed her so much.

The drive out to White Sands seems electric. Isla fills me in on the latest in her life. We have talked on the phone, but this is so different. The phone seems distant, this is so up close and personal. I can glance at her, see her expression, hear her tone, smell her perfume. My senses are on full alert, and I know I need to hold myself back as to not overwhelm her. I hope she will enjoy this place as much as I do.

When we get closer, Isla sees the dazzling white sand dunes off in the distance. She squeals like a young girl heading to a party!

"Yes, that's where we're going. Isla, it's so white and pure."

"I've never seen anything like it," she responds.

Handing her a map with some info on it from the last time I was there with Bobby, Isla starts reading about it. I haven't taken the time to really do that, so it's good to hear it.

"TL, it says here that the White Sands cover 275 square miles. That's huge! It's the largest gypsum dunefield in the world. I'm not sure what gypsum is, but okay. Oh, it says here it's a mineral. And the wind and sun separate the water from the gypsum forming selenite crystals. Then wind and water break down the crystals making them smaller and smaller until they are sand."

"It really looks like snow, you'll see! It's amazing to have this only like 50 miles from Las Cruces."

"Oh, look at this picture! People can sled down these dunes?" Isla asks, excitedly.

"Yes! Don't worry, I brought a sled in the trunk. I came prepared, even though you can buy them here. Bobby and I bought one last time we came. We were probably some of the oldest people out there, but we didn't care. We had fun!"

"I want to have fun!" Isla says with even more excitement.

"We will! During World War II, the U.S. Military tested weapons in the dunefield just beyond the park. The first Atomic bomb was detonated just 100 miles north of here."

"I would not have wanted to be here then!" Isla says with a tone of apprehension.

"Well, no worry about that today."

Pulling into the visitor center, we grab a couple of waters, and then make the drive into the dune area. Finding a good spot for sledding, Isla runs ahead of me, beckoning me behind her. She is a child at heart, I can see that—a free spirit. I look forward to sharing with her the healing I've found in just being here. I haven't talked to her a lot about it all on the phone. I wanted to live it for her, not just have it be words. I run to catch up with her. I feel like a kid today, too.

"Wheee!" Isla screams as I give her a big push down the slope of white sand. If we didn't have our shoes off, it truly would look like snow in a picture. But the morning is warm and wonderful.

"Your turn," she says, carrying the sled back up to me. "I'll push you!" My turn down the slope was a bit slower, digging in deeper with my weight, but no less fun. After many times of this, and exhausting ourselves, we find a picnic table. There aren't too many people here, being a weekday. I know what Isla likes, and I've packed a lunch much like the one we ate outside at the band concert that day in the city. Pulling out the contents, Isla is quiet, watching me...

"Are you okay, Isla?"

"Yes, TL, I am. I'm just taking this all in. And I'm remembering..." she says softly.

"I think I know what you're thinking of."

"I think you do," she responds.

"I want you to know, I haven't talked about all this in depth over the phone, even though we have talked quite often. I've been processing so much in the last nine months. It's been good for me to be here."

"I believe it has, TL. I see a new light in your eyes. Less furrow to your brow. Less stress in your body. Your spirit seems free to be, like a dark cloud has been lifted," she says with compassion.

"I'm glad you can see that in me. I believe that's why I didn't say much on our phone conversations about the healing I've been finding here. I didn't want it to just be words. I wanted it to be real...to be put into action. I wanted you to see it for yourself. But now we can talk about it more, if that's okay with you?"

"It is. Of course. I have been praying for you every day," Isla says, reaching out to touch my hand.

"Thank you. Your prayers are being answered, I believe. Where should I start? I'm not really sure..."

50

Getting up the next morning, I finally pulled up Vic's message. He hadn't come in from the night before. Maybe he couldn't get a ride back from Brentwood. At that point, I really didn't care...although I did. I always cared. That was my problem. My stomach was in knots again, hoping he was okay. Hoping he didn't do anything crazy. Was that wrong of me to just leave him there? Maybe he just stayed with Janice for the night? I listened to his message:

"TL, thanks a lot! Driving off without giving me a way home! I need a ride back. Come and get me! Janice has to work, so I have nothing to do here tomorrow. Call me, Bro. Don't be such a jerk!"

Hmmm, I sat and ruminated on that. Not rushing to do anything. Vic got himself into this mess, I should probably let him figure a way out of it was my thinking. And maybe...this was my window of opportunity? If Vic really was stuck in Brentwood, I could pack stuff up here today and head out tomorrow morning early. Was God giving me an open door to leave? I didn't want to miss it if it was. My heart started pounding. This truly felt like I was escaping, even breaking the law in some strange way. I also knew if Vic found a way back today, and I was in the middle of loading up, that would be a terrible scene. I wondered how I could find out? Would I need to call Vic? I surely didn't want to do that.

Almost on auto-pilot, I just started to load my car. It seemed worth the risk. The trunk first, so it couldn't be seen through the car windows. But the trunk was filling fast. I needed to take less. I made a couple of runs to the thrift store, getting rid of things I really didn't need. Still no sign of Vic, so I kept on. After some time, my heart started to settle down, and a calmness came over me. It felt right. I wondered, was that God saying it's okay? I really didn't know. I just knew I kept moving, kept packing, kept getting rid of stuff.

The neighbor came over about 2:00, seemingly just to chat. She was nice enough, but a bit of a busy-body. "What's going on, TL? You doin' a spring cleaning?" she asked.

"Yeah, you could say that," I answered back, a bit too tentatively. She noticed.

"I'd say it might be more than that. I know you've been here close to a year or so. Is your lease up?" She was being way too nosey.

"It's a good house. I gotta do some things. Sorry I can't stay and talk," I said while walking away slowly but deliberately back into the house. I didn't owe her an explanation, and I couldn't trust her either. Her husband was pretty chummy with Vic. He may have his number and give him a call. I couldn't chance that. I would load the rest later, and just work inside the house.

The phone rang again about 4:00. It was Vic. I didn't answer. I didn't want him to hear anything in my voice. I was too much of a giveaway, always wearing my emotions on my sleeve. I listened to the message when he was done leaving it.

"TL. Come on! Janice has been at work all day, I'm bored stiff. She doesn't even have any good channels here to watch. My phone is dying because I didn't bring my charger and she has a different set up than me. It won't take you super long to come and get me. What are you doing? Call me!"

I could hear the anger in his voice, but part of him knew better than to let me have it full barrels if he was to get a ride. It was sounding like I was really his only way home. I wanted to feel sorry for him, but I knew if I didn't stay strong that day, I might regret it bigtime later. I didn't call him back. I kept sorting through things and packing. I didn't even call Isla. I couldn't. It broke my heart to have to say good-bye to her. I did feel bad about that. She deserved to know. But I knew she would understand, too. We had talked about this very thing.

When the sun went down, and I saw the lights go off next door, I put the rest of my stuff in the car very quietly. Their dog barked, and their lights went on for a few minutes, and then went back out. They usually went to bed early, I was glad for that. Vic had called back one more time, saying his battery was just about gone, and he would have to wait for Janice to get home to get ahold of me again. And he left me her number. I could hear desperation and frustration in his voice. I needed to not focus on that and focus on my own mental health instead.

Packed and ready, I went to bed that night with my mind spinning, and my heart beating too rapidly again. I knew that wasn't good, after the heart scare I'd had. I prayed hard for God to help me be okay with this. After all, it seemed He was giving me the window of time to do this, so I hoped it was in God's perfect plan and not just mine. My prayer was that Vic wouldn't come in during the night...

Before turning off the light, I knew I needed to read my Bible. It might be the only thing that would make sense in the moment. How had my life come to this? It seemed God answered me again when I turned to Matthew 15:18, *"But evil words come from an evil heart and defile the person who says them."*

I prayed, "Father, I pray for my brother. I really do love him, and my dad. I want to have a good relationship with them. Help them to know You, so we can really know one another. This has been an exhausting day, and an exhilarating day, all at the same time. I think I'm really leaving in the morning. It has come to this. Please watch over Isla. I will talk with her soon. Help her to understand, and to not be hurt. I want to spend time with her, but I can't like this. I'm too messed up at this point to be in a relationship like that with her. She needs to know me when I'm healthy, so she can trust me. Help me be that person, not only for myself, but for her, too. Thank you, Jesus. Amen."

I thought I'd be able to go to sleep, but sleep didn't come. Midnight passed, one, then two, and finally I sat up after just dozing off and on, fitfully. I probably shouldn't get my mind going more, but I needed some reassurance that I wasn't the crazy one, so I looked up more things about why it had come to this with Vic.

I read, "They make you crazy and second guess everything. When the narcissist can't control you, they will punish you." That was helping me some, but I kept searching... Another site talked about emotional harm, which includes being self-critical. Self-guilting and being negative about our own abilities...pulling self-love from ourselves. I knew Vic had worn me down in the last year. I also saw how we need to grieve over the parent we never had. I thought about the brother I never had. I thought that counted, too. It went on to say I gotta make Dad and Vic smaller to erase my fear of them. Had I read that before, and forgotten it? There was so much, I knew it was going to take time in New Mexico to not only absorb all I'd discovered so far, but to then implement it into my life. To find that healthy balance. It continued on saying that then I don't have to cut off from them emotionally, but just make healthy boundaries. I remember thinking to myself, make Vic smaller, make Vic smaller. He loomed so large in my mind that night. I wanted to continue to love him and care about him, but I didn't want to allow him to hurt me anymore or run my life.

What I read next was good, that I shouldn't trust the guilt I felt. It talked about my guilt navigator being broken. Wow, that was an amazing realization! Because I felt so terrible! I wanted that power back...I knew Vic shouldn't hold the power to make me feel guilty, or to force me to feel anything. Okay, I thought, I need to go with that. I was realizing I needed to feel things by choice. I was amazed at that concept...not letting emotions run my life anymore. I knew I needed to keep things real in my own mind.

During the long night, I remembered once reading a favorite author of mine...he said something to the effect of not trying to know myself but trying to know Jesus. That reminded me of seeking God's Kingdom first, so everything else can be added after that. Mom always told me the Bible really could keep me on the right track. My plan that night was to purposefully read it more and more in New Mexico.

I clicked through some videos that told me how some always feel overly responsible for everything. I knew that was me! I needed to stop playing god, and KNOW God, fully. I began to realize that not picking Vic up was really the right thing in this instance. He got himself into the mess, he could find his own way home. Plus, I was seeing God's perfect hand on it all. God knew I needed space to leave, and how was I to do that without this window of opportunity? And having just finished with my job, it seemed to be right. Maybe even not sleeping much that night was right, so I could have further encouragement from so many online sources. Something had to override my people-pleasing tendencies.

Somewhere in the night, I remember starting to realize, I'm not the cause of Vic's problem, and I don't need to be the solution. I can't fix this. I think the best way to fix it is to leave. Maybe both of us would find healing in that? I knew if I talked to Vic, he could have convinced me to come and get him. I remember hearing that the correct response, many times, is no response. I wondered if that was God, speaking through people and from places I would never know. Probably, because people like me can't stand up to the harassment from people like Vic—not until I get healthier myself. Maybe some sort of distance in our relationship would always be needed. I hoped not, but...that may be a sense of false hope.

I knew at that point, if I didn't get some sleep, I wouldn't be able to drive in the morning. I tried to shut it all off, and I did get a couple of hours. But when I woke before the sun, I knew the night was over for me. It was time to get up and get on the road. I hoped the neighbor's lights would still be off and their dog would be quiet.

It was time to go...

51

This time, Isla is the one who slowly takes her hand off mine as I begin to share with her. I notice it simply because of the space she is giving me in the moment. It feels right, and healthy. I have no question about her concern and care for me over these past months. She has been there without pressure, but instead in a patient way, waiting on what God is doing. I so respect how she handles life and our relationship. I know I am in the presence of an amazing person, and I hope as I begin to explain all that I've been going through while away from her, it will give her the assurance that drawing close now will be in God's will for both our lives...I believe it is.

"Isla, first of all, I again want to apologize for not officially saying good-bye to you nine months ago. I have never felt good about that."

"TL, we have talked about this, and I understand. You were in a desperate situation that called for desperate measures. I know it took everything you had to leave that morning. It would have been hard for me to say good-bye to you, too. You needed all the strength you could muster to do what you had to do."

"Thank you... And since that time, I know I've talked with you about some of this, but I would like to share with you the things I have learned these last nine months. My search into this started before I left, but it wasn't until I was away from it all that I could really start believing it and living it. Bobby has been a big help for me, too. Simply because, he is a healthy guy to be around, and he shows me what that looks like. I never experienced that type of relationship with my brother."

"I'm so thankful for Bobby, and I look forward to meeting him in person."

"I want you to meet him, for sure. Bobby isn't perfect, no one is, but he's about as healthy of an individual as you can find. He's not super

strong in his faith, but he's growing in that, too. I try to share God with him, hoping maybe I can be an encourager for him in that."

"It's good to hear about the give and take between the two of you," Isla interjects.

"I had to learn how to respect myself, Isla. To know my worth in God's eyes. I lost a lot of that in my childhood. And I know I've shared with you briefly about my dad, right before you got here, but that really is a miracle!"

"It surely is, TL. Your dad finding Jesus gives so many hope for their lost family members."

"My dad sure seemed a lost cause to me. But that's not giving God all the credit He deserves. I mean, think about Paul on the road to Damascus, and how once he saw the 'light,' he was never the same again. It happened differently for my dad, but isn't that the way of God, too. Every person is unique, and so is their story. My dad is even going to come out here with Mom and eat some tacos at my place. I NEVER saw that happening!"

"It's amazing. I'm so happy for you, and him...and your mom," Isla adds. "Your dad's miracle was quick...well, at the end. It was no over-night success story, was it? It took years of hard stuff to get to the good stuff. I wish God would work quicker sometimes. I know your mom hasn't had it easy."

"No, she hasn't. But she's a trooper. And with her cancer scare...she's doing great and the prognosis is very positive. I don't worry about her too much. She will come through this, from everything the doctors are saying. But maybe now my parents will have some really happy years at last. They will finish well. Which brings me to us," I said, turning my face directly toward Isla.

"Oh?" Isla remarks with raised brows.

"Yes. I want to share with you the miracles I've seen here, and hopefully make a good beginning, a new beginning, with you starting today. I sort of left you in the dust as my car peeled out of town those months ago, and I owe you some explanations. You didn't know me very long before I left. Just long enough to know that I truly care about you. But I was having trouble in my care for other people. I had to become comfortable with healthy boundaries. That's what I've been working on. Vic has tried to reach me multiple times, and I've kept that to a bare minimum. It was hard at first, but it gets easier. He's still not changed, and I can't really expect him to until he's ready. In it all, I've learned my worth can't be found in this world alone. I had to start to see myself as God sees me. Jesus came to this earth and died on the Cross for us, He loves us. The Father thinks, He knows, we are valuable, being created in His image. Soaking in that for these last nine months is helping me regain who God created me to be. I don't have to be half a person looking for someone to complete me. I am whole, in Him. Which is why, my dear Isla,

I couldn't be totally with you before. If I depended on you to complete me, that wouldn't have been fair to you. So, thank you for being patient me."

"I'm listening, TL. And I'm hearing you, loud and clear," Isla says with a smile.

"I had to learn to not let people take advantage of me. I had to really see what was good and what wasn't. Vic wasn't good for me, and ultimately, I wasn't good for him. He was very manipulative. He played mind games all the time. I ask myself now, Why couldn't he be honest, and real? But I was having a hard time even recognizing that back then. Maybe because he was so clever, or maybe because I was blind to it. Maybe I didn't want to see it, and I only wanted his love. No matter what, it needed to stop. I know I tried to please him and my dad. I probably would have even wanted to please Great-Aunt Martha if I had seen her more often. I've tried not to!"

"You'll have to tell me more about her," Isla says, laughing.

"Oh, probably not. Unless you like birds a whole lot!"

"Not that much!" Isla responds while munching on her sandwich and smiling at me.

"Bobby has helped me see that relationships can be two-way...need to be two-way. I shouldn't settle for less than that, for the most part. There are exceptions when someone is needing care in a special way, of course— but not the normal person I come in contact with. Vic had no interest in growing into anything but what he was. That's a huge difference between him and Bobby. Bobby is always learning and growing. He's so open to new ideas...we have been growing together. He knows he's got stuff, too, because of his mom. This time has been helpful for both of us. He's realizing now he's had some unhealthy roommates. We are seeing how we don't have to walk on egg-shells with people when things are more balanced in a healthy way."

"It's good to hear that Bobby has gained from all this, too," Isla comments, nodding in approval.

"Vic drained me and left me confused so much of the time. I should have paid more attention to my gut instinct, and not said 'yes' to even rooming with Vic from the very beginning."

"Probably so, but I believe God was teaching you some very good things it was time to learn. Maybe in preparation for...us?" Isla says this while peaking in the basket for more goodies. She knows I like to bring special desserts now.

"You can look around in there...yes, there's a dessert surprise for you."

"Oh goodie," she says, pulling out a big piece of chocolate cake. "This is big enough for the both of us."

"That was the plan!"

"Okay, I'll share, if you insist," she says with good humor, cutting the cake and putting it on napkins for us.

"Sorry I forgot plates for this."

"I don't have a problem eating it this way, or any way," she laughs. "Please go on, Tracy Lynn, I'm sorry, I don't mean to interrupt you with my need for dessert."

"You make me laugh, Isla. That's a good thing. Being here, in this moment, reminds me how important it is to make good choices in life. I can't expect things to change, if I'm not willing to change...starting in my relationship with God. That comes first. The thing is, not to quit...tough stuff in life can either destroy us, which would be the enemy's choice for us, or it can mold us and shape us into what God has for us. When we ask God to help us recognize what's going on, we can be changed for the better."

"I agree, wholeheartedly," Isla says.

"I'm realizing life doesn't revolve around trying to get someone's approval, attention, or love. I wasn't put on planet earth to rescue others, unless specially directed by the Holy Spirit to do something, and with His help. Jesus is the Rescuer. That's His job. Apart from Him, I can do nothing. And by attempting to rescue in my faulty way, I only mess things up...for me, and others. That last Friday I was there, and I cancelled our date in Sausalito, I NEVER should have done that. I should have made Vic be clear with me about what he needed, and then I should have said 'no,' I've got plans for tonight. I learned a big lesson that day. But, it opened my eyes. It was the crow bar that finally got me out of there, and here, so I'm actually thankful for that. It was time to go..."

"God uses many ways to get our attention and show us our need for His help, and not the help of things that aren't good for us. My nephew said something very wise the other day."

"What was that?"

"You know how there are a lot of people who reject Jesus because they don't want to show a need for Him?" Isla asks.

"Yes."

"Well, my nephew said, 'People like to say that if you rely on Jesus, you're relying on a crutch. But most people don't realize we only have one leg.' How amazing is that? He understands this profound truth that so many adults don't. We're all born with 'one leg.' There comes a day when we need to recognize our need for a Savior to help us walk through this life."

"That is GOOD! I, too, had one leg, and am learning to walk with Jesus more and more each day. I wasn't living my life to the full. I was giving up things I wanted and needed, trying to please those around me. There's nothing wrong with being nice, but there is something wrong with breaking your back doing it! Jesus said His yoke is easy, and His burden is light."

"Yes, he did, TL. So true," Isla agrees.

"Isla, I want more relationships that are like what you and I have. Relationships that are sincere, and have a mutual heart-felt sharing involved in it. Being with you today...just the fact that you would make the effort to see me while you're here, and even want to...you show me how much you care. All along, you have kept in contact, asking me how I'm doing, and I hope I've done the same for you."

"Oh, you have, TL. You are very good at caring for others, and I'm so pleased to see you finally taking care of yourself," Isla says.

"Thank you. My restaurant has helped to foster some of this. I know it's what I'm gifted at, serving tacos, and making the customers happy. Even if that doesn't seem like the life for anyone else, it doesn't matter. God makes us all different. Being different is what makes the world go around! I'm happier than I've ever been. This is who I am, although I never thought I'd find me in New Mexico. But the location doesn't really matter. What matters is what God has called us to do. And if it's serving tacos when it's 110 out, so be it!"

"It can get that hot here?" Isla asks astonished.

"Yes. What do you say we finish up here, and I take you over to show you the place? Even if you're not hungry, maybe you could squeeze in one taco."

"I'm sure I could. Plus, we have a little trip back. I'll work up an appetite."

Walking Isla to the car, I can feel such a sense of relief. I can feel growth. I can see Isla possibly being a bigger part of my life now because I have so much more to bring to the table...other than tacos. I don't need her to make me happy. I am full of confidence and joy in who God created me to be. What I would like is to have her by my side experiencing life together like we started doing in the ballpark the day we met. I went in search of a hot dog that day, and God gave me so much more.

52

Putting the last of my things into the only bag I had yet to put in the car, I then tied my shoes, and went into the kitchen. Vic hadn't made it home last night. His bedroom door was still open. I was so relieved. If he had come home, I don't know what I would have done.

The kitchen was dark, but I didn't want to turn the light on. It looked out on the neighbor's side window, and the less evidence that I was up early, the better. I would have made myself a cup of coffee for the trip, but I didn't even want to take the time to do that. My stomach was churning, and if I didn't get on the road soon, I might back out of this.

I got an apple, and with it clenched between my teeth, I tucked in my shirt. I don't know why. I wasn't going to be seeing anyone. It was another habit from the past, I guess. Mom was loving, but also strict about what we wore and how we wore it.

Slinging my bag over my shoulder, I sucked in a deep breath and blew out a long sigh, knowing it was time. I still felt torn, but that just showed me how much I needed to leave. I wondered if maybe I could come back one day? I knew California so well. New Mexico was a mystery to me. I wondered what I would find there? Would Bobby and I get along? Would Vic follow me? Probably not. He had Janice now. She would occupy his time for a bit. My main struggle was Isla...such a good woman. I knew I would truly miss her. But in my heart of hearts, I knew being with her right now would not be fair to her. I knew I had too many pot holes in my soul that needed tending to. I didn't want Isla to have to travel such a rough road with me if she didn't have to.

I figured Vic's phone had died. He hadn't called anymore. Ahhh, the small miracles of God. I'd take them any time I could get them. I put my bag down then, knowing there was one more thing I needed to do before walking out the door. I went back to my bedroom and got down on my knees beside my bed. That wasn't normal for me, but I hoped one day it would be. When I prayed to God that morning, I felt His presence and assurance like never before, even through my fears and doubts. I didn't know why life had to be so hard at that time, but I was also thankful life could also be good. I didn't want to wallow in the sadness I felt. I wanted to be grateful for the good things that might be ahead. While still on my knees, for some reason I thought about the friend at work who was struggling with depression. She had taken some time off to deal with it, and when she came back she was better. But she said the hard part is, 'The last thing you want to do when you feel bad is to feel better.' My heart went out to her when she told me that. I saw the struggle in her eyes. She said her friend came over one of the days she couldn't get out of bed. She was gentle with her at first, asking her if she was sick, or hurting. When she told her 'no.' The friend began to tell her how this was doing her no good, and it was affecting everyone around her. She needed to get up, go for a walk, go to the movie, even take some time off work if needed, but do something, anything but this. When her friend left and didn't come back after saying those things, she told me she got so mad at her. She then got out of bed and went to see her friend. She told her just how mad she was. But what she realized some time later, that was what got her out of bed and back into the land of the living. The anger she had felt was stronger than the sadness that had been consuming her. This enhanced their friendship, it didn't ruin it.

Maybe God had me thinking about that there on my knees that morning for a reason. Maybe He wanted me to see that my need to get healthy was stronger than my need to be the supply for my brother, or anyone. If I was truly addicted to being an addiction, then I had to change. If getting mad at him for what happened on Friday night fueled me to leave today, then so be it.

I finished my prayer with more thanks to a God who cared enough to do what was needed in my life, even though it was hard. Getting up off the floor in that moment for me, was the same as my co-worker getting out of bed. We both needed to walk into wholeness, and healthiness. I found it so interesting the way God used her darkest moment to speak into my life in my darkest moment. I believed God's light was shining on both of us.

The sky grew lighter outside my bedroom window. I knew the neighbors would soon be up, taking their dog out for its morning walk. It was now or never. I chose now.

Locking the front door on my way out, I quietly said, "Good-bye to what I've always known, and hello to what my future holds."

53

"This is it!"

"I'm so excited to see your dream, TL.! I'm so happy for you!!" Isla can barely contain her joy for me as we walk through the doors.

I had longed to share this dream with Isla, and today I finally was. She had seen pics. But it's just not the same. To walk into the restaurant now, smell the food, feel the ambiance, and for her to see the town of Mesilla at last...my heart is full.

"TL, I LOVE this! It's so cute in here! And the location is perfect. You were right!" Isla sounds very pleased.

"Isla, this is Chuck. Chuck, my precious friend, Isla."

"Very nice to meet you," Chuck replies. "My buddy just stepped out for a break, TL. It's been a busy day, but we've been handling it."

"I had no fear. Thank you so much for the time off so I could take Isla out to White Sands. We've come back, not to work, but for a taco. I want Isla to partake in our delicacy here."

"Delicacy, huh?" Isla says with a humorous tone, matching mine."

"Ahhh, yes. Nothing but the finest."

Sitting at a table out front, Isla's eyes light up as she bites into her first taco, quickly ordering a second. With pleasure, I get her one. When she is finished, I take her for a walk around the plaza. She is enjoying the shops, and a bit of the history.

"Look at this, TL, it says this was where the Overland Mail Stage Line went through, St. Louis to San Francisco. That was before the Pony Express. I've heard about the Pony Express, but I didn't even know Mesilla existed until you told me about it," Isla says.

Walking a bit further, Isla reads out loud, "'last major territorial acquisition within the contiguous United States.' There's some history in this town."

"When tourists come for tacos, I need to remember these things, Isla. Sometimes they ask me about the history of this place."

"This is something, TL. This building here is the 'oldest documented brick building in New Mexico.' It makes me wonder what might have taken place in your taco shop a hundred years ago?"

"I wonder. From the rest of the story on this sign, it sounds like there were a lot of murders in this town by robbers. It seems such a quiet place today. Those were different days! Did I tell you that Billy the Kid was tried here?"

"No, you didn't," she responds.

"He was. But he escaped. That was the building over there that they tried him in. We can go in if you'd like?"

"Maybe in a bit. It's so pretty out here. Let's sit on this bench and people watch for a bit. I'm kinda getting lazy with all of today's food in me." Isla is always good natured when she speaks.

"Sure." I can tell something is on her mind, but it isn't a worrisome thing. She's just being a little different than her normal self since we sat down. I could chalk it up to the delicious tacos affecting her this way, but when she starts talking, I know we are heading somewhere unexpected. Especially when she takes my hand in hers. It isn't a casual move, it seems very intentional.

"TL, I am enjoying this time here with you so much. Maybe it's the delicious food, maybe it's the company, maybe it's the sand that looked like snow and the sledding!" Isla laughs at that. "There is something I do need to talk with you about, though, and I'm a bit nervous in saying it. I don't ever want to come across...well, let's just say I want to encourage you with all you've learned, and help you keep healthy boundaries—even with me."

"I don't see that as being a problem, Isla."

"I'm glad for that, but you know, we women can be pushy from time to time. I'm no exception," she says, looking directly at me again.

"Okay, I've been warned. But what would you like to talk with me about? I've done so much talking today. It's only right that I give you the floor now. I'm all ears."

"TL, when I was flying out here for business, I was doing a lot of praying about this visit with you. I know we talked a lot on the phone. But I knew being here with you was going to be different. There's just something about actually spending time with a person, even though technology is so advanced these days. Anyway, I'm stalling here...can you tell?"

"Uh, no, but okay. NO MORE STALLING." We both laugh at that.

"TL, when I got here, I knew I was going to be in meetings with some of the higher-ups at my company. I knew changes were coming, and I might very well be a part of them. Well, I was. They offered me...they

offered me a position in their El Paso office, starting next month."

My heart skipped a beat in that moment, and I felt Isla's grip tighten on my hand. My mind raced ahead, and I had to quickly back it up. I didn't really know where this was going but I surely could have my hopes.

"Okay. Uh, should I ask you what your answer was to them? Or is there more to this?"

"You can ask me. Sure," Isla says, looking directly at me.

"What was your answer, Miss Isla?"

"I didn't know at the time. I told them I had to think about it and consider some things before getting back to them." Isla stops there.

I was so hoping for a more concrete response than that, but I don't want to push her. She seems to be wanting to really take her time with this, and I believe I understand why.

"Have you now had time, and done the considering needed for an answer?"

"I have, TL. I have. But I want to make sure that my answer is what would be best for both of us. I know by taking this new position and moving to El Paso, we would be able to possibly...take our relationship to a deeper level. One of the reasons why I needed to hear you out today, was that I wouldn't want to crowd you if you weren't ready for me to be living nearby."

"First of all, you never would be a 'crowd' to me!"

"Thank you," Isla says, albeit faintly.

"And if this position is good for you, you need never worry that I would stop you in any way. If we are not to be...like this, then that still shouldn't stop you from advancing in your career. But Isla, I want you to know, I would like nothing more than to have you here living near me. I hope you can tell from all that we have discussed today that God has been preparing us for this, even before we knew it was a possibility."

"I have listened very closely today to all that you've been saying, and also through our phone calls since you left. After getting that offer, I knew spending this day with you would help me in my answer to them. I didn't expect this turn of events at work, but I have to tell you, I'm very happy with it. I'm excited to start somewhere new and take on this new role at the company. But even more so, I'm excited that you and I can pick up where we left off nine months ago. I don't believe us meeting at the ballgame was any accident. I can honestly see the two of us together in the future, and I hope that I'm not being that pushy woman now in saying this. I would never rush you..."

"Isla, let me just say, I am in complete agreement with you. And today, I am thrilled beyond words that you could actually be moving here. I want to share a future with you, if you don't mind being in a relationship with a taco guy."

"Hey, they are great tacos! I can tell you this, I will be finding a place *outside of El Paso, on the Las Cruces side, so that I won't be far away when dinner time rolls around."*

"Isla, this is the best news ever! It's not at all what I expected today, but I'm realizing that's the way our God works. He is full of surprises! So if I have any say in the matter, please, please, please give them a resounding YES!"

"Well, it sounds like your vote is in, TL, and I'm in agreement! The two of us soon to be living near one another again! Many nights I've wondered if anything like this would even be remotely possible. I wanted to give you the time and space needed. You have shown me that you really listen to God when He speaks to you about what is happening. I respect you so much for that. You didn't put the responsibility on Vic to be the one to change. You made the decision to walk this out with God, even if it meant walking away from everything you knew."

"And loved." I couldn't help but say it, pulling Isla in close to me. Even in the New Mexico heat, it was good to feel her gladly accept my embrace.

"And it happened, TL. The madness would come to a stop just like God said it would, 'When you do.'"

"We serve a very wise God."

"Yes, we do. I love you, too, TL. I've wanted to say that for a long time now."

"Life seems complete today, Isla. With Jesus in our hearts, you by my side, and a healthy future ahead of us. What more could we ask for?"

"More tacos?" Isla says with great joy!

"That will never be a problem!"

CONCLUSION

You may now be wondering did TL and Isla eventually marry? Have children? Sell so many tacos that they opened a chain of *TL's Tacos* all over the United States? I could tie this story up with pretty little bows and tell you the answer to those questions, but I think not. Let's let this fictional tale end here, while leaving the rest to our imaginations. You be the writer, you finish it however it seems best to you. I will do the same in my own head, because this is *fiction*. But I'd also like to say:
"It's Fiction that tells the whole Truth."
Do TL, Isla, Bobby, and TL's mom, Evon, really exist? How about TL's dad, Will. What about Great-Aunt Martha and Vic, and all Vic's broken-hearted lady friends? Yes, they do, in our everyday world. We know people just like them. We are them. We have different names, live in different places, but all are going through very similar things. You may see people you know in this story...you may see yourself. I do. I know the part I play in these relationships in my own life. I have learned and grown a great deal by writing this book. My hope and prayer is that you will, too.
Change comes to our lives when we acknowledge what's going on and take some sort of action...When *We* Do. If we wait for those we are doing life with to come 'round, be different, and seek God, we could be waiting a very long time. But if we see the changes that might be needed in our own lives, we can start immediately. God's mercies are new every morning...how amazing it is to know we don't have to stay the way we are. God is so willing to work with us on our journey Home where we will meet Him face to face. He never gives up on us, and we shouldn't either.
Maybe some changes started in you before you even got to this page of the book? I hope so. I hope that by the time you're reading this, you've seen things in these chapters that you maybe never noticed before. Maybe you've reached your own conclusion about what it is *You* should do to live

a healthier life, be in healthier relationships, not only with others but with God.

This isn't a perfect book. If, when I started this, my goal was to write a masterpiece, it would have never been written. I was too overwhelmed with this project. I had a ton of research notes and my keyboard in front of me that loomed like a very large mountain—It seemed so hard in the beginning to chip away at the enormity of it. Each chapter felt like jumping from rock to rock in a dry riverbed, with no connection between them. Where was the rushing Living Water of the Holy Spirit I had experienced with earlier novels? But still, there was something driving me forward with this project. And when even that "drive" started to dry up, God then sent loving friends to urge me on to keep writing.

This book is about 86,000 words today. It wasn't until about 60,000 words that the water started trickling in the dry riverbed of writing this. But when it did start, the excitement grew, and I began to enjoy what was flowing onto these pages. Our pastor recently spoke about perseverance— to not stop short while waiting on God and create our own *Ishmaels* in life. We must wait and seek the *Isaac* God has planned for us. This book took that waiting, that perseverance to complete. Is it everything it could be? I doubt it! When is a book really finished? I could go back and make changes in it every day until forever. But then you wouldn't be reading it. And if it touches your life the way it is, and the way it has mine, then praise be to God for that. If any healing is found within these pages, then *Yay God!*

If we are seeking perfection in our jobs, in our crafts, in our giftings, and most especially in our relationships, it's not going to happen. Our Lord, Jesus Christ, is the only Perfect Person to ever walk the face of this earth. The things He did are the only perfect things that happen. Even His death on the Cross was perfect, making a way for all of us to have forgiveness and an eternal life with Him. But our fleshly imperfection shouldn't stop us from being all God created us to be. He is the Great Creator. He designed us. We have to now allow God to do His work in us and through us, and then we aren't to hide it under a bushel. It must be shared. That's why I'm sharing this imperfect work with you even in great fear and trembling. But share, I must.

As the months went by, about eight of them, I plowed through the mountain before me in writing this book. It seemed to me an act of obedience when I would take myself to my laptop and start in...not knowing where I was going, just that I was going. Now I pray any light that shines from our Savior through this project touches hearts and minds for renewal and restoration. Believe and be healed, because by His stripes we have been. It's up to us to walk in that healing each day...when *we* do, He *will*, because He has!

Fiction was never my thing. Oh, years ago, perhaps. But those romantic novels I read...uhhh, were the kind I'm not much interested in now. Not since I've come to know Jesus as my Best Friend. So I stopped reading them. And then many, many years later I started writing them, only in a different way. The desire of my heart is to write fiction with so much Truth running through it that maybe it could be life-changing for someone.

My first three novels, the ROSIE series, seem to have prepared me for this book on narcissism. ROSIE was my first fictional attempt at telling the Truth...the Truth of the Gospel through story form. (Hey, didn't Jesus do that?) ROSIE one, two, and three, started off with the first book being easy to write, with two and three becoming more challenging. First it was, "Write what you know." Then in the second book it was "Write what you research." Then came ROSIE 3, "Write what you don't want to write about." And now we're here, combining all three...where did Rosie go? Oh, that's right, she stopped in and prayed for TL. That was fun!

Where did this all start? I didn't even think much about *narcissism* until a friend introduced me to the word a couple years ago by using it frequently. It was eye-opening. In talking with my friend, Lynn, about this subject in Tracy, California, one day, it seemed it was to be a book. (Hence the character's name.) That very day, after leaving the restaurant, we saw the eagle-shaped cloud in the blue sky pictured on the cover of this book. That picture has not been altered other than to take the bugs off the windshield, remove a telephone pole and a construction site below it. How could I not think of the verse in Isaiah 40:31 (NET):

But those who wait for the LORD'S help find renewed strength;
they rise up as if they had eagles' wings,
they run without growing weary,
they walk without getting tired.

I don't believe this book is *for* the narcissist or even *about* the narcissist, as much as it is for and about the *co-dependents*...the weary who need renewal and strength. It's for those blinded to the actions of a narcissist that need awakening to the truth of what is going on, so one day they will rise up and soar above such abuse as if they had eagles' wings.

I heard a VERY powerful song just this past week by a new musical artist, Kyle Tredway. The song, "Till I Don't," captures narcissism succinctly in just over three minutes. It's taken me thousands of words to write what he says in these last nine words of the song: "You're just something that I need...till I don't."

Being invited by our friend, Paul, to another concert just two days later, I heard over and over in this artist's lyrics the effects of narcissism. The result of what Kyle was singing about showed up in her songs when she sang about broken hearts, abandonment, confusion, shame, and such. Why are there so many love songs about sadness? Yes, it draws us all in, it makes for an emotional experience...but why is it happening? Could it be narcissism? I'm hearing those sad songs in a different light now.

This cruelty toward another was not God's design. But it is certainly Satan's goal to steal, kill and destroy all he can before the return of our Lord Jesus Christ. Recognizing what our enemy is doing, bringing his tactics, schemes, and viciousness into the light can turn it around and thwart his plans of ruination aimed at all of us. Seeing Satan's destructive ways more clearly can help us live more fully in the wonderful plans of our loving Father. That's what this book is about—exposing the darkness so we can all find healing in God's brilliant, magnificent light of Love.

Thank you to all who encouraged me to keep facing the mountain that stood before me until the Living Water of the Holy Spirit was rushing down from that mountain, through the once dry riverbed of the Rio Grande in New Mexico, and out into the open ocean of healing possibilities with our God.

This is the picture taken in Tracy, California, out of the front windshield of the car. A minute later, this cloud formation was gone, blown away by the wind of God, just as it had been delivered to us on that day. God is ever present in each moment of our lives. Let's look up and see that God is good!

Original photo used for the book cover.

ACKNOWLEDGMENTS
GIVING THANKS

Without the guidance of the Holy Spirit, the love of my heavenly Father, and the strength of my Lord and Savior, Jesus Christ, there would be no, "When You Do," in book form or in real life. I need You, I need You, I need You!! Thank You!

Jim, here we are again with what God has given us to share. Together, we are a team, making a cord of three strands that cannot be easily broken. Thank you for all your hard work and love during this season of writing for however long it lasts. You are always there to "Stop everything work on your problem." I love you.! And I know TL is using your chicken taco recipe!

Son, Jimm, thanks for your input on the cover! We appreciate your eye for detail and design.

Connie Fulmer Dixon, once again, your encouragement and help are deeply appreciated. You stick with me through each phase, always happy to be there to read and edit. Thank you for your faithfulness to me.

To my Beta readers, Lynn and Denise. Thank you! You are not only the greatest of friends, you hold me accountable, and always surround me with your encouragement and love. Our times together are always amazingly blessed!

Bob, thanks for being a Beta reader, even when it's not your kind of book! I appreciate your perseverance and corrections.

To my best friend, Deb, and her wonderful husband, Alan, thank you! We had an awesome time in New Mexico with you. I loved our hike, Deb, into the Organ Mountains, exploring and experiencing the dry riverbeds, the sanatorium site, and so much more. Doing "research" with both of you was a blast! Thank you for showing us Mesilla and so much more.

To my brother, Rick, and wife, Cindy, our stop in Chino added to the experience of this journey for TL. Thanks for your love and hospitality. We enjoyed the time spent with you and your amazing grown kids!

Norma, you've been telling me for a long while now, "Not Capable." Those words have sunk in, and are seen in the pages of this book. Thank you for the wisdom shared.

Cheryl, one of my favorite characters in this book is Isla, your new granddaughter's name. When I first heard it, I knew her beautiful name would be used. I just didn't know how or where. Now I do. I have cherished our friendship through the years.

Allie, this book would not be here today without the conversations we have had. You are healing and learning to live life without your mom. I appreciate how you allow me to pray with you through the process of grief.

Dina, our many conversations have added elements to this book that were very much needed. Thank you for being you, for sharing your life with me, and for always doing such a beautiful job! What you do allows me to do what I do.

Pastor Rick, your sermons always add to what I write. What you teach from the pulpit speaks the Truth of Jesus into all our lives, and it carries on into our every day and into the giftings God has given to each of us. May God bless you and Cindy for leading our church well.

Roxanne, my beautiful niece, our times together are a treasured part of my life. Thank you for allowing me to quote you in the pages of this book, and for being so open with me. My generation is so different than yours, but I hope and pray we can continue to learn from one another. And to my nephew, Max, you are quoted in here, too. Thank you for those wise words.

Joan, my author friend, and so much more. I'm proud of what you and Debbie have accomplished with your book. Many years ago when that pastor spoke those words over us, about Living Water flowing through our hands, we didn't know we would be writers. Thanks for loaning me a book that spurred this one on, and for the many conversations about God and life. Keep it flowing!

Jackie, in Florida, God makes a way for us to connect when needed. I find it so amazing how God put an illness on my mind for one of my characters, then has me call you for info, I tell you what I'm writing about, you give me the name of a man I need to listen to, I do, and he adds more depth to one of my characters in a profound way. God is fun! Thanks for your friendship and help!

Kyle, your music is awesome! May God bless your gift far into the future!

Drue, our times together are always faith-building and inspirational to me. Iron sharpening iron in the truest sense. Thank you for all you do for me and so many others in this life. I know your daughter, Diana, and my son, Phil, must be friends in Heaven...as we all await that glorious reunion.

To my Wednesday Morning Bible Study group from the Rock Church, and my Writers' Group on Saturdays, so many blessings come out of our times together. Let us never give up meeting together as some have been known to do. Those times are invaluable as we grow and learn together. Thank you!

ABOUT THE AUTHOR

dianecshore.com

Diane C. Shore lives in San Ramon, CA with her husband Jim of more than 40 years. They are enjoying these years together after raising three sons, and now being the grandparents of six. Writing and sharing stories about God is Diane's passion. God continues to lead her and show her new ways of how He expresses His love toward us each day. Whether it is sitting one-on-one with someone, or speaking to a group, Diane is excited to boldly proclaim the Good News of Jesus Christ and how He works in our daily lives.

FICTION BOOKS BY DIANE C. SHORE

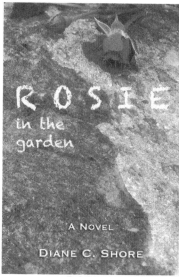

ROSIE I
ISBN: 978-0990523192

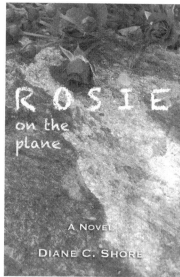

ROSIE II
ISBN: 978-0-990523185

ROSIE III
ISBN: 978-1732678507

NON-FICTION BOOKS BY DIANE C. SHORE

ISBN: 978-0990523161

ISBN: 978-0990523130

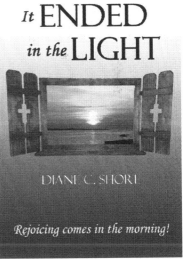

ISBN: 978-0990523109

ISBN: 978-0990523147

dianecshore.com

Made in the USA
Columbia, SC
06 August 2021